DRAKULYA

The Lost Journal of
Mircea Drakulya, Lord of the Undead

With selections from Bram Stoker's

"Journals of Jonathan & Mina Harker"

Edited and amended from original documents

by

Earl Lee

See Sharp Press ◆ Tucson, Arizona ◆ 1994

For information write to See Sharp Press,
P.O. Box 1731, Tucson, AZ 85702-1731.

Lee, Earl, 1954–
    Drakulya : The lost journal of Mircea Drakulya, Lord
of the Undead / by Earl Lee ; with selections from Bram Stoker's
Journals of Jonathan & Mina Harker ; edited and amended from
original documents. — Tucson, AZ : See Sharp Press, 1994.

ISBN 1-884365-02-7

    1. Vampires — Fiction. 2. Dracula, Count (Fictitious
character) — Fiction. I. Title. II. Stoker, Bram, 1847-1912.
Dracula. Selections.

813.54

First Printing

Cover and interior design by Chaz Bufe. Cover graphic © Clifford Harper.
Typeset in Century Old Style and Old English. Printed on acid-free paper
with soy-based ink by Thomson-Shore, Inc., Dexter, Michigan

For John C. Holmes and Charles Oliver,

in memory

ACKNOWLEDGEMENTS

In the years since 1972, when I first began work on this project, a number of people have offered their assistance and advice. It would be impossible to name all of them, friends and relatives who worked on this project, including Kathy DeGrave, Chaz Bufe, Lynea Search, Lori & Erik Smith, Terry Schmitz, Judy DeGrave, Terrell Tebbetts, Bonnie Buhrow, Dan Pezze, Nicki Neil, Scott Forschler, Gene DeGruson, and many others. I would like to take this opportunity to say thanks to all of you for your time and your trouble on what probably seemed to be an impossible task.

The main inspiration for this book remains, of course, an expatriot Irishman, Mr. Bram Stoker. I have taken the liberty of quoting heavily from his work and adapting as necessary to fill my needs. Stoker's original work is quoted in a heavily edited form and makes up substantial parts of chapters 11, 12, 19, 22, 24, 48-60, 72 and 73. As an aside, I might mention that in the years since 1966 when I first discovered Stoker's novel, I found it odd that Stoker chose to kill off his monster on November 7th, the day before my birthday. Some years later, after I had begun my novel, I discovered that my chronology was off. Dracula actually died on my birthday, Nov. 8th. Later I discovered the reason Stoker chose this date—Bram Stoker's birthday is also Nov. 8th.

I would like to thank the following for permission to reprint their copyrighted materials:

Random House for permission to reprint from *The Encircled Serpent* by M.O. Howey published by David McKay in 1926; from *The Stranger* by Albert Camus, translated by Stuart Gilbert and published by Knopf in 1954; from *The Immoralist* by Andre Gide, published by Random House in 1970; from *If It Die* by Andre Gide, published by Random House in 1935; and from *Light in August* by William Faulkner, published by Smith & Haas in 1932.

Taplinger Publishing Co., Inc., New York, for permission to reprint from *Linda Goodman's Sun Signs* by Linda Goodman, copyright 1968.

Reed Book Services, London, for permission to reprint from *Egyptian Art* by Francesco Abbate, Octopus Books, 1972.

Hanuman Books, Madras and New York, for permission to reprint from *The Lie of the Truth* by Rene Daumal, copyright 1989.

Johns Hopkins University Press for permission to reprint from *Night Battles* by Carlo Ginzberg.

Sun Publishing Co. (PO Box 5588, Sante Fe, NM 87502) for permission to reprint from the *New Dictionary of Astrology* by Sepharial.

Scarborough House for permission to reprint from *The Truth about Dracula*, copyright 1974 by Gabriel Ronay, originally published by Stein & Day, Inc.

Librarie Droz, Geneva, for permission to reprint from *Michael Servetus: a Case Study in Total Heresy* by Jerome Friedman.

The Peters, Fraser, & Dunlop Group Ltd. for permission to reprint from *The Natural History of the Vampire* by Anthony Masters, published by Putnam in 1972.

HarperCollins for permission to reprint from *Vampire* by Hanns Heinz Ewers, published in 1934; from *Jesus the Magician* by Morton Smith, published in 1978; and from *The Nag Hammadi Library* by James M. Robinson, Editor, published in 1977.

Most of the verse used in the Renfield chapters is taken from Nathaniel Lee, a Restoration playwright. Several different editions exist and all his plays are in the public domain.

Generally speaking, the use of quoted material as chapter headings is considered "fair use" when the quoted material is less the 250 words. I have made a serious effort to contact all the publishers of books dated later than 1925. Several responded with letters stating that I did not need their permission to reprint the material as they considered it "fair use." Others stated that it was "fair use" but asked that I add a permission statement anyway. I am only too glad to comply with those requests.

— The Author.

PRINCIPAL CHARACTERS

MIRCEA DRAKULYA, son of Prince Drakul of Wallachia, elder brother of Prince Vlad, later called The Impaler.

JONATHAN HARKER, Englishman and real estate broker.

MINA MURRAY HAWKINS, Assistant school mistress & part-time actress, she is engaged to Jonathan and is a friend of Miss Lucy Westenra.

LUCY WESTENRA, heiress, daughter of Mrs. Westenra.

ARTHUR HOLMWOOD, suitor to Miss Westenra and son of Lord Godalming.

QUINCY MORRIS, suitor to Miss Westenra and wealthy Texan.

DR. JOHN SEWARD, suitor to Miss Westenra and an old friend of Miss Mina Murray Hawkins.

JOHN RENFIELD, alleged lunatic and resident of Dr. Seward's sanitorium.

PROFESSOR JOACHIM HEINRICH VON HELSING, scientist and expert in diseases of the blood, once a teacher to Dr. Seward.

PETER HAWKINS, Stepfather of Mina Murray Hawkins and employer of Jonathan Harker

In a conversation related by William Oldys, the Doctor visited the Poet in his cell in Bedlam, where the Poet recited two lines that he had just composed:

"I've seen an unscrewd Spider Spin a Thought
And walk away upon the Wings of Angels."

—"What say ye to that Dr.?"

—"Ay marry Mr. Lee that's superfine indeed. The Thought of a winged Spider may catch the sublime Readers of Poetry sooner than his Web, but it will need a Commentary in Prose to make it intelligible to the Vulgar."

Every moving thing that liveth shall be meat for you: even as the green herb have I given you all things. But flesh with the life thereof, which is the blood thereof, shall ye not eat.
—Genesis 9:4

1

I am called Drakulya. If the legends the peasants tell of me can be believed, I must certainly be the most singularly evil being that has ever lived. In their crude imaginings, my nights are filled with one long, eternally varied debauch—a teeming mix of lust, seduction, and violence. After all, how else could one endure four centuries of life?

Once, long ago, I lived among them as their Prince, an armored demi-god astride a chalk-white charger awash to its haunches in human blood. But now I am reduced to a mere night-thing, furtive and darkly passing among them, to fall upon an unwary milk-girl now and again to refresh myself. Luckily I am not dependent on their misshapen lumpish brains for my existence. And death has forced me beyond concern for my reputation . . . even beyond good and evil—which are to me no more different than the sunset and the dawn.

Four centuries separate me from that day, long ago, when I slipped from this mortal life, as a snake sheds its skin, and disappeared from the world of men. Since that day my body has been maintained whole, intact and unspoiled through the ages— without nourishment . . . except, of course, for the regular consumption of small amounts of human blood.

There was a time at the beginning of my "life" as one of the un-dead when there were a few people I trusted. There were those among the living with whom I tried to share my new world—to let them see through un-dead eyes. With these few friends, I described the energy that flooded my limbs, and the sharp, almost painful triumph of my senses—to bathe in moonlight, to hear the roaring of the sun! And for a time they were able to understand, at least partially, what I felt.

But finally there came a time when I went beyond their mortal understanding. There came a time when all they could see was a slow decay into the dissolute and degenerate. Soon they began to avoid me, as if my presence were painful to them. My very touch became terrifying to them and my words . . . were nothing! Nothing issued from my mouth except the rank odor of blood. I called each one "friend" but there was no answer.

And each of them—Janos Hunyadi in 15th century Transylvania, Joseph de Harmathea in 18th century Paris, and finally even this young Englishman, Jonathan Harker—they each turned against me, plotting with my enemies to destroy me. They hated me, for mine was the voice of awakening into eternal night. I taught each of them the secrets of the Children of the Night; each of them hunted as the wolf hunts. For only those who kill as the wolf kills are truly counted among the Just, truly ready for the awakening from death—to live on in the bodies of the living.

They have dined with me, eaten the immortal flesh & drunk the eternal blood of the Christ. But they, even after consuming His flesh, could not believe the strange miracle that they saw with their own eyes. They witnessed the wonders and were transformed into New Men. But they came to betray the blood. . . .

These are the betrayers who have forced me to live in isolation among rude and barren folk, for even though they hounded me to the very gates of my castle, they could not destroy me. Instead they died. Though not without leaving behind their agents—a network of silently invisible "watchers" whose gigantic web extends beyond these mountains, so that should I attempt escape, they would know the moment I left Borgo Pass.

But they did not cast their nets widely enough, for the last of these betrayers, this Jonathan Harker, provided the means for my escape—to London.

And I will escape, as my ancestors escaped the mass-murder and cremations at Montsegur, as I escaped the tender mercies of St. Bartholomew on that day the waters of the Arges flowed red with blood. I will escape beyond the reach of my old enemies—to London!

Tiresias spoke, after drinking the dark blood . . . "Any ghost to whom you give access to the blood will hold rational speech with you."
—*The Odyssey*, Homer

2

During the past few years my thoughts have turned more and more toward England. This island fortress holds a strange, unexplainable attraction for me.

England, the pale and distant land surrounded by the sea, a European island whose vast chalk cliffs have resisted the pounding of ocean waves for countless ages. Those chalk cliffs, when seen from the sea, possess a perfect whiteness unlike that of any living thing. As one approaches the shore, however, it becomes obvious that there is not so much colour in those cliffs as a visible absence of color. And the rocks themselves have a peculiar odor and brittleness like that of old bones.

This island is quite different from the villages and towns of my homeland. My people are earthbound and inseparable from the Carpathian mountains of Transylvania. Even their clothes smell of animal feces and moldy hay.

I remember well the night in March when I first decided to go to England. I was walking through the streets of Bistritz when, in the darkness just before sunrise, I found a young woman sitting in the graveyard of a small stone church that had fallen into ruin.

She wore a plain dress of a dark scarlet color that was without decoration or embroidery of any kind. Her hands held a bunch of flowers, rue I think, whose white petals were strewn across her lap and also across the yellowed marble of the bench on which she sat. I was struck by the expression on her face—her eyes were open in a blank stare, her lips were set, her skin was of a white, chalk-like pallor, set off by a black gauze veil.

I could not say why she sat in that place—there was nothing here, only the gnarled old oaks, birches and hemlocks, casting their shadows over fallen tombstones. There had once been here a shrine to some local saint, but it had been long since abandoned. She paused often to look toward the gate, as though she had come here to meet someone, perhaps someone she loved, as though she had come here many times to meet him, only to be disappointed.

As I stood watching her through the gateway of the churchyard, the sky began to glow in the east. I could see the tip of the sun shining over the trees. As I turned to leave, I saw her look up at me. I hesitated. She stood up and shaded her eyes with her hand.

This silent stranger influenced me in some way other than through my senses. The way she stood, the darkness of her eyes, the light of the sun glowing on her cheek, all combined to create in me an emotion that I dare not mistake for love. I drew in her presence as the green grass draws in the morning dew.

"Come to me," I felt her say. "I wait for you alone."

I was filled with awe, for I had seen in those few seconds what I never before beheld with bodily eyes; like a vision of eternity, I saw in her eyes a new thing. I saw London.

And on one day
They'll break apart with spears this harmony—
And then my sleeping and long hidden corpse,
Cold in the earth, will drink hot blood of theirs.
—Oedipus at Colonus, Sophocles

3

The French philosopher Voltaire once said that the red mark which a lover leaves on the throat of his beloved is a sign of great significance. It states to all who see it "I was here"—like a dog urinating against a tree—a sprinkling Gules on a field d'Argent.

I drew the first blood of my un-dead existence more than four centuries ago. Draining the blood from the veins of a living human being is a very difficult process. The best method is that of biting the throat of the victim in a manner like that of a kiss. In this way, two small and almost unnoticeable punctures can be made in the delicate flesh of the throat, and small quantities of blood can be taken quite easily.

But the act of drinking human blood involves much more than a simple kiss. I feel that by this kiss the opening of an entry to the soul is made, so that my soul pours itself into the bodies of those who have become my prey, at the same time that the precious fluid of their vital life flows into my body, giving me new life.

The first victim of my need for human blood was a dying soldier. It was from him that I learned an important lesson: piercing someone's flesh with your teeth, like dying, should be done very quickly, or it becomes a messy process.

Using my teeth to pierce the delicate skin of the throat requires that I come into close contact with my victim. For those few moments while I am bent over my victim, just before my lips and teeth touch the throat, the thought often passes through my mind that I could be easily destroyed. At this close proximity I could be the one being drained, rather than the one feeding.

Nor did the monster mean to delay it, but, starting his work,
he suddenly seized a sleeping man, bit into his bone locks,
drank his blood from his veins . . .
  —Beowulf

4

One may wonder why, after considering the journey for so many years, a chance encounter with a young woman in a churchyard would cause me to travel to England. The truth is that this encounter was the culmination of other events that as a whole compelled me to make my journey. The fact that she and I had been together in the same place for a few short moments was tied by invisible threads to countless other encounters in other places, extending far into the past.

When I saw her in the churchyard, I felt myself being carried back through time a thousand nights, through an endless stream of nocturnal encounters. At the moment when she noticed my presence, I saw the shock of recognition in her eyes, the recognition of who and what I was.

I moved slowly among the tombstones to the place where she stood. Despite the sunlight which began to close around us, I embraced her; I touched her ear and then the flesh of her throat with my lips, and we stood quite still for some moments. When finally the light touched us, surrounded us, I released her from my embrace and lowered her slowly to the ground, where she lay, quite still.

My body was flooded, satiated with life, but it lasted for only a few moments. I saw then what I most fear of all things—I saw her life slowly drain from her, so that without medical help she would surely die; and I saw myself standing over her like one damned.

I lifted her and carried her to the home of a young doctor I knew. I stood next to her bed as he examined her—the paleness, the weakness, the marks of violence on her throat. After several minutes he turned to me, saying, "You know what has happened to her." I did not answer. He went on, "She has been attacked by an animal—a wolf or wild dog." The sound of anger in his voice convinced me that he was not telling the truth—trying to protect my feelings, as if they needed protecting. Making no answer, I walked into the hallway, put some money on the table, and left.

When I returned the next night, she was gone—taken by coach to a hospital in Buda-Pesth. I learned her name, too—Mina Murray—and also that she was a young English assistant schoolmistress on a traveling holiday with her English friends and her fiance, a Mr. Jonathan Harker.

By the time I was able to reach Buda-Pesth, she had already set out with her friends for Exeter, by way of London, where she was to see a blood specialist. I was able to get her fiance's address in

Exeter, but that was all. I wondered what kind of man he was to deserve such a woman.

As the sun rose in the East, I walked along the river bank, saying over and over again—Mina! Mina! Until the remnant of a tear began to form in my eye. I knew then that I was going to follow her, to England if I must.

'Tis now the very witching time of night,
When churchyards yawn and hell itself breathes out
Contagion to the world: Now could I drink hot blood,
And do such bitter business as the day
Would quake to look on.
—*Hamlet*, Shakespeare

5

Before proceeding further with the story of my strange journey to England, I am sure that you, my friends, are a bit curious about how I became one of the un-dead. I'm sure my story will be instructive.

People have, over the ages, learned to associate dying with pain, both physical and emotional. Those who die a blessedly peaceful death, free of anguish, are by far outnumbered by those who die violently. A being like myself, who has visited the scene of countless deaths in my role as either vampire or voyeur—even I who know Death as an intimate—even I am filled with anger at the wastefulness of Death. The mere sight of one of those Medieval sketches of a skeleton brandishing a huge sickle fills me with despair. I am, however, comforted by the fact that my final death will be no more than the sensation of a pin pricking my heart, as compared to the pain of my first dying.

On that day, long ago, I felt the searing pain of a Boyar's lance finding its way with almost magical inspiration into my own breast. And I felt myself falling to earth, my strength let out of me like water pouring from a cracked jug.

My men fled when they saw me fall from my horse. I was alone. Pain flooded my body until there was no more room for feeling. I saw Hunyadi's soldiers standing over me, "le chevalier de blanche fort" no longer, covered with blood, my clothing soiled and stinking from the release of my bowels. I felt distant from my body in a curious way.

Odd details became filled with meaning—the rough leather apron the soldier wore, the way the light gleamed off the spathe of his dagger, which looked more like a trowel than a knife. The last thing I remember is the slow, almost reverent way he bent down over me . . . the feeling of separation, followed by nothing and the sense of being nothing. And the sensation of nothingness is more despairingly beautiful and terrible than any pain of which the mere body is capable.

I felt my tortured body desire the final release of death, the sensation of being cut off and set adrift in the night of a frozen polar sea. But it did not come. Instead I still felt myself attached, by some ubiquitous umbilical cord, to my former life. I was not allowed to rest, for the cord pulled me forcibly through wave after endlessly beating wave of bone-chilling coldness and pain . . . until, suddenly, I was pulled headfirst back into this world like a cork being dragged under the surface of the water. Yet, I doubt that anyone can blame me for thrashing my limbs against the cold, for putting off—even for a moment—my return to that dark and unholy sea, or for being tempted to exist by whatever power it was that had restored me to "life" among the living.

I found myself then returned to my body, a heavy warmth poured itself into me, like syrup. I felt the weight of life wrap itself around me, suffocating me with its vital heat. My senses—touch, taste, sight—were restored, like the strange gifts of an oriental hareem. I reached out my hand and the sacred fount of life welled up within me.

Perhaps you can understand the terror I felt as my life-energies were suddenly restored to my lifeless corpse. I was . . . I was so very cold. Slowly my limbs regained their movement. My senses were restored, but they were far more acute than they had ever been before, so much so that I could clearly make out the stone walls of my tomb in the total darkness of the underground vault. I felt the dampness and smelled the wine that had leaked onto the floor of the vault and heard the praying mutter of a priest through the stone ceiling over my head. But I thought then that these perceptions were due to the sudden return of senses to a sense-less body, rather than owing to a new supernatural acuteness.

The knots of my winding sheet slipped loose as my fingers touched them. I pushed away the wreath of roses and lilies, and made my way to the stairway leading out of the vault. There I found the tomb of my father.

My father's name being Drakul, and mine being Drakulya, my first accomplishment as a child was learning to distinguish between his name and mine. But now on my first waking from the sleep of death into my un-dead existence, I, in the stony confines of my tomb, found his coffin near the door-posts, with the name DRAKUL clearly visible, carved in wood. He was freshly dead. I had not known of his death in battle, and the shock of this discovery confused my sense of who I had been before—a prince of Wallachia, eldest son of Drakul the Dragon, now Drakul the Dead . . . now Drakul the murdered king.

My thoughts turned to the battle we had been involved in against our enemies and how I might return to my men, but that was all. For in that moment I looked to my father's coffin and saw that it was adorned with a crucifix of stone.

A sudden weakness spread through my body and I collapsed on the floor of the vault. As I lay there, my mind was filled with a strange scene from my childhood, a memory I had tried to suppress of Turkish soldiers using a tent-peg and mallet to "convert" a priest they had captured. It was a horrible sight that I and my brother Vlad were forced to watch. I turned my eyes from the scene in horror, but Vlad watched with a childlike fasci-nation, his hands toying with the small silver crucifix he wore.

I don't know how long I lay there on the floor of the vault, but some time later I was able once again to stand, as long as I kept my face averted from the crucifix. I climbed up a narrow stairway and pushed aside the wooden planks that were fitted into the opening over my head. I pulled myself up through the hole.

The only light came from the candles behind the altar, but I recognized the church as one that stands just outside Targoviste, not far from where I had been wounded with the spear. It was a wooden-frame church, called the Church of the Hill, that had been built on the stone foundation of an old visigoth church dedicated to St. Nicholas of the Wines, so called for the pleasant vineyards that cover these hills. It was in the stone vault of the church that my father and I had been buried.

I left my tomb that night and made my way out into the world of men. And in the world of men I discovered that I was no longer a man, but merely a ghost who somehow was leading a posthumous existence. And that night a dying soldier provided me with my first blood.

You cannot understand what it means to become an un-dead creature, and you should pray that you never will. You can no longer see yourself in shadows or in mirrors because you have changed. Now you are something else, reflected only in the eyes of those who are your prey.

At last by fatall course they driven were
Into an Island spatious and brode,
The furtherest North, that did to them appeare:
Which after rest they seeking far abrode,
Found it the fittest soyle for their abode,
Fruitful of all things fit for living foode,
But wholy wast, and void of peoples trode,
Save an huge nation of the Geaunts broode,
That fed on living flesh, and drunke mens vitall blood.
—The Faerie Queene, Spencer

6

On the night that I escaped from my tomb—struggling free of my burial garments—cast out from my true place, I made my way out of the chapel and down the steep hillside to the vineyard, hiding among the ripe bunches of grapes.

Naked and helpless, I lay there in the darkness for some time. I don't know how long, though it seemed a long time. It was as I lay there that I noticed the sound of a horse-drawn cart approaching. I waited. As it drew near I saw an old gypsy woman driving it.

She was small and wrinkled, dressed in the familiar costume. I made no sound, but when the cart drew near, she stopped and looked to where I lay hidden in the darkness. My skin shone a silvery color, mottled by shadows in the vague moonlight.

She helped me into the back of the cart and covered me with some wolf-pelts. She took me to her camp, not far away, and built a small fire. There two young women joined us, carrying wood for the fire. They were gypsies, too, and looked like they might be her daughters. But neither spoke. Instead they sat by the fire and poked at the hot embers with a branch of ivy that they had stripped of leaves. They avoided my gaze, out of modesty I supposed, as I was lying near the fire, naked except for the wolf-pelts.

I asked her how she had found me, and she answered that the song of the white wolves—called "the Children of the Night"—had told her about me and where she could find me. They told her, too, that I was "mulo"—a living corpse.

I asked her how she could be sure that I was the one she was told to look for. She answered by pointing a crooked finger at the scar on my chest—a huge, inflamed gash running from my neck to my waist, and a second gash running from my left side to my right side—so that they formed a crude cross-like scar that was centered over the place where the spear had entered my chest. At first I thought that these cuts had been made by someone in order to remove the spear, but these were obviously too long, and the colouration of the scars—like scarlet cords against the pale silvery whiteness of my skin—led me to believe that they were made before my death. One of her daughters touched the wound—I thought for a moment that she meant to put her fingers into it and I drew back from her touch. But the wound had already healed over quite well. She was the oldest of the two daughters, and as she touched the scar on my chest she repeated a phrase—"Hav co kar! Hav co kar!"—that seemed more the Romany tongue than Wallach.

I then turned to the old woman and asked how it could be that a man who was dead could be restored to life. She looked at me and said that I was not the first, and that as I was a descendant of Barsabat the Great, Prince of Wallachia, I carried within me the original seeds of the "Beyonders." She said that the Beyonders had relations with the daughters of the boyar, the men of old, and that, for this reason, their children carried within them two souls, one mortal and one immortal, and that the cuts on my chest were where my heart—and with it the mortal soul—had been taken out.

"Our time has come upon us and our blood must be sacrificed to the dragon for the sake of this night-child and for the redemption of all the Children of the Night." For a moment I looked into her dark eyes and saw there a resolve so strong that I became afraid. She smiled and pointed toward the elder of the two daughters, called Shovihani, who wore the heavy, dark costume of the Romany gypsies. As I watched, Shovihani tied about her waist a leather apron, into which she thrust a broad silver knife.

By this time it was nearly morning. The ritual had to be begun before the sunrise and deep in the forest, where the canopy of trees created a land of perpetual shadows. Her huge iron kettle was sitting on the fire, steam slowly rising from the surface of the water. She had been sitting near it for some time, fingering the beads of her rosary and muttering prayers rapidly over the fire.

She stopped, the beads falling limply against her withered breasts, and dipped her hands in the water, half stirring it, lifting her cupped hands and pouring the water back on itself—pausing only to bite into a piece of raw garlic. She took a white cloth from her daughter and dipped it in the water. Her daughters used the wet cloth to bathe my skin and wash away the dirt and dried blood.

She turned away from me as they completed their task. Then she pulled aside a blanket of grey wolf-pelts stitched together with leather thongs. There, lying in a basket, I saw the dessicated corpse of a she-wolf and living within the corpse, resting within the cavity of the rib cage, were the Children of the Night. I saw them for the first time—a pair, male and female—in the she-wolf's body, where the old gypsy had hidden them before coming to find me. "I have placed the Holy Ones in the basket, and from the basket to this holy place I bore Them. I have eaten the flesh and drunk the blood of Our Lord Jesus Christ, and I have been proven worthy. Hav co kar!"

She took them and washed them gently, as her face expressed the religious feeling of . . . an exact translation of this is impossible, but the words "joy" and "grace" are close. She was quite careful in washing their feet. When she finished she held each one over a broad, shallow bowl and twisted each one firmly, from left to right, so that the head separated from the body quite easily.

It is extremely difficult to describe exactly what happened at this point, except to say that she used a small knife—resembling a modern surgical knife—to cut small strips of flesh that then fell into the bowl. To this she added a wineskin of dark red Burgundy, or Sangria. Soon the strips of flesh seemed to curl of their own, like serpents. We each drank from the bowl. The two young women drank also, but only after we had already drunk most of the wine and flesh.

By this time the sun was already above the horizon and I was beginning to feel quite warm, my body flooded with warmth, with languid life. I lay back against a tree and closed my eyes.

I saw the sun through my eyelids and felt its rays touching me through the tiny breaks in the forest canopy, the mottled pressure of light coming to rest here and there on my skin. The sensation was pleasant, but distracting. And then I felt myself floating upward toward the sun, and then into the sun. At first its roaring was painful to my ears, deafening. But as I penetrated to its core, it became only a quiet hissing that was almost unnoticeable.

After floating in these currents, I was drawn back again. In the fraction of a second I was within my body again, oblivious to everything except the sound of my own heartbeat. I was absorbed by the sound, by the beating, which grew louder and louder until the beating surrounded me, smothering and absorbing me.

It was as if suddenly my whole body had become one gigantic heart with vast quantities of blood flowing through me—thousands of gallons—as if I were the great heart of some alien metropolis. It was a sensation unlike anything I have ever experienced, my body expanding and contracting in some eternally ordained rhythm.

Then, without warning, I was stabbed through with dozens of sharpened barbs, as though I were wrapped in thorns. I felt, once again, the spear tip pressing against my chest and my body falling to the earth as great gouts of blood poured from my wounds; great rivers of blood spouted in a gory flood from my chest until the earth was bathed in blood.

It went on and on, endlessly, as the great streams of blood without measure poured onto the earth, enough to stain the oceans of the world. I felt, once again, the sensation of death, of being dragged beneath the surface of the sea . . . of drowning. I gasped for air but was forced below the surface of the sea again, like an insect at the mercy of some ancient mischievous child. When I could stand it no longer, I ceased struggling and fell back against the earth. I closed my eyes and dreamed this strange dream:

I was standing in a peaceful vale, before an orchard of apple trees. There was a beautiful woman standing by the trunk of a tree, one arm embracing the trunk and the other around the neck of a small child, a boy about two or three years old. They had not seen me, and I moved quickly, on all fours, behind a hedge row. I was different . . . not human and not animal. More than human, I had taken the shape of a she-wolf and the life and the soul of the she-wolf. I had become the she-wolf and I experienced everything she was. I say "was" because the woman and child wore a style of clothing I hadn't seen in several years. And the child looked very much like me.

As the wolf, I dived toward my prey, snatching at the arm of the boy . . . myself . . . I remembered my childish impressions of the attack, as it happened to me nearly twenty years ago, at the same time, so that I was caught suspended between two memories of the attack.

At that moment there appeared a knight riding a black horse. His round shield was bright yellow. He charged after me on his mount and the point of his lance pierced my flank. When he withdrew the point, my side began to glow with a clear white light that spread through my body. I felt as if I were being torn to pieces by wild beasts . . . or like a white flower whose petals were being torn off one by one and tossed into a stream . . . the bits of consciousness were swept away by a flood of darkness . . . and then the dark . . . .

I was helpless, too weak to move. I heard a woman's voice say, "He was young and strong, there is enough here for us all!" And I felt their weight bearing down on me, and voluptuous pleasure being drawn from me like wet, knotted ropes. I wanted to surrender to it, but some indescribable fear possessed me. I tried to rouse myself to the surface of consciousness, but the weight held me under. I fought against it, struggling to throw off the terrible pressure. I clawed desperately with both hands for something to hold on to, my mouth open, gasping for breath, until suddenly I broke through into the air. I sat up, bolt upright, and threw off the weight that held me down.

The sunlight fell across my eyelashes like drops of dew. I was once again in the small clearing. The old woman was dead, her naked body fallen and bent like drapery. I covered myself with the blanket of wolf pelts and moved over to where she lay. There were marks of violence about her throat and blood smeared all over her breasts—and blood on my face and chest also. Around her throat was a garrote made from wolf-gut. I could not tell if she had died from loss of blood from the throat wounds or by the tightened garrote that cut into the flesh of her throat. I touched her, and she fell over like a sack of meat. It was only then that I saw the gaping X-shaped wounds on her abdomen where she had been disemboweled.

The two women were gone, leaving behind their shoes. Their wagon was gone too. And I was alone with the knowledge she had given me of how animal spirits can be transferred from the dead to the living, from the unliving to the undying. I, Drakulya, only-begotten of myself—for me this was the beginning of eternity.

I made my way through the forest to a peasant's hut and stole a blanket in which to wrap the corpse and a rope so I could hoist it into a tree—safe from scavengers. From there I went to a nearby village, careful to hide my identity, for anyone who knew me could easily turn me over to Hunyadi's men. I knew that my younger brothers Vlad and Radu were in safe hands, so my first thought was for my own escape.

With throats unslaked, with black lips baked,
We could not laugh or wail;
Through utter drought all dumb we stood!
I bit my arm, I sucked the blood,
And cried, A sail! A sail!
—*The Rime of the Ancient Mariner,* Coleridge

7

It can truly be said of me that my destiny was forged on the anvil of history. In my case the Fall of Constantinople was to my life like a boulder falling into a pond. For centuries the Turkish Sultan had expanded his empire westward, and after the failures and setbacks of recent crusades, the Turks were poised at the doorstep of Europe, ready to smash the Byzantine Empire into the dust. It was because of this danger that the Order of the Dragon had been formed. Both my father, Prince Drakul of Wallachia, and Janos Hunyadi, vizier of neighboring Transylvania, were invited to join the order. The main purpose of the order was to defend certain holy relics that had to be removed from Constantinople for safekeeping. The Turks knew that Constantinople was the doorway to Europe—and conquest!

I was with my father as a Christian knight defending Constantinople. When the city fell to the Turks, we retreated in defeat, having given an account of ourselves with honour. Hunyadi, on the other hand, had led his troops in a foolish charge on the Turkish position and had precipitated the collapse of our battle line. My father was angered by Hunyadi's folly, for, with the fall of Constantinople, Wallachia would surely become the next battleground.

Prince Drakul argued that Hunyadi should be stripped of his command. Many agreed and were on the verge of placing Hunyadi in chains. It was only because the Holy relics were, by an earlier agreement, to be hidden by Hunyadi that he was spared. Hunyadi never forgave my father. This is why he supported our enemies. My father's death was his revenge. My murder, followed shortly by my father's assassination in the marshes outside Bucharest, had become only the slightest of ripples in the pond of history.

After a few days I was able to reflect on what had happened to me. It is still not clear to me, even now, what happened after I fell from my horse, wounded by the spear. From what I was able to piece together, I was taken by the traitorous boyar to a hill just outside Targoviste and hung upon a cross, still living. The boyar believed me dead, and left me there as a lesson to any who might be tempted to oppose Hunyadi's rule.

Later that night a priest and two peasants came to the place where I had been crucified and bribed the guards who had been left to watch over my corpse. Another body was put on the cross in my place, and I was removed to the Church of the Hill, above an ancient Roman vineyard in the foothills of the Carpathians.

The priest who brought me to this church was a Spaniard, a Catholic priest from the town of San Gresancte in the Pyrenees. He had been forced to leave Spain and had since travelled to Wallachia as a holy penitent in a sort of self-imposed exile. Several years earlier an outbreak of the plague had killed all the other priests who lived in Targoviste, and only he had survived as the sole representative of Rome. Over the years some of the towns-people of Targoviste had come to believe that he was a dabbler in the Black Arts, and his superiors in Rome suspected him of some unspecified heresy.

Indeed, he was a student of the Occult, a searcher like many others for the Philosopher's Stone—which he believed could be created through the proper mixture of the fire of a Phoenix Aegyptus and the blood of Ouroboros the Dragon. As a part of his experiment, he needed the fresh corpse of a prince of royal blood. My body was therefore for him a god-send, a "Gott-sonder" as he described it in his Germanic dialect.

That night he performed the ancient ritual, drawing off a small amount of my blood to be used to create the ELIXIR VITALE described in his alchemical text. With this he mixed the blood of a prostitute who had been murdered by her lover and, of course, a small quantity of sacramental wine, which, as one knows, is vital to any proper Satanic ritual. This he poured into a metal bowl and heated over a flame for several hours until nothing was left but a dried residue. This was then scraped out with a knife and put into a mortar, where it was reduced further into a powder by a vigorous application of the pestle. The resulting dark red powder, he claimed, could be added to wine or to unleavened bread, or even sprinkled over one's food—with the effect of allowing the supplicant to retain his youth for many years, or even decades . . . perhaps even centuries. After he finished his experiment, he had my body placed in an empty tomb in the vault beneath the altar. The hole was then hidden by tightly-fitted planks that matched the wooden flooring of the church.

After my father's assassination in the marshes near Bucharest—stabbed through the eye with a boyar's lance—the evil usurper, Janos Hunyadi, proclaimed himself Prince of Wallachia. Two days later, my father's mutilated body was brought to the church by loyal boyar—they had heard of this priest's "noble" efforts to provide me with a decent burial—and they placed his body in the vault, near mine.

When, the next morning, the priest found the planks removed and my body missing, he assumed that he had been betrayed and fled. By an indirect route, he escaped to the monastery of Snagov and joined the monastic order. It was only many years later, when my brother Vlad was buried there at Snagov, that I met the priest. It was then that he told me the story of what had happened to me and how my body came to be in the vault.

But first on earth as Vampire sent,
Thy corpse shall from its tomb be rent;
Then ghastly haunt thy native place,
And suck the blood of all thy race;
There from thy daughter, sister, wife,
At midnight drain the stream of life;
Yet loath the banquet which perforce
Must feed thy livid living corse.
—*The Giaour,* Lord Byron

8

My new life began with stealing some clothes from a peasant's hut and later joining a gypsy caravan. It was they who taught me to survive by passing invisibly through the clutches of local authorities.

Years passed, and my name was slowly forgotten.

The arch-betrayer, Janos Hunyadi, had returned to Transylvania after placing one of the Danesti family on the throne of Wallachia. This new prince was only mildly interested in the strange rumors about the "ghost" of Mircea Drakulya. He preferred to ignore the stories, perhaps assuming that they referred to my brother Vlad who was then living in Moldavia with my Uncle Bogodan.

Some years later, after Bogodan's assassination, Vlad was forced to flee for his life to Transylvania and throw himself on the tender mercy of Hunyadi, our old enemy. By this time Hunyadi was becoming increasingly suspicious of his Danesti protege and so allowed young Vlad's presence at his court.

It was during this time that Hunyadi effected his last and greatest betrayal by revealing the secrets of the Order of the Dragon to one who was clearly unfit—my brother Vlad. Hunyadi certainly knew of my brother's great cruelty, and yet despite this, or perhaps because of it, Hunyadi revealed to him the secrets of the Order—secrets whose value Vlad clearly knew.

And after Hunyadi died, felled by the plague during a long siege, Vlad saw his chance, crossing the border into Wallachia and seizing the throne. This was the beginning of Prince Vlad's rule over Wallachia.

Wallachia was a small country that lay between the moslem sultan in Constantinople and the Christian lands of Europe, and particularly the land of Transylvania. Because our country was placed between two gigantic forces, after the fall of Constantinople it had become the battleground for both empires. As the latest of a series of short-lived Princes, Vlad's first concern was to consolidate his hold on the throne by executing as many of his enemies as were foolish enough to fall into his hands. And Prince Vlad also staged an elaborate funeral for me—as he, too, had heard the strange rumors about the "ghost" of Prince Mircea Drakulya, . . . who was now a "blaut-sagar."

Finally, Vlad came to use the knowledge foolishly given him by Hunyadi—the list of towns where the holy relics were hidden, the relics that had been taken from Constantinople before it fell to the Turks. Years earlier, our father, Vlad Drakul, and the other knights of the Order of the Dragon had taken these relics—a dozen long boxes—and hidden them in secret crypts all across eastern Transylvania. I, myself, had been with my father at the siege of Constantinople when the relics were removed from the city for safekeeping; and I had participated, as part of a small group of nobles, in their removal to Transylvania.

At the time, my father and I had both objected to placing the relics in an area controlled by Hunyadi. And I think he never forgave us for objecting to his being placed in control of their safety. Vlad was such a sharp contrast to the typical Crusader knight that Hunyadi no doubt derived some secret pleasure in telling Vlad of their existence. By making Vlad a member of the Order, Hunyadi betrayed his oath in spirit while keeping the letter of it intact.

Crossing the border into Transylvania with a large army, Vlad attacked the city of Brasov, looting the Church of St. Bartholomew and burning the homes in the area around it. His men then set up thousands of wooden stakes around the church and proceeded to impale countless numbers of citizens there, while Vlad sat at a large table in the center of this bedlam, eating his lunch and carefully observing the carnage around him. As he ate, his soldiers tortured the people one by one—until his victims gave up the secret location of the hidden crypt in their city.

Other cities were destroyed, too, in this same way, as Vlad swept across the countryside like a scythe, until the feast day of St. Bartholomew, August 24, when Vlad's men entered the town of Amlas and burned it to the ground, and then, to complete the crime, impaled almost twenty thousand people on blunted pikes—men, women, and children. And those who were not impaled died equally horrible deaths.

One by one the city's elders were tortured, until one of them gave up the location of the hidden crypt. Some of Vlad's men found the relics—stone, loaf-shaped sarcophagi, each with a long wooden box placed within it. Every one of the sarcophagi bore the distinctive design of a human head with a crucifix rising from its forehead—eyes wide, mouth open, a look of astonishment—like the ancient oracles of Greece.

Legends say that by possessing these relics, one can gain power over life and death itself. And this was the reason for Vlad's interest in the relics of Constantinople.

After the sack of Amlas, a small group of soldiers escorted two wagons to Vlad's capital at Bucharest. Vlad himself traveled with his army and conducted the wagons—containing a dozen large wooden boxes and their relics—to a hiding place in the mountains.

But this was only the beginning of Vlad's reign of terror. The life of every person in Wallachia was dependent on his whims, and his terrible cruelties were beyond description.

It was during this period of Vlad's rule that I came to truly understand death. Many times I dealt with Vlad's soldiers, coming often, too often, near arrest as I bartered with Vlad's henchmen for the lives of my people. It took all my ingenuity, as I passed myself off as the son of a Wallachian nobleman, or alternately as a favorite cousin to the Ottoman Sultan. I helped many to escape across the border. Where intimidation and forgery failed, the promise of bribery—or "backsheesh"—usually succeeded. So, by the end of his terrible reign I had exhausted my meager resources and was penniless.

This living hand, now warm and capable
Of earnest grasping, would, if it were cold
And in the icy silence of the tomb,
So haunt thy days and chill thy dreaming nights
That thou wouldst wish thine own heart dry of blood
So in my veins red life might stream again,
And thou be conscience-calm'd —see here it is—
I hold it towards you.
—*This Living Hand,* John Keats

9

Years later, Vlad was forced to flee from the invading Turks and was captured and imprisoned by King Matthias of Hungary. During his long confinement, Vlad demonstrated his penchant for cruelty by torturing and killing small animals provided him by his jailers. Yet, eventually, Vlad ingratiated himself with King Matthias, who placed him at the head of an army that recaptured the throne of Wallachia for Vlad.

Vlad's last reign was short, only a few months. He was eventually killed in battle by the Turks; and his severed head was taken back to the Sultan Mohammed as proof that "the Impaler" was finally dead.

According to his last wishes, his corpse, the sacred Person of Prince Vlad of Wallachia—at least what remained of it—was taken by his men to the island monastery of Snagov for burial. The monks, in turn, following the secret written directions of their princely benefactor, handed his body over to a Spanish priest. This was the same priest who had stolen my body almost thirty years before.

I had followed the wagon bearing Vlad's body to the island. Hiding in the boat, I went with it and watched, disguised as a soldier, as the monks carried his coffin into the chapel at the edge of the lake. The priest was waiting there also, the instruments of his trade spread out over the altar.

That night, at the stroke of midnight, he tried to resurrect the corpse of Vlad Drakulya. Lifting the chalice filled with wine and blood, he cried out, "O Logos, Power of the World, O Greatest of the Most High, O Ruler of Men and Angels, Master of all Powers, the Archons, and the Daemons. Remember me, for I was with you in the beginning. O Breaker of the Darkness, remember me; Master of the Primordial Waters, remember me; O Master of the Waves, remember me; O Breaker of Walls, O Mover of the Deep, remember I was with you when you swallowed the soul of the Chrestus; I was with you at the dismemberment; I fought with you against the enemy and it was I who brought him before you in chains. I your servant have brought before you one of your own. He was cast down by his enemies and his soul cast down into darkness. Restore him, O Great One, that he may serve you again. Release him from the bonds of death. Restore him to life and show him to me."

The priest then took the knife from its jeweled scabbard, placing the scabbard on the altar. Moving to the coffin, he placed the blade against the chest of the corpse. Cutting a hole in the abdomen, he then poured the mixture of blood and wine into the wound. And then began the waiting.

From my hiding place, I could see his growing frustration. "Why do you not heed me!" he croaked, flailing his arms against the sky. "You may not deny me, for I have given you everything. All that I have has been sacrificed. All! All!" Pulling the hempen rope belt from his waist, he fashioned a scourge and then pushed the coffin off the altar so that the headless corpse fell to the floor.

In his mad rage, he began whipping the corpse, while crying out, "O Rex Mundi! Give me his soul! You cannot deny me this. It is signed and delivered into my hands." Seizing the chalice, he threw the last of the blood and wine into the flames of the brazier and uttered a curse, flaying the corpse again and again with his rope.

But this time there were unexpected consequences. For as the mixture of blood and wine sizzled in the flames, a powerful storm erupted over the lake, and the island was punished with blasting wind and hail. The monks were used to the fury of these winter storms, but the huge waves crashing against the very walls alarmed them.

A dozen of the monks broke into the chapel and found the old priest cringing against the altar. They seized the body of Vlad Drakulya and carried it out into the courtyard where a flaming pyre had been hastily built. With all their strength, they hurled the corpse into the flames. I looked on, stunned.

A flash of lightning shattered the enormous bell-tower. In the wake of the thunder and the sound of the tower collapsing into the lake, I leaped from my hiding place in the shadow of a buttress. I screamed, "What are you doing!" at the group of monks. As they gawked at me, one of the monks clutched his chest and collapsed—the others broke into a mad scramble to escape, believing me to be the resurrected spirit of their prince, Vlad the Impaler.

I ran into the chapel and seized the old priest. Upon seeing me burst through the doors, he fainted, luckily, so that I had no trouble carrying him from the chapel. As the walls cracked and then imploded from the weight of the water, we reached the safety of a low stone wall. The Chapel of the Annunciation collapsed on its foundations as the rain and wind poured over us. I hid in the wreckage of the bell-tower, pinning the priest under my arm so that he would not escape me.

Minutes became hours, until the storm slacked, its fierceness dying away as rapidly as it came. The moonlight illuminated the rocks before me on the beach as I dragged and half-carried the priest to the shore. The lake waters had receded and there, half-floating and half-submerged at the foot of an ancient oak, was the enormous wooden door of the monastery—as it had been pulled from its hinges and then deposited against the tree by the rising and receding waters of the lake. I pulled the door free of the roots and carried it to the water's edge. It was easy to push off from the shore and let the wind carry us across the lake.

The huge door possessed an intricately carved representation of St. George slaying the dragon. A gift, no doubt, of my father. The monks were justly proud of this door, and they were greatly angered when they discovered the next morning that the door had fallen into the lake and floated to the opposite shore. There it was found by a group of nuns who appropriated it for the door of their convent. And with the door they had found an elderly Spanish priest, who, looking like a drowned rat, they adopted instantly as their new Father Confessor.

From that day forward Mircea Drakulya ceased to exist, even as a ghost. Instead there was only the horrible blood-sucker, Vlad Drakulya. I adopted my brother's identity, realizing that the fear he had instilled in the people as "The Impaler" would serve me as a weapon against my enemies. The memory of Mircea Drakulya, dead now for thirty years, was already dim in their memories. But Vlad was still fresh and bloody in their common existence. His name inspired fear and trembling. And I vowed to keep his memory ever fresh in their minds.

Over the years I have been hunted by many who sought to destroy me. They were not afraid of the common, run-of-the-mill variety of blood-sucker. But as "Vlad the Impaler" I was not an ordinary vampire, and even the most courageous of vampire-hunters gave me a wide berth once they were made to recognize who I was. And so it is using his identity that I have managed to survive for the last four hundred years.

Although I have made many journeys to other parts of the world, I never stayed long. For I always returned to my castle in the mountains and to the hidden "treasure" that my father and I took from Constantinople before it fell to the Turks, the treasure stolen by my brother Vlad and brought to this castle.

In the years that followed Vlad's death, I wandered across Europe. I found myself drawn to the site of every revolution, even the failed revolution in France that descended into horror and destruction. In 1848 and in the following reaction, I found myself on the barricades with Bakunin and a few others, especially the nihilists, who seemed to me to have taken revolution as their religion. I have within me the spirit of Gnosis, the knowing and naming of things that carry destruction. Those who fought with me saw the forces at work in my soul, and as the revolutionary spirit died—hardening into channeled reactions against the oppressions of king and priest—I finally withdrew into my secret citadel, an abandoned castle above Borgo Pass.

In these most recent years, I spent my days and nights nurturing the secrets that I would one day carry into the very heart of my enemies. I would go to London.

It is because he betrayed the sacred treasure of Constantinople that I came to hate and despise this Englishman, Jonathan Harker. In past years I had revealed the secret of my coffins to only a few others—Miguel Servetus, Michel de Montaigne, Mikhail Bakunin—and they had been both drawn and repelled by what they had seen. They stood on the edge of the abyss. But none of them had betrayed me.

I had felt a kinship with Harker, for Mina's sake, and had arranged with Mr. Hawkins that Jonathan be sent here to me. Yet after all I did for him, even revealing the secrets of my castle to Harker, he repaid my generosity by trying to destroy me. It was not just Harker's offense against my hospitality during his stay at my castle that made him my enemy.

And what was my crime that he could prove in the eyes of a court? Nothing more than waylaying a real estate agent. Harker came to my castle to sell me some property in England, but I planned to make him one of my own. Yet he spurned this great gift and chose instead to join my enemies.

"Fearful and ghastly to me—eh sir, I never saw a face like it! It was a discoloured face—it was a savage face. I wish I could forget the roll of the red eyes and the fearful blackened inflation of the lineaments."
"Ghosts are usually pale, Jane."
"This sir was purple. The lips were swelled and dark; the brow furrowed; the black eyebrows widely raised over the bloodshot eyes.
Shall I tell you of what it reminded me?"
"You may."
"Of the foul German spectre—the Vampire."
—*Jane Eyre*, Charlotte Bronte

10

From "1887 field notes—Prof. Von Helsing"*

One evening in the spring of 1887 in a village near Bistritz, a carriage came to rest before the door of an inn, and two men then descended from the coach. The first was a short English physician named Sir William G_____; the second was myself—a gentlemen from Dantzig, Prof. Joachim Von Helsing. We went to the inn and were admitted into the silence of a dining room.

In the middle of the room on a round table burned half-a-dozen candles of various lengths in odd candle holders, illuminating the area of the table in a murky half-light that threatened to go out with every draft. On the table amid the candles was situated a pine box containing the remains of a young woman.

Standing over the coffin was an elderly Greek Orthodox priest. His black robe, grey-flecked hair, and sable beard were almost invisible in the darkness, so that all that could be seen of him was the pale whiteness of his forehead glowing in the candle-light and the slow motion of his hands as he turned the pages of a small prayer book from which he read.

We stood for several minutes in the darkness near the doorway, watching the scene in silence. Finally we removed our hats and coats, hanging them on wall-pegs, and moved toward the coffin in the middle of the room. I was the first to speak: "Sir William, would you be so kind as to examine the throat of the deceased."

The doctor bent over the coffin, from which the lid had been removed, and placed two fingers on the cold flesh of the corpse, just below two small puncture marks on the throat.

"My superficial examination reveals two small, ragged punctures on the throat, probably made by a sharp instrument."

Von Helsing: "Please feel the the skin and the flesh of the face."

---

*Prof. Von Helsing's field notes were purchased by the National Academy of Sciences in Leningrad from a private collector. The notes are written in a secret cipher and were only recently decoded and translated from the original German.

Sir William touched the face and stated, "Cold, clammy, but pliable. Also very pale, white. She cannot have been dead for more than a few hours."

"She has been dead for two weeks."

"Two weeks? Rigor mortis should have set in. And considerable decay of the tissues."

Von Helsing: "The people in this village believe that this woman was the victim of a vampire. Those punctures on her throat are where the vampire drained the blood from her body. It is also believed that this woman will, in turn, rise from the grave and become one of the un-dead, unless she is prevented from doing so. The villagers have already sent for a young man who lives near here, a dhampire who will destroy the evil that possesses this body."

Sir William examined the throat wounds more closely. "Do you seriously believe that a cup, or even a handful of blood, could restore life to this dead body?"

"Not life. Rather a semblance of life. I wanted you to see the body before the dhampire arrives tommorrow."

"The doctor of dead souls?" Sir William said as he smiled.

Von Helsing: "Don't laugh. This man is one of the few who know the rituals that will free the soul of this poor woman from her un-dead body. His profession has been passed on from generation to generation for many centuries. It is said that he is a direct descendent of Vlad the Impaler, the Son of the Dragon—Drakulya —who was, it is believed, a vampire of the fifteenth century."

At this point the innkeeper entered the room and offered us whatever comforts it was within his power to provide. After a brief discussion we were shown to a small room on the upper floor. The two lamps in the room were quickly lit and the innkeeper's wife dispatched to prepare food and drink for the two travelers.*

---

*It is perhaps interesting at this time to point out that Sir William was a prominent neurologist and surgeon—a self-made man who by skill and tenacity had become one of the wealthiest physicians in London. I, Professor Joachim Heinrich von Helsing, M.D., D.Ph., D.Litt., etc., etc., of the Wallenburg Institute in Dantzig—am a novelist, archeologist, botanist, folklorist, physician and chemist, who often serves as a police consultant in criminal cases involving the unusual or bizarre. I am also the author of nearly one hundred books, including a history of Poland, a book of folk tales, and a treatise on the occult.

After we finished our meal, I began searching through the pockets of my great-coat and produced several old, yellowed sheets of paper which I then handed to Sir William. "These letters and other documents should give you some idea of what we face."

"But you cannot deny, Von Helsing, that you are lacking somewhat in physical evidence."

"What do you call this?" I asked, gesturing in the direction of the coffin in the room below them.

"A corpse, undeniably, with two small punctures in the flesh of the throat—probably made by some small animal—nothing more."

"You refuse then to admit the possibility of the existence of the vampire?"

"I do."

Thus the conversation went on, well into the night, until I drew from Sir William a promise to remain in the village until the arrival of the Dhampire. We two travelers then went to our beds and slept soundly until morning.

Early on the following morning, we sat for a while in the dusty brightness of the inn, as the windows had been opened to allow sunlight and air into the small dining room. Sir William was the first to speak:

"Professor Von Helsing, do you really believe that a man can prolong his life for years, even centuries, by consuming human blood?"

"No, my friend, a man cannot, of course. But the thing who has caused the death of this poor girl is not a man—or, at least, is no longer a man, although he once was human."

"And this girl, Professor; I can see no way that her flesh could be preserved in this way . . . unless . . ."

"Unless she is not truly dead, but only in a false death. Which is why I asked you to examine her. You are the specialist in physical paralysis and the wasting diseases of nervous origin."

"This is not a typical wasting illness, although nerve damage could cause paralysis. Perhaps this could be a disease-induced catatonic trance, or perhaps toxin-induced."

I reached into my coat and produced a small notebook, saying, "Please consider this carefully. Imagine a virulent disease, similar in nature to hydrophobia, communicated by saliva into the blood stream. The onset of the disease is marked by a wasting illness until death results . . . or a semblance of death, a catatonic paralysis which is the effect of disease-produced toxins. The victim appears dead . . . to all appearances is dead. But then something happens. The body resists; in some cases the patient recovers and throws off the disease. And yet something else has happened, a physiological change in the structure of the cell tissues."

"A metamorphosis, a new form of life, no longer human, or not quite human, but capable of resisting all human diseases. Is that what you mean?"

"Remember, too, that all accounts of attacks by these . . . living dead . . . report that those who return from the dead are younger, stronger and more vital than they were before the onset of their disease."

"Then you think that the aging process itself is arrested, or even reversed."

"Yes, Sir William, so now you know why I wanted you to see this," I pointed toward the coffin, "and why I have suggested to you what I have chosen to call 'The Wallenberg Hypothesis,' and why I am giving you this copy of my experiment reports."

"I don't understand. Why are you giving this to me?"

"I have carried the hypothesis as far as I can using books and chemicals, human cadavers and animal subjects. I do not have access to . . . human subjects for experimentation."

"You realize what you are asking of me? To introduce a disease of this type into a healthy subject!"

"Surely you have access to subjects who will not be . . . missed. At your hospital you do have a fair population of the insane."

"Von Helsing, you realize, too, what would happen if these experiments were discovered."

"Please, Sir William, you are recently retired. And I have discovered from my inquiries that you have very powerful and influential friends who could shield you, who would have to shield you, if what we are doing became known."

"I would need samples of blood and of the diseased tissues."

"I have taken the liberty of arranging for their delivery in London."

"You must realize that there may be other factors: genetics, environment, mental state, or some other characteristic that we will be unable to isolate."

"My friend, every primitive society on the face of the earth from Polynesia to Ireland, from Mexico to India, knows or has known of the existence of the living dead. Therefore, it seems clear to me that whatever other factors may be involved, they cannot be unusual or rare—quite the contrary."

"You have thought this out very carefully."

"Sir William, you are about seventy years of age; I am in my late sixties. What do we lose in the attempt? Against that, what do we stand to gain?"

"And yet, the effects of the disease—I don't relish immortality as a mindless, ravening beast."

"I believe that adverse effects are negligible, and most are easily attributed to complications: general bad health, mental weakness, premature burial with asphyxiation and loss of oxygen to the brain, and so on. But these complications can be avoided, especially if the subject is easily suggestible and can be prepared through hypnosis. All of this is detailed in my report."

"There is, Professor, one final problem: assuming that we succeed, how do we then get access to human blood in order to survive as a living dead."

"This is the easiest of all; after all, we are doctors and there are a variety of means available to us . . . besides the obvious alternative."

At this, Sir William grimaced visibly. Then I led my friend out to the back of the inn, where a group of peasants were loading a box on a wagon. The wagon was being packed with ice and straw in preparation for its journey to London.

"And how shall I contact you, Professor, when the experiment has been completed?"

"You can reach me through my agent, Mr. Peter Hawkins, in Exeter."

"And how much can I tell him . . . without his realizing what we are doing?"

"Do not worry. Hawkins will do whatever I wish, and he knows enough to keep quiet. You see, I know a great deal about his conections in Ireland, enough to send him to prison, or the gallows. I trust him implicitly, for that reason. Indeed, I am sending him to Transylvania next year to gather a specimen . . . the blood and tissue samples for my experiments."

"I will contact him then in about six months."

"Good. I will expect a full report."

Sir William left to go to the train station and begin his return trip to London. I followed later that day.

We find some book naturalists—Olassen and Povelson—declaring the Sperm Whale not only to be a consternation to every other creature in the sea, but also to be so incredibly ferocious as continually to be athirst for human blood.
—*Moby Dick*, Herman Melville

11

From Jonathan Harker's Journal*

3 May 1889. It was on the dark side of twilight when we got to Bistritz, which is a very interesting old place. Being practically on the frontier—for the Borgo Pass leads from it into Bukovina—it has had a very stormy existence, and it certainly shows marks of it. Fifty years ago a series of great fires took place, which made terrible havoc on five separate occasions. At the very beginning of the seventeenth century it underwent a siege of three weeks and lost 13,000 people, the casualties of war proper being assisted by famine and disease.

---

*A heavily edited and expurgated version of this journal was published as a "novel" in 1897 by Mr. Bram Stoker.

Drakulya had directed me to go to the Golden Krone Hotel, which I found, to my great delight, to be thoroughly old-fashioned, for of course I wanted to see all I could of the ways of the country. I was evidently expected, for when I got near the door I faced a cheery-looking elderly woman in the usual peasant dress—white undergarment with long double apron, front, and back, of coloured stuff fitting almost too tightly for modesty.

When I came close she bowed and said, "The Herr English-man?" "Yes," I said, "Jonathan Harker." She smiled, and gave some message to an elderly man in white shirt-sleeves, who had followed her to the door. He went, but immediately returned with a letter:

"My Friend Harker, Welcome to the Carpathians. I am anxiously expecting you. Sleep well to-night. At three to-morrow the coach will start for Bukovina; a place on it is kept for you. At the Borgo Pass my carriage will await you and will bring you to me. I trust that your journey from London has been a happy one, and that you will enjoy your stay in my beautiful land. — Drakulya"

I took some time to walk through the village, which seemed very quiet in that evening. The strangest figures I saw were the Slovaks, who wore big cowboy hats, great baggy dirty-white trousers, white linen shirts, and enormous heavy leather belts, nearly a foot wide, all studded over with brass nails. They wore high boots, with their trousers tucked into them, and had long black hair and heavy black moustaches. They are very picturesque, but do not look prepossessing. On the London stage they would be set down at once as some old Oriental band of brigands. They are, however, I am told, very harmless and rather wanting in natural self-assertion.

Three of them stood together near a gateway. The first, the apparent leader, had a single birch-colored wooden leg. The second had lost an eye in a fight and the missing orb had been replaced by a artificial one, the color of pine sap. The last stood leaning against an oak tree, his shirt open to reveal an odd tattoo on his stomach that seemed to represent a tongue. I could see, though, that the tattoo actually disguised an old scar. Each of these strange warriors had, it seemed, lost a fight and been marked by his opponent as a reminder, or a warning.

I saw this proven by their reaction to a young man, a gypsy, who was dressed even more strangely than they were. I was told that the clothes he wore were certain identification of the clan of gypsies to which he belonged. The blue woolen blouse he wore had on its breast the insignia of his family—a dragon—and was tied at the waist by a long belt made of hemp, with the insignia now partially hidden by an open fleecy white sheepskin vest, covered with embroidery and pierced coins. His pants were of a rough, yellow cloth which ended over the straps of a pair of goat-skin boots.

On this particular evening, the Slovaks had begun dancing a funny comic-opera dance in the street. Yet, when the young gypsy walked through the market place toward them, the dancing stopped and the crowd of Slovaks parted to make a path for him, and they even made an odd little bow as he passed.

Curious, I followed the gypsy to an inn, where he knocked at the door and was admitted into the dining room. I followed him inside and saw him walk directly over to a coffin, resting on a table, and examine the corpse of a young woman, bending the limbs to see that they were flexible and examining the throat. As he worked, the expression on his face did not change. His features were strong and clearly drawn. His skin was dark, accentuated by the solid blackness of his hair—even his eyebrows and his moustache were pitch black. His face with those heavy sensual lips and black penetrating eyes displayed a kind of indifferent look to those who tried to meet his gaze. He turned from the coffin and regarded the people in the room for some moments. Finally, he spoke:

"I am Bifrons."

He turned to the inn-keeper and the priest who presided over this wake, though it was more a vigil, and he said, in Latin, "Do you have all the things I requested?" My own school-boy Latin was quite good, so I had no trouble following most of what he said to the priest.

Soon the inn-keeper dragged a large wooden box out from under a table and opened it. Inside was a variety of talismans: garlic, the branch of a wild rose, a long knife, and a sharpened wooden stake and hammer.

Beginning his work, the gypsy removed the stake and hammer from the box and walked over to the coffin. The room was in semi-darkness, so that it was difficult for most of the observers to see what then occurred. But I had taken up a place on the landing of the stairway and could see all that happened. As I watched, the gypsy—called a "dhampire"—leaned over the coffin, placing the point of the stake over the heart of the corpse, and uttered a strange prayer:

"Thou Tetragrammaton, O great Unmanifest,
Through Darkness lead us to Light,
Through Death lead us to Immortality.
O Thou Terrible! Thou Living God,
From the land where there is no day
Has this one been brought unto me;
Night and day are nothing to us;
Eternity has become for ever barren;
Her death sleep is broken. Shall she sleep again?
Call it what you will, she is awake
Now! I give sleep to her whose it was;
The Sleeper I have given sleep for ever
Through your hand, All Destroyer.
To Death I have given death for ever
Through your will, Almighty God."

At least this is how I translated the prayer from his rough Latin.

Then, after finishing the prayer, he moved over the corpse and, with one blow of his terrible hammer, he drove the stake through the corpse's heart. He followed this heavy blow with a second and a third, until blood began to flow quite freely from the mouth of the corpse and from the wound in her chest.

Next the dhampire took a leather apron from the innkeeper and put it on over his clothing. He took the huge knife in both hands and raised it over his head, so that all could see the light gleaming from its blade. He said, "From unjust men deliver me!" At this point several of the peasants pointed toward me and began a furtive gesturing, the two-fingered gesture like cow's horns. I ignored their insults, even when an old man began shaking his keys in my general direction.

The dhampire did not seem to notice the disturbance. He placed the knife against the woman's breast and began cutting, with a single long stroke, a deep gash in the chest of the corpse, running from the collar bone down along the center of the chest to the stake, and then further down to a point just above the left kidney. This he followed with a second cut by pulling the knife across the chest with both hands, plough-like, so that the two wounds began to resemble a crudely formed "X" like the cross of St. Andrew. No one seemed at all surprised by this gruesome desecration of the corpse.

The innkeeper held out a brass basin filled with water, and the dhampire washed the blood from his hands and said, "I will wash my hands among the innocent—SIBI CONSCIA RECTI."

He turned then once again to his work and placed both hands on the stake. Gripping it tightly, he whispered, "I will take the bread of heaven and call upon the Name of the Lord—PANEM CAELESTEM ACCIPIAM—for the blessings of the earth, the water, the air, and the fire; so that all these agree."

Using all of his strength, he twisted the stake loose from the corpse, so that blood poured from the gaping wound and along the gashes cut in the chest of the corpse. Soon a puddle of dark blood, mixed with a brackish-looking fluid the color of grey amber, had collected in the bottom of the coffin. The dhampire collected a small amount of this fluid in a shallow bowl of beaten silver. He took the stake then and used it to make the sign of the cross in the direction of the north, the south, the east, and the west. He washed the blood from the stake and handed it to the innkeeper.

Then the innkeeper gave him the branches of a wild rose bush. The dhampire held these over the coffin and shook them, while repeating—"eloi, eloi"—as petals fell from the bush into the coffin. After a few moments, he handed the branches to the innkeeper and said, "And the heavens were made flesh to rise up among us."

The people in the room began to push forward, forming two lines. They began to file past the coffin on each side. Holding their eyes averted, each one took a handful of petals from the rose bush and dropped them in the coffin as they passed, and then returned to their places to make way for the others to come forward.

When they had all returned to their places, the dhampire reached into the coffin and took from it a petal in each hand. These he held out before him, saying, "This is her body," and placed a rose petal in his mouth. He placed the second rose petal on his tongue and said, "This is her blood," and then he drank the dark blood that he had collected in the silver bowl. I was appalled by this gross parody of the Latin mass.

The dhampire stood for some minutes over the coffin. Motioning the others back from the table, he completed his work by placing a branch of the wild rose in the coffin. Fitting the lid on the coffin, he sealed it with four nails that had been blessed by the priest; one at each side and one at the head and at the foot of the coffin.

It was then that the innkeeper came forward and finished nailing shut the coffin. As the nails were being driven, the dhampire went to a table and sat down. Filled with disgust, I left the inn and returned to my room at the Golden Krone Hotel. I did not eat, but went straight to my room and to bed.

4th May 1889. I found that my landlord had got a letter from Drakulya, directing him to secure the best place on the coach for me; but on making inquiries as to details he seemed somewhat reticent, and pretended that he could not understand my German. This could not be true, because up to then he had understood it perfectly; at least, he answered my questions exactly as if he did. He and his wife, the old lady who had received me, looked at each other in a frightened sort of way. He mumbled out that the money had been sent in a letter, and that was all he knew. When I asked him if he knew Drakulya, and could tell me anything of his castle, both he and his wife crossed themselves, and, saying that they knew nothing at all, simply refused to speak further. It was so near the time of starting that I had no time to ask any one else, for it was all very mysterious and not by any means comforting.

Just before I was leaving, the old lady came up to my room and said in a very hysterical way:

"Must you go? Oh! young Herr, must you go?" She was in such an excited state that she seemed to have lost her grip of what German she knew, and mixed it all up with some other language which I did not know at all. I was just able to follow her by asking many questions. When I told her that I must go at once, and that I was engaged on important business, she asked again:

"Do you know what day it is?" I answered that it was the fourth of May. She shook her head as she said again:

"Oh, yes! I know that! I know that, but do you know what day it is?" On saying that I did not understand, she went on:

"It is the eve of St. George's Day. Do you not know that tonight, when the clock strikes midnight, all the evil things in the world will have full sway? Do you know where you are going, and what you are going to?" She was in such evident distress that I tried to comfort her, but without effect. Finally she went down on her knees and implored me not to go, or at least to wait a day or two before starting. It was all very ridiculous, but I did not feel comfortable. However, there was business to be done, and I could allow nothing to interfere with it. I therefore tried to raise her up, and said, as gravely as I could, that I thanked her, but my duty was imperative, and that I must go. She then rose and dried her eyes, and taking a crucifix from her neck offered it to me. I did not know what to do, for, as an English churchman, I have been taught to regard such things as in some measure idolatrous, and yet it seemed ungracious to refuse an old lady meaning so well and in such a state of mind. She saw, I suppose, the doubt in my face, for she put the rosary round my neck, and said, "For your mother's sake," and went out of the room.

I had my dinner and am writing up this part of the diary from my notes whilst I am waiting for the coach, which is, of course, late; and the crucifix is still round my neck. Whether it is the old lady's fear, or the many ghostly traditions of this place, or the events of last night, I do not know, but I am not feeling nearly as easy in my mind as usual. If this book should ever reach Mina before I do, let it bring my good-bye. Here comes the Coach!

*There was—somehow in the clouds on which the moon was shining—
hidden in the mystery of glowing whiteness—delivery from the torpor;
there was the Infinite Well-Being. Then he saw—flying past him like a
falling star in a November night—a small red strip on her chest between
her breasts. A tiny wound, less than an inch long
—and a single drop of blood oozed from it.*
—*The Vampire*, Hans Heinz Ewers

12

From Jonathan Harker's Journal

5 May 1889. The grey of the morning has passed, and the sun
is high over the distant horizon, which seems jagged, whether
with trees or hills I know not, for it is so far off that big things and
little are mixed. I am not sleepy and, naturally, I write till sleep
comes. There are many odd things to put down, and, lest who
reads them may fancy that I dined too well before I left Bistritz,
let me put down my dinner exactly. I dined on what they call
"robber steak"—bits of bacon, onion, and beef, seasoned with red
pepper, and strung on sticks and roasted over the fire, in the style
of the London cat's meat! The wine was Golden Mediasch, which
produces a queer sting on the tongue, which is, however, not
disagreeable. I had only two glasses of this, and nothing else.

When I got on the coach the driver had not taken his seat, and
I saw him talking with the landlady. They were evidently talking
of me, for every now and then they looked at me, and some of the
people who were sitting on the bench outside the door—which
they call by a name meaning "word bearer" or "spit and whittle
corner"—came and listened, and then looked at me, most of them
angry. I could hear a lot of words often repeated, queer words, for
there were many nationalities in the crowd; so I quietly got my
polyglot dictionary from my bag and looked them up. I must say

they were not cheering to me, for amongst them were "Ordog"—
Satan, "pokol"—hell, "stregoica"—witch, "vrolok" and "vlkoslak"—
both of which mean the same thing, one being Slovak and the
other Serbian for something that is either were-wolf or vampire.

(Mem., I must ask the Count about these superstitions)

When we started, the crowd round the inn door, which had by
this time swelled to a considerable size, all made the sign of the
cross and pointed two fingers towards me. With some difficulty I
got a fellow-passenger to tell me what they meant; he would not
answer at first, but on learning that I was English, he explained
that it was a charm or guard against the evil eye. This was not
very pleasant for me, just starting out for an unknown place to
meet an unknown man; but every one seemed so fearful and
upset. I shall never forget the last glimpse which I had of the inn-
yard and its crowd of stilted figures, all crossing themselves, as
they stood round the wide archway, with its background of rich
foliage of oleander and orange trees in green tubs clustered in the
center of the yard. Then our driver, whose wide linen drawers
covered the whole front of the box-seat, cracked his bog whip over
his four small horses, and we set off on our journey.

I soon lost sight and recollection of ghostly fears in the beauty
of the scene as we drove along, although had I known the
language, or rather languages, which my fellow-passengers were
speaking, I might not have been able to throw them off so easily.
Before us lay a green sloping land full of forests and woods, with
here and there steep hills, crowned with clumps of trees or with
farmhouses, the blank gable end to the road. There was everywhere a bewildering mass of fruit blossom—apple, plum, pear,
cherry; and as we drove by I could see the green grass under the
trees spangled with the fallen petals. In and out amongst these
green hills of what they call here the "Mittel Land" ran the road,
losing itself as it swept round the grassy curve, or was shut out by
the straggling ends of pine woods, which here and there ran down
the hillsides like tongues of flame. The road was rugged, but still
we seemed to fly over it with a feverish haste. I could not
understand then what the haste meant, but the driver was
evidently bent on losing no time in reaching Borgo Pass. I had
been told that this road is in summertime excellent, but that it had

not yet been put in order after the winter snows. In this respect it is different from the general run of roads in the Carpathians, for it is an old tradition that they are not to be kept in too good order. Of old the people would not repair them, lest the Turk should think that they were preparing to bring in foreign troops, and so hasten the war which was always ready at the loading point.

Beyond the green swelling hills of the Mittel Land rose mighty slopes of forest up to the lofty steeps of the Carpathians themselves. Right and left of us they towered, with the afternoon sun falling full upon them and bringing out all the glorious colors of the beautiful range, deep blue and purple in the shadows of the peaks, green and brown where grass and rock mingled, and an endless perspective of jagged rock and pointed crags, till these were themselves lost in the distance, where the snowy peaks rose grandly. Here and there seemed mighty rifts in the mountains, through which, as the sun began to sink, we saw now and again the white gleam of falling water. One of my companions pointed as we swept round the base of a hill and there opened up the lofty, snow-covered peak of a mountain, which seemed, as we wound on our serpentine way, to be right before us:

"Look! Isten szek!—God's seat!"—and he crossed himself. As we wound on our endless way, and the sun sank lower and lower behind us, the shadows of the evening began to creep round us. This was emphasized by the fact that the snowy mountain-top still held the sunset, and seemed to glow out with a delicate cool pink. Here and there we passed Czechs and Slovaks, all in picturesque attire, but I noticed that goitre was painfully prevalent. By the roadside were many crosses, and as we swept by, my companions all crossed themselves. Here and there was a peasant man or woman kneeling before a shrine, who did not even turn round as we approached, but seemed in the self-surrender of devotion to have neither eyes nor ears for the outer world. There were many things new to me: for instance, hay-ricks in the trees, and here and there very beautiful masses of weeping birch, their white stems shining like silver through the delicate green of the leaves. Now and again we passed a leiter-wagon—the ordinary peasant's cart—with its long, snake-like vertebrae, calculated to suit the inequalities of the road. On this were sure to be seated quite a

group of home-coming peasants, the Czechs with their white, and
the Slovaks with their coloured sheepskins, the latter carrying
lance-fashion their long staves, with axe at end. As the evening fell
it began to get very cold, and the growing twilight seemed to
merge into one dark mistiness the gloom of the trees, oak, beech,
and pine, though in the valleys which ran deep between the spurs
of the hills, as we ascended through the pass, the dark firs stood
out here and there against the background of late-lying snow.
Sometimes, as the road was cut through the pine woods that
seemed in the darkness to be closing down upon us, great masses
of greyness, which here and there bestrewed the trees, produced
a peculiarly weird and solemn effect, which carried on the
thoughts and grim fancies engendered earlier in the evening,
when the falling sunset threw into strange relief the ghost-like
clouds which amongst the Carpathians seem to wind ceaselessly
through the valleys. Sometimes the hills were so steep that,
despite our driver's haste, the horses could only go slowly. I
wished to get down and walk up them, as we do at home, but the
driver would not hear of it. "No, no," he said; "you must not walk
here; the dogs are too fierce!" And then he added, with what he
evidently meant for grim pleasantry—for he looked round to catch
the approving smile of the rest—"and you may have enough of
such matters before you go to sleep." The only stop he would
make was a moment's pause to light his lamps.

I took advantage of the slower pace to record my thoughts and
experiences of the day in my journal — "Make hay while the sun
shines."

When an hour or so later it grew dark, there seemed to be
some excitement amongst the passengers, and they kept speaking
to the coachman, one after the other, as though urging him to
further speed. He lashed the horses unmercifully with his long
whip, and with wild cries of encouragement urged them on to
further exertions. Then through the darkness I could see a sort of
patch of grey light ahead of us, as though there were a cleft in the
hills. The excitement of the passengers grew greater; the crazy
coach rocked on its great leather springs and swayed like a boat
tossed on a stormy sea, so that I had to hold on to the door frame.
The road grew more level, and we appeared to fly along. Then the

mountains seemed to come nearer to us on each side and to frown down upon us; we were entering the Borgo Pass. One by one several of the passengers offered me their "blessings," that strange mixture of fear-meaning gestures which I had seen outside the hotel at Bistritz—the sign of the cross and the guard against the evil eye. Then, as we flew along, the driver leaned forward, and on each side the passengers, craning over the edge of the coach, peered eagerly into the darkness. It was evident that something very exciting was either happening or expected, but though I asked each passenger, no one would give me the slightest explanation. This state of excitement kept on for some little time; and at last we saw before us the pass opening out on the eastern side. There were dark, rolling clouds overhead, and in the air the heavy, oppressive sense of thunder. It seemed as though the mountain range had separated two atmospheres, and that now we had got into the thunderous one. I was now myself looking out for the conveyance which was to take me to the Count. Each moment I expected to see the glare of lamps through the blackness; but all was dark. The only light was the flickering rays of our own lamps, in which the steam from our hard-driven horses rose in a white cloud. We could see now the sandy road lying white before us, but there was on it no sign of a vehicle. The passengers drew back with a sigh of gladness, which seemed to mock my own disappointment. I was already thinking what I had best do, when the driver, looking at his watch, said to the others something which I could hardly hear, it was spoken so quietly and in so low a tone; I thought it was "An hour less than the time." Then turning to me, he said in German worse than my own:

"There is no carriage here. The Herr is not expected after all. He will now come on to Bukovina, and return tomorrow or the next day; better the next day." Whilst he was speaking the horses began to neigh and snort and plunge wildly, so that the driver had to hold them up. Them, amongst a chorus of screams from the peasants and a universal crossing of themselves, a caleche, with four horses, drove up behind us, overtook us, and drew up beside the coach. I could see from the flash of our lamps, as the rays fell on them, that the horses were coal-black and splendid animals. They were driven by a tall man, with a great black hat and a scarf, which seemed to hide his face from us. I could only see the gleam of a pair of very bright eyes, which seemed red in the lamplight, as he turned to us. He said to the driver:

"You are early tonight, my friend." The man stammered in reply:

"The English Herr was in a hurry," to which the stranger replied:

"That is why, I suppose, you wished him to go on to Bukovina. You cannot deceive me, my friend; I know too much, and my horses are swift." As he spoke he smiled, and the lamplight fell on a hard-looking mouth, with very red lips and sharp-looking teeth, as white as ivory. One of my companions whispered to another the line from Burger's "Lenore": "Denn die Todten reiten schnell" ("For the dead travel fast").

The strange driver evidently heard the words, for he looked up with a gleaming smile. The passenger turned his face away, at the same time putting out his two fingers and crossing himself. "Give me the Herr's luggage," said the driver; and with exceeding alacrity my bags were handed out and put in the caleche. Then I descended from the side of the coach, as the caleche was close alongside, the driver helping me with a hand which caught my arm in a grip of steel; his strength must have been prodigious. Without a word he shook his reins, the horses turned, and we swept into the darkness of the pass. As I looked back I saw the steam from the horses of the coach by the light of the lamps, and projected against it the figures of my late companions crossing themselves. Then the driver cracked his whip and called to his horses, and off they swept on their way to Bukovina. As they sank into the darkness I felt a strange chill, and a lonely feeling came over me; but a cloak was thrown over my shoulders, and a rug across my knees, and the driver said in excellent German:

"The night is chill, mein Herr, and my master Drakulya bade me take all care of you. There is a flask of slivovitz (the plum brandy of the country) underneath the seat, if you should require it." I did not take any, but it was a comfort to know it was there all the same. I felt a little strangely, and not a little confused. I think had there been any alternative I might have taken it, instead of prosecuting that unknown night journey. The carriage went at a hard pace straight along, then we made a complete turn and went along another straight road. It seemed to me that we were simply going over and over the same ground again; and so I took note of some salient point, and found that this was so. I would have liked to have asked the driver what this all meant, but I really feared to do so, for I thought that, placed as I was, any protest would have had no effect in case there had been an intention to delay. By-and-by, however, as I was curious to know how time was passing, I struck a match, and by its flame looked at my watch; it was within a few minutes of midnight. This gave me a sort of chill, for I suppose the general superstition about midnight was increased by my recent experiences. I waited with a feeling of suspense.

Then a dog began to howl somewhere in a farmhouse far down the road—a long, agonized wailing, as if from fear. The sound was taken up by another dog, and then another and another, till, borne on the wind which now sighed softly through the pass, a wild howling began, which seemed to come from all over the country, as far as the imagination could grasp it through the gloom of the night. At the first howl the horses began to strain and rear, but the driver spoke to them soothingly, and they quieted down, but shivered and sweated as though after a runaway from the sudden fright.

Then, far off in the distance, from the mountains on each side of us began a louder and a sharper howling—that of wolves—which affected both the horses and myself in the same way—for I was minded to jump from the caleche and run, whilst they reared again and plunged madly, so that the driver had to use all his great strength to keep them from bolting. In a few minutes, however, my own ears got accustomed to the sound, and the horses so far became quiet that the driver was able to descend and to stand before them. He petted and soothed them, and whispered something in their ears, as I have heard of horse-tamers doing, and with extraordinary effect, for under his caresses they became quite manageable again, though they still trembled. The driver again took his seat, and shaking his reins, started off at a great pace. This time, after going to the far side of the pass, he suddenly turned down a narrow roadway which ran sharply to the right.

Soon we were hemmed in with trees, which in places arched right over the roadway till we passed as through a tunnel; and again great frowning rocks guarded us boldly on either side. Though we were in shelter, we could hear the rising wind, for it moaned and whistled through the rocks, and the branches of the trees crashed together as we swept along. It grew colder and colder still. The keen wind still carried the howling of the dogs, though this grew fainter as we went on our way. The baying of the wolves sounded nearer and nearer, as though they were closing round on us from every side. I grew anxious, and the horses shared my fear. The driver, however, was not in the least disturbed; he kept turning his head to left and right, but I could not see anything through the darkness.

Suddenly, way out on our left, I saw a faint flickering blue flame. The driver saw it at the same moment; he at once checked the horses, and, jumping to the ground, moved to where he could see my face. I pretended to sleep, cradling the flask of brandy in my arms. Satisfied that I was sound asleep, he slipped from his seat and disappeared into the darkness. I did not know what to do, the less so as the howling of the wolves grew closer; but while I wondered the driver suddenly appeared again, and without a word took his seat, and we resumed our journey.

I think I must have fallen asleep and kept dreaming of the same incident, for it seemed to be repeated endlessly. And now looking back, it is like a sort of nightmare. Once the flame appeared so near the road, that even in the darkness around us I could watch the driver's motions. He went rapidly to where the blue flame arose—it must have been very faint, for it did not seem to illumine the place around it at all—and gathering a few stones placed them into a bag he carried with him. Once there appeared a strange optical effect: when he picked up a stone, it began to burn in his hand with a ghostly flame. His fingers did not appear to obstruct it, for I could see its ghostly flicker all the same. This startled me, but as the effect was only momentary, I took it that my eyes deceived me straining through the darkness. Then for a time there were no blue flames, and we sped onwards through the gloom, with the howling of the wolves around us, as though they were following in a moving circle.

At last there came a time when the driver went further afield than he had yet gone, and during his absence, the horses began to tremble worse than ever and to snort and scream with fright. I could not see any cause for it, for the howling of the wolves had ceased altogether; but just then the moon, sailing through the black clouds, appeared behind the jagged crest of a beetling, pine-clad rock, and by its light I saw around us a ring of wolves, with white teeth and lolling red tongues, with long sinewy limbs and shaggy hair. They were a hundred times more terrible in the grim silence which held them than even when they howled. For myself, I felt a sort of paralysis of fear. It is only when a man feels himself face to face with such horrors that he can understand their true import.

All at once the wolves began to howl as though the moonlight had some peculiar effect on them. The horses jumped about and reared, and looked helplessly round with eyes that rolled in a way painful to see; but the living ring of terror encompassed them on every side; and they had perforce to remain within it. I called to the coachman to come, for it seemed to me that our only chance was to try to break out through the ring, and to aid his approach I shouted and beat the side of the caleche, hoping by the noise to scare the wolves from that side, so as to give him a chance of reaching the trap. How he came there, I know not, but I heard his voice raised in a growl of imperious command, and looking towards the sound, saw him stand in the roadway. As he swept his long arms, as though brushing aside some impalpable obstacle, the wolves fell back and back further still. Just then a heavy cloud passed across the face of the moon, so that we were again in darkness.

When I could see again, the driver was climbing into the caleche, and the wolves had disappeared. Not only this, but the driver had apparently lost his boots in the darkness—as I could see the whiteness of his feet and blood from various cuts on his soles as he stepped up into his seat. In his rush to return to the coach he had no doubt cut his feet on the stones. This was all so strange that confusion came upon me, and I was afraid to speak or move. The time seemed interminable as we swept on our way, now in almost complete darkness, for the rolling clouds obscured the moon. We kept on ascending, with occasional periods of quick descent, but in the main always ascending. Suddenly, I became conscious of the fact that the driver was in the act of pulling up the horses in the courtyard of a vast ruined castle, from whose tall black windows came no ray of light, and whose broken battlements showed a jagged line against the moonlit sky.

"You fastened yourself on me to have easy times and grow fat on my life blood, I tell you. Was that it? I believe you are the greatest miser in the world, or else why . . . ?"
"No. I am only poor," interrupted Captain Whalley.
—*The End of the Tether*, Joseph Conrad

13

On the night of St. George's Eve, 1889, I took Jonathan Harker into my home. He was my guest. Nay, he was my friend! But he soon became my betrayer—the Judas Iscariot who spurned my hospitality and finally even attempted to take my life; I still carry the scar on my forehead! But on this night I welcomed him to my castle, my hand held out to him in greeting.

"Welcome to my house! Enter freely and of your own will!"

I grasped his hand warmly, but he looked uneasy.

"Welcome to my home! Come freely. Go safely. And leave a little something of your happiness with me when you go."

"Count Dracula?" he said, thus Anglicizing the pronunciation of my name. I bowed politely.

"You may call me Drakulya. I bid you welcome, Mr. Harker, to my home. Come in. The night air is chill, and you should eat and rest." I carried his baggage, over his protest. "Nay, sir," I said, "you are my guest. It is late. My servants are not available. Let me see to your comfort myself."

I carried his bags through the long passageway to his bedroom and left him there to perform his toilet. In the next room I, meanwhile, prepared his meal: salad, some goat cheese, a plate of roast chicken—seasoned lightly with paprika—and a bottle of white wine.

After he had dined, I offered him a cigar, though not taking one myself—I do not smoke—and we relaxed in the large, red velvet cloth chairs near the fireplace. We talked long into the night. I had a thousand and one questions about his trip, about the many difficulties of travel in a foreign land. And about London.

"I have come to know your great country through these books, Herr Harker," gesturing to the library shelves, thickly packed with books of every kind—politics, history, botany, law—and dozens of newspapers. "They have given me many hours of pleasure. I long to pass through the crowded streets of mighty London, to enter the whirling rush of humanity—to share its life, its change, its death. I soon shall be among the huddled masses. I will pass through the streets to enter the lighted chambers set for dining. The theatre, the halls for dancing, the evening parties—these will be mine in the night!" I paused to refill his wine glass. "But in the day-time, then my young friend, I fear that I will be as nothing, a mere foreigner—a stranger in a new land."

As we talked late into the night, and well into the early morning hours, I asked Harker about his fiancee, Miss Mina, and about his family and the origin of the name Harker. "It signifies," I suggested, "one who goes before . . . a herald, a kind of John the Baptist. Or perhaps it alludes to the cock, the herald of the morning, which has its origin in the word gallu, gaullus, gaul, gules or gull." This notion seemed to puzzle him, and he quickly changed the topic of conversation.

I noted that this Jonathan Harker had a quality of genuine, child-like honesty about him that was quite refreshing. Though common in his taste and opinions, his eyes suggested something below the mere surface of a middle-class English solicitor. Each time he spoke of his fiancee, Mina, I knew from his expression that he did indeed love her with all the emotion with which he was able. He did love her, though not in the way I did. It was this that made us true friends, although he did not yet know it. I felt close to him, through her. And in the last minutes before dawn, while he described for me the pleasures of London night-life, I quite innocently allowed my hand to come to rest on his arm.

Suddenly there came across his features a look of bewilderment as he drew back from my touch. At that moment we heard the distant roll of thunder, followed by the howling of wolves—"Listen to them—the Children of the Night—they are riding on the thunder-claps. They weep in the darkness. They are so lonely, so very alone. And yet . . . would you like to see them. To hear them. What music they make! Do you hear them? Do you hear?"

His eyes traveled to the window.

"Ah, sir, you dwellers in the city cannot enter into the passions of the hunter." He looked at me, a curious expression on his face. "But you must be tired. Your bedroom is ready, and you shall sleep as late as you wish. I have to be away on business until evening; so sleep well and dream well!"

I brought Harker to his room; and through the window I could see the horizon as the sun's red canopy thrust itself above the trees of the Carpathian mountains, silhouetted by wispy clouds.

————————————

"Go and give your cousin a kiss," said my mother, as I came into the drawing room. I went obediently up and she drew me towards her; but at the sight of her bare shoulder and its dazzling whiteness, some sort of craziness possessed me; fascinated by her dazzling shoulder, I gave it a great bite with my teeth. My cousin screamed with pain and I with horror. She began to bleed and I to spit with disgust.
—*If It Die,* Andre Gide

14

Even though there are times when I can lose myself in pure instinct, I can do so only under certain conditions. It is only at night, after the sun goes below the horizon, that I can really feel myself exempt from all my cares and escape the powers of the world. At night, when the wind calls me to explore the darkness, I can free myself from consciousness and roam the dark fields with the undiluted joy of a simple creature of the night.

But when the sun once again begins to appear on the horizon and the cock crows to announce the coming of the dawn, I feel the burden of life begin once more to oppress me. During the day I am bound by my social self, cordial and easy-going, lacking the will to be anything more than a man. The anxieties that result from my commerce with men cannot compare to the pleasures that greet me in my dark solitude. When I am among men, I know that my real life has passed; I am constantly aware that I am leading an un-dead existence.

When I am among men, I must think and act as a man. For if I were to reveal myself to be one of the living dead during the day-time, when my vast powers are at their lowest ebb, I would quickly be destroyed—seized by a mob of angry peasants and dropped on the nearest sharpened pale. It is for this reason alone that I allow myself to be abused by others. This offering-up of myself, at a time when my powers are no greater than those of any ordinary man, is to me more frightening than any of the dangers of my night-time existence.

It is only during the day that I feel endangered by mankind. Luckily, the peasants of my country believe that the un-dead are bound to the hours of the night-time. They believe that if the rays of the sun should strike me, I would be utterly destroyed. Little do they know that it was I, and I alone, who originated this belief. Little do they realize that it was I, Drakulya, who first circulated this story almost two centuries ago.

The peasants ardently believe in this and countless other silly superstitions about the un-dead. They no doubt feel secure in their beliefs, and I, in my own way, help reinforce these beliefs at every opportunity. They do not even suspect that it was I who created the rules for this child's game and that I can break those rules at any time I choose.

Yet I do not break my rules. I respect my law and do not overstep the bounds I have set for myself as I search for prey. Because of my respect for these limits, I have engendered in the peasants a careful respect for my law—a respect not untainted by fear. There are few people in my country who would dare to leave the safety of their hovels after dark. Those that venture out after sun-down know that they risk a rather unpleasant encounter with a stranger who will ask of them, "Have you aught to quench my thirst?"

Often when I go out among men I find myself drawn to the most crowded streets and the most brilliantly lighted houses. I go there seeking warmth, and I often find it. And when I go to parties I often teach my new friends to drink deep before I depart. The enjoyment I get from large crowds is perhaps not so hard to understand. Sometimes as I walk through the crowds, I see, out of the corner of my eye, someone in the crowd I seem to remember. I detect amazing resemblances to people I once knew, people now long dead. I realize that all of this may be merely an illusion that my mind is creating in order to bridge the gap between myself and my past. Of late, finding the features of the dead in the faces of the living has become a common occurrence.

Joseph has with him in his sarcophagus two white and silver cruets, filled with the blood and sweat of the prophet Jesus.
—*Historia de Rebus Britannicus,* Maelgwyn of Avalon

15

On the evening of his arrival, I had, disguised as a servant, driven my calash to Borgo Pass to fetch Jonathan from his coach. As we traveled along through the deserted forest that evening, Harker had seen the ghost-flame along the side of the road. When he asked about it the next evening, I told him of the legends of St. George's Eve, when pieces of buried Szygny gold are said to push themselves up through the crust of soil and give off a phosphorescent silverish glow, like that of St. Elmo's fire.

Disguised as a coachman, I had driven Harker to my castle. And during the long trip, I had stopped several times while he slept to gather up the gold in a blanket and hide it under the seat of the calash. Now, in the morning light, I lifted the moist and heavy bundle onto the table and untied the corners of the wolfskin blanket. Inside the blanket, covered with bits of black earth and rotten wood, was a heaped-up pile of gold, my new found treasure—Romany gold once used by the Hapsburgs and Romanoffs to pay their assassins, *In Specie*, and later captured by the Szekely and buried in the forest, where it lay forgotten. Until the ghost-flame revealed it to me through the darkness.

I, myself, have seen this curious flame before. Many years ago, an army decimated the city of Amlas and a huge pit was dug as a common grave for the dead. I helped carry the corpses to the pit. At night the death pit was illuminated in just such a way, as the rotting corpses gave off gaseous putrefactions that burned with a pure blue flame.

A dozen years later I came back to the blood-soaked soil of Amlas. On the night of St. George's Eve, I wandered out to the mass grave and searched for the ghost flame. Just as the legend said, I found the treasure—Gules on a field d'Argent. For only the soil made sacred by the blood of innocence can bear the tears of the Children of the Night. Blood where there is no blood, tears lighted by spiritual fire and flame, wolves prowling in darkness, and, of course, the dead.

*Anything approaching the change that came over his features I have
never seen before and hope never to see again. Oh I wasn't touched. I
was fascinated. It was as though a veil had been rent. I saw on that ivory
face the expression of somber pride, of ruthless power, of craven terror—of
an intense and hopeless despair. Did he live his life again in every detail
of desire, temptation, and surrender during that supreme moment of
complete knowledge? He cried out in a whisper at some image, at some
vision. He cried out twice, a cry that was no more than a breath.
"The horror! The horror!"*
—*Heart of Darkness*, Joseph Conrad

16

Eventually we came around to discuss the terms of the purchase
of the estate at Purfleet. This, after all, was the purpose for
Harker's visit. When I asked him how he had found such a place,
he said, "In Purfleet, at a cross-road, I found the type of place you
described to Mr. Hawkins. The estate is called Carfax Abbey and
dates from about the 13th century. It contains, in all, some twenty
acres, completely surrounded by a high wall built of heavy stone
and in serious need of repair. The gates are of heavy old oak and
fretted with iron-work, all eaten through with rust. The house is
quite large and was, in medieval times, a monastery with a large
bell tower of stone that is immensely thick, with few windows and
those heavily barred with iron cross-pieces. It adjoins the chapel."
He handed me a description, adding, "The house has been added
to, over the years. There are few houses close at hand, one being
an old tuberculosis sanitorium only recently formed into a private
lunatic asylum."

I replied, "I am glad that it is old and big, and that there is a
chapel from the old times. You have done well, Harker. It is just
as I visualized it. There I may find a final resting place among the
blessed dead. We love not to think of our bones lying with the
common dead. We Szekely are a close race; we have the strength

of all the dead ones who live in us. The race of the Szekely have a long and glorious history, Herr Harker."

I handed him a mug of hot rum, mixed with egg-batter and sprinkled with ground nutmeg, and we walked over to the large chairs near the fireplace. "The Szekely are the descendants of Roman frontier soldiers, the 'Beyonders'—the guardians whose duty it was to defend the borders of the Empire from the invading armies. It was they who turned back the double-headed axe of the Ugric tribes—the Norse Berserkers who fought with the fury of the were-wolf. It was the Szekely who shattered the ranks of Attila the Hun, fighting with lance and shield against the heavy battle mace of the Golden Horde. Ah, young sir, after the fall of Constantinople, the Szekely—and the Drakulya as their heart's blood, their brains, their swords—were all that stood between the sickle blades of the Sultan Mohammed and the throats of Western Christendom." I handed him a new history of the East that I had just brought back from Bucharest. "The Turkish army was like a mighty river swollen with spring rains, which, if it finds any breach, pours through in torrents of destruction. But when the army of the Sultan came upon the Drakulya he found a force equal to his. But not in numbers, no, for the Sultan's army outnumbered the soldiers of the Drakulya many times over. No, my dear Harker, the soldiers of the Drakulya were their equals because they fought as free men, whereas the Turks are a gang of slaves."

Pointing to the portrait of my brother over the fireplace, I continued, "And it was one Vlad Drakulya, the Kaziklu Bey—the Impaler—who struck terror into the hearts of the Turks, attacking their camp in the dark of night, in what they came to call the 'Night of the Terror.' He drove his cavalry into the heart of the enemy, like a foaming wave, up to the very tents of the Sultan. It was only the foolhardy courage of a few of the Sultan's men that stopped the Drakulya from taking the Sultan in his tent." Placing my hand on the mantle, I turned away from Harker, in a purely theatrical gesture. "When the Turks recovered from this shock, they rallied and drove back the Drakulya. When morning came they set out in pursuit of this Drakulya to the outskirts of his capital of Targoviste. And there they came upon such horrors as to make strong men quail, for the city was a scorched and

smoking ruin, everything of value carried away—the wells
poisoned, the crops destroyed—and far worse . . . they found in a
meadow before the gates a forest of wooden stakes, and impaled
on the stakes were twenty thousands of captured Turkish soldiers,
along with the rotting corpse of the Sultan's ambassador, Hamsa
Pasha Bey of Nicopolis."

I brushed a streak of dust from the frame of the portrait. "When
the Sultan saw the black birds wheeling in a dark cloud over the
forest of stakes, it is said that fear entered his heart, as he
abandoned the pursuit to his generals and fled. Meanwhile, the
Impaler retreated to his castle high up in the Carpathians. The
Sultan's army pursued him there and laid siege to his castle. After
many months the defenders were on the verge of starvation, and
finally surrendered. Although not before Prince Vlad escaped over
the mountains into Transylvania."

I turned to Harker, who swallowed the last of his drink. "This
Vlad Drakulya returned many years later to again fight the Turks
and was himself finally slain and his severed head taken to the
Sultan as a trophy. Yes, my friend Harker, this was a Drakulya
indeed!" With a grimace, Harker interrupted. "But he killed thousands of people . . . he was a monster . . ."

I handed him a history book written by the Hungarian,
Arminius Vambery, and published in London. "No, my friend. He
is that Drakulya about whom the Germans tell such tales of his
terrible cruelties, which are merely empty lies told to frighten
children. But, in fact, he was the greatest of Christian knights, in
battle most awesome, and is worthy to be the subject of a true
history, his having been the sole support of his countrymen
against the invading Turks; and on the day of his death, in battle
with the Infidel, he slew sixty-five Turks before being treacher-
ously slain by three assassins disguised as his own men!"

My voice wavered. "I can assure you of one thing, Herr Harker,
Drakulya's countrymen do not think of him as the monster you
describe. He is a national hero, a legend. It is believed by many
of the peasants that Drakulya still lives, in an enchanted castle
high up in the Carpathians, while others say that Drakulya's grave
is in the mountains and that he has gone into the next world,
where he was healed of his wounds and restored by a life-giving

drink given to him by the Queen of Death, so that he could become king among the dead; but all agree that someday, when his nation is in the hour of its greatest peril, he will again return from that place to which he has gone, and he will again be alive."

I am the bread of life . . . I am that living bread, which came down out of heaven: if any man eat of this bread he shall live for ever; yea, and the bread which I will give is my flesh, for the life of the world. . . . Except ye eat the flesh of the Son of Man and drink his blood, ye have not life in yourselves. He that eateth my flesh and drinketh my blood hath eternal life; and I will raise him up at the last day. For my flesh is true meat, and my blood is true drink. He that eateth my flesh and drinketh my blood abideth in me and I in him.
—John 6:48-56.

17

The next night, we finished our meal and in the late evening I took Harker into my library to show him some of my most prized possessions. "Here, for example, is a fine little book on Glastonbury. The author claims to tell the secret of the Holy Grail. But like all pretenders to secret wisdom, she has mistaken the thing for what it contains. After all, what is the value of a blessed vessel, if it does not contain the sacred blood of Christ? It is the blood that is important, not the thing that holds it. It is always the blood that is important. Remember that, my friend.

"And here, my friend Harker, is a magazine with the latest lecture of your great scholar, Walter Pater. Granted that he is discerning, but like the author of the book on Glastonbury, he has managed to grasp only a part of the truth. His lecture 'A Study of Dionysus' is quite clever, and he appears even at times to suggest that he knows the truth, but he really only touches the hem of Truth. He tantalizes us, he mocks us. Does he know the secret? Is he simply guessing? How could he know?

"Take for example this reference to the poplar, the oak-tree and the pine, who are as nurses to the infant Dionysus, who is 'the spirit of fire and dew.' Now what can we make of this? And the miracle of the sacred water which flows from the smitten rock? How are we to take this? And his reference to the Pythian oracle and the coffin of Dionysus that was kept nearby, as the giver of ecstacy? Does he suspect that the Holy Grail and the coffin of Dionysus were instruments with a common purpose? And likewise the coffin of Osiris? If he were to know these things, then he would be truly wise—a marvel to all who heard his words.

"Has he studied the ancient Welsh legends? Does he know of Bran the Blessed? Has he made a study of the Holy Book? Does he know that the Prophetic Head of Moses was of the same nature as the Blessed Head worshipped by the Templars?

"He states here that Dionysus drank the blood of goats, he sprang from the dead body of Semele and was nourished in the thigh of Zeus. Can one read these things and still not understand? How can men today, who have based their science and philosophy, their government, and even their literature on the inventions of the ancient Greeks—how can modern men believe that the Greeks would say such things of Dionysus unless these same Greeks had witnessed these things with their own eyes?

"Truly, it has been said by a wiser man than I, that those who know the great secrets do not tell, and those who offer to tell secrets do not know. And those who might, like the ancient Greeks, speak openly of the great secrets are not believed, for to believe might bring madness. . . . Ah, my friend, some things must always be hidden from mankind.

"But the greatest secret of all lies below us, hidden in the darkest vault of my castle. It is best we leave it hidden there, forgotten, like those Knights who placed it here so long ago. Yes, my friend, of what purpose is the Grail, except to hold the sacred blood. . . . To what purpose is my life, except to serve that great secret?

"One day I will find one who is worthy, one who can bear this secret after I am gone. Like Keats' famous urn, I too the unravished, may then be ravished by death. And return again to the dust from which I was made."

What was bothering M., what he strongly opposed, was "putting the dead
in civilian clothing," as he accused James Whale of having done in
Frankenstein, "making the fruit of the grave dress just like you and I."
He wanted to show the skin graftings, the putrefactions all over G.'s
white-horrid body, and not alone for their shock value either. "Perhaps I
was thinking of your Herman Melville."
—*The Late Great Creature*, Brock Brower

18

The next evening, remembering that I would have to see to the comfort of my guest, I went to his bedchamber. I found him standing in front of a table, wearing his pants and an undershirt, his suspenders hanging limply to each side. He was bent over a basin of cold water and was scraping the cold lather from his face with a straight razor.

I came up behind him, placed my hand on his shoulder, and started to speak. But before I could utter a word, I saw hanging on the wall a small pocket mirror. I stopped, startled by an object whose presence I had banned from the castle many years before. But after my initial shock and annoyance, I looked into the mirror. There I saw something I had managed to avoid for many years. I saw, reflected in the glass, my own face.

When I came up behind Harker and saw my face reflected in the mirror, I was overcome by a sense of disgust. It was not the face I once had, as my features changed greatly after I died. Rather I saw myself as what I had become: I saw the face of my brother, Vlad. After his death, I had become Vlad, and the memory of the monster that he really was came rushing in, filling me with contempt and loathing. I am not that man, and the possibility of his existing today—living in the same world that I live in—filled me with rage.

I pulled Harker toward me, and my hand went to his throat. As his body was wrenched to face me, I saw that Harker had nicked himself with the razor and blood was flowing quite freely down his neck. And I changed my mind.

But at that moment my hand brushed the silver chain around his throat and a crucifix fell out of his shirt. I turned away from it, but not in time. For the sensations came to me again of what it was like to die. Frustrated, I snatched the small pocket mirror, turned to the window, and hurled it out, while giving some pointless excuse about the vanity of mirrors, and watched as it fell into the chasm below, shattering on the rocks into a thousand tiny fragments.

Harker was shocked, and I relieved. His face revealed his horror and I stuggled to retain my composure. I returned to my room then, muttering an oath and planning revenge. Harker would soon learn the secret of Castle Drakulya. But it was a secret that he would purchase with his soul.

In time Harker would become one with me, body and soul, so that he would call upon me as "lord, lord" and I would answer him "my son, my son," as I will have begotten him as my true son. His earthly father will be of no importance to him; only I, his true father, will be able to claim him.

One sees, too, how large Joseph of Arimathea now looms in the fabulous history of Britain. . . . Richard Bere, who became abbot of Glastonbury in 1493, raised the ceiling of the crypt under St. Mary's chapel, which occupied the site of the old church of wattles, and dedicated the subterranean chapel to St. Joseph. A stone image of the patron was set up, and pilgrims resorted thither in great numbers. A new coat of arms was adopted: on a white field, sprinkled with blood drops, is set a green 'raguly' cross, and beneath the arms of the cross are the two cruets of St. Joseph.
—*The Grail*, Roger Loomis

19

From Jonathan Harker's Journal

10 May, Morning. After my journey to the castle, I did not report the strange behaviour of the coachman to his master. After all, I planned to return to Borgo Pass and did not feel I could risk offending the coachman. Now, however, I begin to suspect that the Count was himself the coachman, for since my arrival here I have seen absolutely no other servants. I believe the Count lives here alone and deliberately misled me.

The Count is a very peculiar man. He spends most of the evening lecturing me on history or asking me questions about London. This has all been very trying for me, staying up all night and sleeping only a fitful and restless sleep during the daylight hours, until I am unsure of myself and what I am doing here. What is most peculiar is that one evening after showing the Count a small photo of my fiancee, Mina Murray, I placed the photo in my wallet and returned it to my room. But the next evening the photo had disappeared. I mean to ask the Count to return it, but I have difficulty, dependent as I am on his good will and afraid to risk his displeasure. This strange event, combined with others, including the Count's terrible fury last night and the destruction of my pocket mirror, lead me to wonder if I have fallen into some sort of trap.

For the last several days I have been ill. I suspected food poisoning and complained vigorously to the Count—to no avail. I wonder that a man of such wealth cannot afford to get fresh meat from the local peasants.

At sunset I came up from my room to find the Count sitting in his great chair, gazing at the photograph of Mina. I asked for its return, but he simply laughed and said that his was the greater need—he would keep the photo. Overcome with anger and frustration, I went to the dining room and ate alone. Thank God no lecture tonight.

12 May, Later. Tonight. I cannot write the unspeakable. The horror of this place. And him. The Fiend. He has put something into my food. And this is not the first night. I know that now, for tonight I became ill after supper and went to my room where I disgorged the whole mess of his pottage into my bedpan. I was dizzy and ill, and I fell back on my bed in exhaustion as a chill came over me and a cold sweat broke out on my skin. I was lying on my back when the fiend entered my room, quietly at first and then moving to my bed like a sudden rush of cold air. I could not resist him as he grabbed my nose and forced a noxious potion down my throat. I struggled weakly, but I could not overcome his irresistible grip. Within moments I felt the poison take effect as my limbs began to jerk uncontrollably. I wanted to vomit, but he held me helpless on the bed. Soon the room began to spin and I blacked out. When next I woke, he was gone. This was no dream.

He had left me alone in my room. After a little while, not hearing any sound, I came out and went up the stone stair to where I could look out towards the South. There was some sense of freedom in the vast expanse, inaccessible though it was to me, as compared with the narrow darkness of the courtyard. Looking out on this, I felt that I was indeed in prison, and I seemed to want a breath of fresh air, though it were of the night. I feel this nocturnal existence tell on me. It is destroying my nerve. I start at my own shadow, and am full of all sorts of horrible imaginings. God knows that there is ground for my terrible fear in this accursed place! I looked out over the beautiful expanse, bathed in soft yellow moonlight till it was almost as light as day. In the soft light the distant hills melted with the shadows in the valleys and gorges of velvety blackness. The mere beauty seemed to cheer me; there was peace and comfort in every breath I drew. As I leaned from the window my eye was caught by something moving a story below me, and somewhat to my left, where I imagined, from the order of the rooms, that the windows of Drakulya's own room would look out. The window at which I stood was tall and deep, stone-mullioned, and though the stones were weatherworn, it was still complete; but it was evidently many a day since the wooden casement had been there. I drew back behind the stonework, and looked carefully out.

What I saw was the Count's head coming out from a window below me. I did not see the face, but I knew the man by the neck and the movement of his back and arms. In any case I could not mistake the hands which I had so many opportunities of studying while listening to his lectures—a habit I retain from my school days. I was at first interested and somewhat amused, for it is wonderful how small a matter will interest and amuse a man when he is a prisoner. But my feeling of curiosity changed to repulsion and terror when I saw the whole man slowly emerge from the window and begin to crawl down the castle wall over that dreadful abyss! He was face down with his cloak spread out around him like great wings. At first I could not believe my eyes. I thought it was some trick of the moonlight, some weird effect of shadow; but I kept looking, and it could be no delusion. I saw the fingers and toes grasp the corners of the stones, worn clear of the mortar by the stress of years, and by thus using every projection and inequality move downwards with considerable speed, just as a lizard moves along a wall.

What manner of man is this, or what manner of creature is it in the semblance of man? I feel the dread of this horrible place overpowering me; I am in fear—in awful fear—and there is no escape for me; I am encompassed about with terrors that I dare not think of . . . . But then the greatest horror of all. The Greek wine that he gave me earlier began to churn in the pit of my stomach—my whole abdomen stretched and twisted—and I found myself leaning against the window as if to retch, and then moving my whole body out the window, so that I myself was climbing down the wall after him. As we came to ground I saw him transform, with his face becoming a wolfish muzzle, and I too as my nails became claws and I went on all fours as part of his pack. We went down the valley after the sheep, and we fell on them and tore their bodies with our teeth. The taste of blood was good, mixed with wool and flesh.

I woke the next morning in my own bed. I began crying, for the first time in many years. God! God! God! Why have you forsaken me!

Later. I endorse the last words written; this time there is no doubt in question of what I saw. I shall not fear to sleep in any

place where he is not. I had placed the crucifix over the head of
my bed—I imagined that my rest would thus be freer from dreams;
and there it has remained. But I had not imagined that my
nightmares had all too real a cause.

---

*From its wounds there fell upon the snow three red drops of blood. These
brought Parzival great distress, from the trueness of his love. When he
saw the blood-drops on the snow which was so white, he thought, "Who
created this color so pure? Condwiramurs, this color does in truth
resemble you. . . . Condiwiramures, here lies your image, for the snow
offered the blood its whiteness, and the blood reddens the snow.*
—*Parzival,* Wolfram Von Eschenback

20

I drew the nets slowly, very slowly around Harker as he struggled
helplessly to escape and finally was forced to turn in on himself,
like a starving wolf who chews his own paws for the mere taste of
blood. The time was drawing near; he had found the doors
throughout the castle locked against him—no exit, save for the
shear face of the castle wall and the chasm below.

"My dear Harker, have you written to Mr. Peter Hawkins since
your first letter?"

"No, I have not."

"Or to any other?"

"No, no one. I have written to no man since I wrote to Mr.
Hawkins."

"Or no woman either?"

"No, I have said so."

"Very well," putting a hand on his shoulder, "then write, my
young friend, to your employer and to your beautiful fiancee, Miss

Mina, and say that you will remain here with me for another month."

"Do you wish me to stay?"

"I desire it. It suits my needs that you should remain with me. Is this not understood in my agreement with your employer? Indeed, it shall be so." Harker could not refuse, although his face betrayed his true feelings on the matter. His horror and disappointment were evident in every line of his face.

"I pray you, Herr Harker, in your letters speak only of our business. I am a private man, and I value my privacy above all." And handing him the blank paper, "It will no doubt please your friends to know that you are well. Is it not so? And that you look forward to getting home to them."

He sat at the desk and wrote his letters, as I requested, while I wrote also to my bankers in Buda-Pesth and to Herr Luetner in Varna, the owner of the ship "Demeter." When he finished I collected his letters and said, "Forgive me, but I have much to do this evening and tomorrow. You may use your time as you will. But be advised, my young friend—nay, let me warn you. Do not leave your rooms or by any chance go to other parts of the castle that I leave unused . . . I fear that parts of the castle are infested by rats. It is not safe." I closed the door behind me and went to my own rooms. Once there, I opened the letter to his fiancee. It was clear and straightforward, stating his wish to see her soon. The letter to his employer was more convoluted:

Mr. Peter Hawkins
Exeter

Dear Sir,

I have nearly completed the arrangements for Count Drakulya's purchase of Carfax Abbey in Purfleet. I hope to soon be leaving for Bistritz and hope to be able to see you soon.

Please give my love to Mina when you next see her. I am sure that you recall all the obligations you owe her, as I am honoring mine to you. I hope too that your gout is much better and that you are getting about and able to travel. I look forward to seeing you soon.

Best Wishes,
Jonathan Harker

Tucked neatly into the folds of this letter was a small note written in some strange cryptographic hand that I was unable to decipher. So I destroyed the note and replaced the letter to Hawkins in its envelope. I placed the letter to Mina and the letter to her step-father, Mr. Hawkins, in the post the next day.

Several days passed, and Harker's voice could no longer conceal his growing anxiety, an anxiety reflected in his letter. I found the evidence of his search—doors left ajar, the dust of many years disturbed. Finally the time was right. I left a single door unlocked, a door leading to a part of the castle that he had not yet explored.

Artists of the early and mid-Victorian period were not great respecters of persons. In their quest for knowledge of anatomy, a group of artists including Gibson went grave robbing. They came across, recorded Gibson, a "very beautiful girl about sixteen; her face was full and round. How sweet and innocent she looked in death! She was shrouded in white linen and sprinkled over with bits of red wool like flowers."
—*The Worm in the Bud*, R. Pearsall

21

It was to my purpose to introduce Jonathan Harker to the secrets of the Order of the Dragon. This was the military order to which my father once belonged, though in recent years a "new" Order has been resurrected from the ashes of the old—this New Order of the Dragon is little more than an aristocratic social club changed remarkably in its purpose and methods from the old Order—no longer a military order in any sense, but now having something more in common with a mystical order like the Lesser Mysteries of the Children of Knossus—an exotically austere society into which I, myself, had been initiated while living in

Paris during the last century, some years before my retreat into the Carpathian mountains—nor was the New Order unlike some religious societies, like that of the Brothers of the White & Rosy Cross, whose main rituals involve chewing the red petals of a rose and the white petals and green buds of the poppy, in an elaborate ceremony, with the incarnation of the Thrice-Greatest-Hermes in the form of a high priestess of Thoth thrown in for dramatic effect.

The day finally arrived. I found him wandering aimlessly along a stone passageway. Past the private rooms, he had ventured down the long, circular stairway and through the underground tunnel to the old chapel. There in the ancient chapel were fifty great wooden boxes of earth.

I came up behind him as he stood in the doorway and took him by the arm. "The time has arrived, Herr Harker, for you to see the great secret that you were sent here to discover, to see the secret with which I have been entrusted for so many years." I then gestured to the boxes that lay before us. "The contents of these boxes were brought to this land centuries ago, shortly before the fall of Constantinople, and the secret of their location entrusted to a few crusader princes, warriors like Janos Hunyadi, Drakul of Wallachia, and a few others. These boxes were brought here from their hiding places some years after the Turks seized Constantinople and here they have remained for all these many years. They represent a sacred trust that has fallen to me to protect. It was a precarious trust, for this region is plagued by wars and rumors of wars. But the latest invasion of the Balkans by the armies of the Czar has convinced me that these remains must be transported to a safe country."

Harker's expression was strained. I continued, "Do you know, Herr Harker, that there has been no successful invasion of England since 1066 by Prince William the Conqueror. Ah, yes. You see, I am a student of history."

Harker's eyes traveled to the windows and to the gate and the stairway to the crypts. He said, "But why all of this? Why?"

Before us lay fifty boxes. Some of them were quite old—brought away from Constantinople by The Order of the Dragon before the city fell to the Turks. My brother Vlad had stolen these boxes from the Order before his death and hidden them here in the

mountains in this old forgotten fortress. And to the original
number, I had added three dozen more.

I led Harker by the arm to the box that lay nearest us. "Do you
wish to see what treasure was brought away from Byzantium
before its fall? Do you wish to see the prize of Menelaus? To see
the secrets for which so many thousands have died? Tell me, Herr
Harker, is she not beautiful? Would not any man wish to have her
kiss him as she will?"

I lifted the lid of the box so that he could see its contents quite
clearly. An inexpressible look of recognition passed over his features. He gave a low moan, turning away his face from the sight.
I gripped his arm to steady him. "Yes, here they are. Look upon
them here where they lie. They sleep yet, my dear Harker, but
you may look upon them as you wish—there is no harm in this."
I led him like a child to the next box and opened it. "You have
looked upon the daughter, chaste and fair. Here lies her mother,
Brunissande." He covered his face with his hands. "And there," I
pointed to a far box, "a sister, the dark and beautiful Stephania
l'Amoureuse, whose black hair is such that she could tempt St.
Michael from his heavenly perch were he to look upon her."

I brought him to her also, and began to raise the lid, but the
look on Harker's face was enough to convince me that he was not
ready for so great a shock to his sense. "This one, my friend,
bears a remarkable resemblance to your beautiful fiancee, Miss
Mina. You may look upon her, or you may not, as you will. Here,
I will hold your arm to steady you. . . . Do you wish to look? No,
indeed you do not. It is just as well. However there is one more
here that you should look at in order to truly understand the
importance of what you have seen."

I led Harker to a nearby box, one of the original dozen brought
here from Constantinople. I lifted the lid of the box and Harker
looked at the bearded face covered with a mask of beaten gold.
"You may count yourself among the very few, dear Harker. You
are among the chosen. For this is the body of Jeshua ben Joseph,
the Prophet of Many Names. His was the body figured in the
famous Shroud of Turin."

There was, of course, one slight ommission in the Shroud, as
this corpse, like all the others in this crypt, bears the same cross-

shaped wounds on the breast. Harker started like a frightened deer, "Surely not . . . it can't be." In answer, I took Harker's arm by the wrist and thrust it into the box so that he could feel the wound in the side, and thus confirm his discipleship with his own hand. Harker could no longer doubt the truth of his senses.

I led Harker then over to the last box, number 49, and slowly raised the lid. There lay the remains of Vlad Drakulya, Prince of Wallachia, my brother. I had stolen his corpse from his grave many years ago. The signs of the funeral pyre were still evident as the fingers and toes were little more than charred stubs. Keeping his corpse here, among the blessed dead, was a mistake. But I was both foolish and sentimental—I could not bring myself to finish the cremation begun four hundred years ago. I had taken his identity, but I could not bring myself to destroy Vlad's corpse.

Harker's reaction to the dessicated flesh was predictable. He reached a spot near the wall and, leaning against it, vomited. A few minutes later I took his arm.

"Now you have seen what your employer, Mr. Hawkins, sent you to see, my friend. In a few days you will leave my home, never to return. You may describe for Mr. Hawkins and those he works for all that you have seen here. By then it will make no real difference, for I will be gone. But I would take care and speak to no one else of what you have seen here. Not knowing you, they might think you mad."

I released my hold on his arm, as he turned away and stumbled toward the stairs. Lowering the lid of the box, I soon followed him, locking the heavy doorway to his apartments.

Harker found his way to the rooms in a remote part of the castle, a bedchamber that had once belonged to my wife, Helena. It was here that I found him asleep. I left him there and returned to the crypt.

*Now though the magic horn of Bran, translated as the "cors" of the
Fisher King, could be taken, and was taken, to refer to the corpse of the
Fisher King, it could also be interpreted as the body in possession or
keeping of the Fisher King. What if the body was the most sacred of all
bodies, that of the crucified Christ? Then it was a reasonable inference
that the Fisher King was Joseph of Arimathea, who according to
Scripture begged for the body of Christ, took it down from the cross, and
kept it in his sepulchre until the third day.*
                              —*The Grail,* Roger Loomis

22

From Jonathan Harker's Journal

16 May, Later. God preserve my sanity, for to this I am reduced.
Safety and the assurance of safety are things of the past. Whilst I
live on here there is but one thing to hope for, that I may not go
mad, if, indeed, I be not mad already. If I be sane, then surely it
is maddening to think that, of all the foul things that lurk in this
hateful place, the Count is the least dreadful to me; that to him
alone I can look for safety, even though this be only whilst I can
serve his purpose. Great God! Merciful God! Let me be calm, for
out of that way lies madness indeed. I begin to get new lights on
certain things which have puzzled me. Up to now I never quite
knew what Shakespeare meant when he made Juliet say to
Romeo:

"Take here this Tablet with this ribbon strung,
And see it still about thy bosom hung—
By whose eternal virtue never fear
To suffer thus again, nor perish here, etc."

For now, feeling as though my own brain were unhinged or as if the shock had come which must end in its undoing, I turn to my diary for repose. The habit of entering accurately must help to soothe me.

The Count's mysterious warning, that I avoid the East wing of the Castle at all cost, frightened me at the time; it frightens me more now when I think of it. Because of my defiance he may dare even more. He has a deadly hold upon me.

The Count was absent from the castle on some business and I had, out of a perverse desire, wandered into the East wing of the castle and entered a private room by forcing the door latch with a piece of wire I had found earlier that evening. I sat on the bed, a bed that apparently belonged to a young woman in ages past.

When I had written in my diary and had fortunately replaced the book and pen in my pocket, I began to feel sleepy. The Count's warning came into my mind, but I took a pleasure in disobeying it. The sense of sleep was upon me, and with it the obstinacy which sleep brings as an outrider. The soft moonlight soothed, and the wide expanse without gave a sense of freedom which refreshed me. I determined not to return to-night to the gloom-haunted rooms, but to sleep here, where, of old, ladies had sat and sung and lived sweet lives whilst their gentle breasts were sad for their menfolk away in the midst of remorseless wars. I drew a great couch out of its place near the corner, so that as I lay, I could look at the lovely view to east and south, and unthinking of and uncaring for the dust, composed myself for sleep. I suppose I must have fallen asleep; I hope so, but I fear not, for all that followed was startlingly real—so real that now sitting here in the broad, full sunlight of the morning, I cannot in the least believe that it was all sleep.

I was not alone. The room was the same, unchanged in any way since I came into it; I could see along the floor, in the brilliant moonlight, a long accumulation of dust. In the moonlight opposite me were three young women, ladies by their dress and manner. I thought at the time that I must be dreaming when I saw them, for, though the moonlight was behind them, they threw no shadow on the floor. They came close to me, and looked at me for some time, and then whispered together. Two were dark, and had high aquiline noses, like the Count, and great dark, piercing eyes that seemed to be almost red when contrasted with the pale yellow moon. The other was fair, as fair as can be, with great wavy masses of golden hair and eyes like pale sapphires. I seemed somehow to know this face, and to know it in connection with some dreamy fear . . . the hardness of her features . . . the sharp angles of her face seemed familiar, but I could not recollect at the moment how or from where. All three had brilliant white teeth that shone like pearls against the ruby of their voluptuous lips. There was something about them that made me uneasy, some longing and at the same time some deadly fear. I felt in my heart a wicked lust, a burning desire that they would kiss me with those red lips. It is not good to note this down, lest some day it should meet Mina's eyes and cause her pain; but it is the truth. They whispered together, and then they all three laughed—such a silvery, musical laugh, but as hard as though the sound never could have come through the softness of human lips. It was like the intolerable, tingling sweetness of water-glasses when played on by a cunning hand. The fair girl shook her head coquettishly, and the other two urged her on. One said:

"Go on! You are first, and we shall follow; yours is the right to begin." The other added:

"He is young and strong; he shall serve for us all." As she spoke she smiled, and the moonlight fell on a hard-looking mouth, with very red lips and sharp-looking teeth, as white as ivory. I lay quiet, looking out under my eyelashes in an agony of delightful anticipation. The fair girl advanced and bent over me till I could feel the movement of her breath upon me. Sweet it was in one sense, honey-sweet, and sent the same tingling through the nerves as her voice, but with a bitter underlying the sweet—a bitter offensiveness, as one smells in blood. I could smell the perfume on her skin and inhaled the fine particles of face powder that seemed to fall from her skin.

I was afraid to raise my eyelids, but looked out and saw perfectly under the lashes. The girl went on her knees, and bent over me, simply gloating. There was a deliberate voluptuousness which was both thrilling and repulsive, and as she arched her neck she actually licked her lips like an animal, till I could see in the moonlight the moisture shining on the scarlet lips and on the red tongue as it lapped the white sharp teeth. Lower and lower went her head as the lips went below the range of my mouth and chin and seemed about to fasten on my throat. Then she paused, and I could hear the sound of her tongue as it licked her teeth and lips, and could feel the hot breath on my neck. Then the skin of my throat began to tingle as one's flesh does when the hand that is to tickle it approaches nearer—nearer. I could feel the soft, shivering touch of the lips on the super-sensitive skin of my throat. I closed my eyes in a languorous ecstacy and waited— waited with beating heart.

But at that instant, another sensation swept through me as quick as lightning. I was conscious of the presence of the Count and of his being as if lapped in a storm of fury. As my eyes opened involuntarily I saw his strong hand grasp the slender neck of the fair woman and with a giant's power draw her back, her blue eyes transformed with fury, her white teeth champing with rage, and her fair cheeks blazing red with passion. But the Count! Never did I imagine such wrath and fury, even to the demons of the pit. His eyes were positively blazing. The red light in them was lurid, as if the flames of hell-fire blazed behind them. His face was deathly pale, like chalk, and the lines of it were hard like drawn wires; the thin eyebrows that met over the nose now seemed like a drawn bar of blackness. I could not make out his cruel mouth—it was a smear of red amid the deathly whiteness of his face. His cloak was one solid piece of disordered blackness. With a fierce sweep his dark form merged brutally with hers and then, with the thrust of his arm, he hurled the creature from him, and then motioned to the others, as though he were beating them back; it was the same imperious gesture that I had seen him use with the wolves. In a voice which, though low and almost a whisper, seemed to cut through the air and then ring round the room, he said:

"How dare you touch him, any of you? How dare you cast eyes on him when I had forbidden it? Back, I tell you all! This man belongs to me! Beware how you meddle with him, or you'll have to deal with me." The fair one, with a laugh of ribald coquetry, turned to answer him:

"You yourself never loved; you never love!" On this the others joined, and such a mirthless, sad, soulless laughter rang through the room that it almost made me faint to hear; it seemed like the pleasure of fiends. Then the Count turned, after looking at my face attentively, and said in a soft whisper:

"Yes, I too can love; you yourselves can tell of it from the past. Is it not so? Well, now I promise you that when I am done with him you shall kiss him at your will. Now go! go! I must awaken him, for there is work to be done."

"Are we to have nothing to-night?" said one of them, with a low laugh, as she pointed to a leather bag which had been thrown upon a nearby table. For answer he nodded his head. One of the fiends jumped forward and opened it. If my ears did not deceive me there was a gasp and a low wail, as of children suddenly thrust into a darkened room. The creatures closed round, whilst I was aghast with horror; but as I looked they disappeared, and with them the dreadful bag.

Then the horror overcame me; and I sank down unconscious.

Whales, mighty whales have felt the wound—
Plunged bleeding through the blue profound.
—*Clarel,* Herman Melville

23

I found Harker sleeping in his room and took the opportunity to administer the strongest dosage I thought he could tolerate of my potion—a vile, noxious little brew I call "The Blood of the Drakulya." By now Harker had experienced a dozen different variations on this potion, each one with a different base. The most amusing by far was a potion whose basic ingredients derived from

South American vampire bats. After a small taste, Harker began to squeak and gibber and climb the stone walls of his room chasing imaginary mice.

At the last, I placed a cup of warm blood on the table near his bedstead. The moment the smell of blood reached the air, I saw him turn toward the table and move toward the blood. In seconds he pounced on the cup, dipping his tongue into the blood like a kitten drinking cream.

Harker had proved himself imaginative and open to any possibility I might suggest. His mind and body twitched and churned with each new experience. His dreams were filled with bats, and wolves, and bears, and all manner of wild experiences. I had even taken him with me into the forest at night to roam with the wolf pack. Harker was a fine hunter who fell readily on the swine and sheep, tearing at them with his teeth. He seemed a born killer, and it was all I could do to keep him from attacking the local peasants who were foolish enough to leave their homes at night.

Harker the were-wolf! He shall bear watching once he returns to London. I would hate to see him go berserk in the midst of a crowd, tearing at the throats of his fellow Englishmen—at least not without me there to help him.

Behold the handmaid of the moon. In sleep the wet sign calls her hour, bids her rise. Bridebed, childbed, bed of death, ghostcandled. Omnis caro ad te veneit. He comes pale vampire, through storm his eyes, his bat sails bloodying the sea, mouth to her mouth's kiss.
—Ulysses, James Joyce

24

From Jonathan Harker's Journal

30 June, morning. These may be the last words I ever write in this diary. I slept till just before dawn, and when I woke threw myself on my knees, for I determined that if Death came he should find me ready.

At last I felt that subtle change in the air, and knew that the morning had come. Then came the welcome cock-crow, and I felt that I was safe. With a glad heart, I opened my door and ran down to the hall. I had seen that the door was unlocked, and now escape was before me. With hands that trembled with eagerness, I unhooked the chains and drew back the massive bolts.

But the door would not move. Despair seized me. I pulled, and pulled, at the door, and shook it till, massive as it was, it rattled in its casement. I could see the iron bolt shot into place. It had been locked after I left the Count.

Then a wild desire took me to obtain that key at any risk, and I determined then and there to scale the wall and gain the Count's room. He might kill me, but death now seemed the happier choice of evils. Without a pause I rushed up to the east window, and scrambled down the wall into the Count's room. It was empty, but that was as I expected. I could not see a key anywhere. I went through the door in the corner and down the winding stair and along the dark passage to the old chapel. I knew now well enough where to find the monster I sought.

The great box was in the same place, close against the wall, but the lid was laid on it, not fastened down, but with the nails ready in their places to be hammered home. I knew I must reach the body for the key, so I raised the lid, and laid it back against the wall; and then I saw something which filled my very soul with horror. There lay the Count, but looking as if his youth had been half renewed, for the hair and moustache were changed to dark iron-black; the cheeks were fuller, and the white skin seemed ruby-red underneath; the mouth was redder than ever. Even the deep, burning eyes seemed set amongst swollen flesh, for the lids and pouches underneath were bloated. It seemed as if the whole awful creature were simply gorged with blood. He lay like a filthy leech, exhausted with his repletion. I shuddered as I bent over to touch him, and every sense in me revolted at the contact; but I had to search, or I was lost. The coming night might see my own body a banquet in a similar way to those horrid three. I felt all over the body, but no sign could I find of the key. Then I stopped and looked at the Count. There was a mocking smile on the bloated face which seemed to drive me mad. This was the being I was helping to transfer to London where, perhaps for centuries to come, he might amongst its teeming millions satiate his lust for blood and create a new and ever-widening circle of semi-demons to batten on the helpless. The very thought drove me mad. A terrible desire came upon me to rid the world of such a monster. There was no lethal weapon at hand, but I seized a shovel which the workmen had been using to fill the cases, and lifting it high, struck, with the edge downward, at the hateful face. But as I did so the head turned, and the eyes fell full upon me, with all their blaze of basilisk horror. The sight seemed to paralyse me, and the shovel turned in my hand and glanced from the face, merely making a deep gash on his cheek. I felt his voice reaching into my very mind, saying: "You, Jonathan Harker, shall be my means of escape from this dying land. I will find a new world, bloated and teeming with life. I will escape . . . to London!"

I knew then that my life was all that stood between this monster and my darling Mina. I took then the shovel, gripping it tightly in both hands, and brought it down with the full force of my weight behind it across his throat. The dull edge cut through the flesh of his neck and blood began to spurt out. I raised the shovel again, and this time brought it down again across his throat, severing the arteries and windpipe. In a final blow I felt the blade shear through his throat and strike his spinal cord with a sharp crack! I had severed the monster's head clear away from his body. The shovel fell from my hands, falling across the box, and as I pulled the handle away, the flange of the blade caught the edge of the lid. The coffin lid fell over and hid the horrid thing from my sight. The last glimpse I had was of the bloated face, fixed with a grin of malice which would have held its own in the nethermost hell.

As I reached for the shovel, I grew suddenly dizzy and lost my balance, falling against the shovel blade so roughly that I cut a serious gash in my forehead. The blood streamed into my eyes and I was forced to sit and wipe away the blood with my sleeve before I could plan what I should do next.

I thought and thought what should be my next move, but my brain seemed on fire. Count Drakulya was destroyed! This at least was a victory over evil. But I began to wonder, with a despairing feeling growing over me, how I could escape this tomb. As I waited I heard in the distance a gypsy song sung by merry voices coming closer, and through their song the rolling of heavy wheels and the cracking of whips; the Szygny and the Slovaks of whom the Count had spoken were coming. With a last look around and at the box which contained the vile body, I ran from the place and gained the Count's room, determined to rush out at the moment the door should be opened. With strained ears, I listened, and heard downstairs the grinding of the key in the great lock and the falling back of the heavy door. There must have been some other means of entry, or someone had a key for one of the locked doors.

Then there came the sound of many feet tramping and dying away in some passage which sent up a clanging echo. I turned to run down again towards the vault, where I might find the new entrance; but at the moment there seemed to come a violent puff of wind, and the door to the winding stair blew to with a shock that set the dust from the lintels flying. When I ran to push it open, I found that it was hopelessly fast. I was again a prisoner, and the net of doom was closing round me more closely.

As I took my journal from my pocket to write there was, in the passage below, a sound of many tramping feet and the crash of weights being set down heavily, doubtless the boxes, with their horrible freight. There is a sound of hammering; it is the boxes being nailed down. Now I can hear the heavy feet tramping again along the hall, with many other idle feet coming behind them.

The door is shut, and chains rattle; there is a grinding on the key in the lock; I can hear the key withdraw: then another door opens and shuts; I hear the creaking of lock and bolt.

Hark! in the courtyard and down the rocky way the roll of heavy wheels, the crack of whips, and the chorus of the Szygny as they pass into the distance.

I am alone in the castle—a prisoner! But I shall not remain here; I shall try to scale the castle wall farther than I have yet attempted. I may find a way home from this dreadful place.

And then away for home! away to the quickest and nearest train! away from this cursed spot, from this cursed land, where the devil's children still walk with earthly feet! I will escape this cursed land. I will go to . . . London.

At least God's mercy is better than that of these monsters, and the precipice is steep and high. At its foot a man may sleep—as a man. Good-bye, all! Mina!

Marie taught me a new game. The idea was, while one swam, to suck in the spray off the waves and, when one's mouth was full of foam, to lie on one's back and spout it out against the sky. It made a sort of frothy haze that melted into the air or fell back in a warm shower on one's cheeks. But very soon my mouth was smarting with all the salt I'd drawn in; then Marie came up and hugged me in the water, and pressed her mouth to mine.
—*The Stranger*, Albert Camus

25

Letter, John Seward to Mina Murray

17th January 1889

My Dearest Mina,

The worst I fear is true, and like a good doctor I have taken the advice "Physician heal thyself" to heart. I have, before this, had some experience as an intern in the "Hermetical arts" but the suggestion you made in your last letter I found less than amusing. I only wish this ailment could be treated so easily—well, that much less work for the leech-gatherer, I say—Thank heaven we've advanced beyond that!

I feel I owe you an apology for the bitterness of my recent letters. It was my natural reaction to blame you for what has happened. I realize now that much of the blame should fall on my own unworthy head. It was I who was unable to make a decision, and I who forced you to continue our relationship beyond the natural span of days.

You will be glad to hear that I am responding quite well and hope to be completely free of lice within the span of a few days. I wish you equal success at your end. The extreme pain combined with the embarrassment makes one wonder if perhaps the treatment is worse than the problem. The hospital interns usually recommended a visit to the laboratory to see the little vermin under a microscope, but memory serves me well enough. Also the copy of that Roman poet's book, "The Remedies of Love," you sent me has lost much of its humor in the translation, Q.E.D.

Since moving to Purfleet and taking a position with the local sanitorium, my life has changed considerably. The life of a poor intern in London is an endless round of work and more work, broken up occasionally by a few hours of sleep or a hasty bite of food. My friends sometimes found release from the endless rounds in drunken orgies. Oblivion was never a possibility for me, however, not even as a student. So all I could do was stop my ears to the noise of the world and plod on like a dray-horse.

My mother warned me against "fallen" women, but in this matter I'm glad I chose to decide for myself. You were the only brightness in the gloom that palled my existence, making life bearable, cherishing the few sparks of feeling I had left within me. The debt I owe you for that little happiness cannot be repaid.

Purfleet is a small, pleasant town where people come for short visits. In London I always felt as though each second of happiness had to be stolen from my duties at the hospital or from my medical studies. In Purfleet, however, there is always more than enough time, too much in fact. The days wear on endlessly—I can read, write, perform experiments—my work with the patients is rewarding; they are grateful for any small attentions and return simple faith and devotion for kind and fair treatment.

Though there will always be those who declaim against "new-fangled" ideas, the changes in the way we treat the insane are all to the good. Gone are the days when doctors were obliged to exorcise "evil spirits" and "bad humours" through tortures disguised as medical treatment—no more dark rooms, bonds, whippings, and ice baths. When we force these poor creatures to accept—with gratitude—blood-lettings, starvation, and enemas thrice-daily, we should stop to ask ourselves who indeed are the madmen.

At my own sanitorium I have begun a new regimen of walks, vapour baths, mustard plasters, & massages. The patients each have a moderately warm & lighted room, white cotton clothing for summer and grey woolen for winter. Their diet consists of fresh water, unkneaded barley bread, fish, diluted wine, boiled vegetables, sardines, radishes, cheese, milk, and limes & other fruit. More important even than diet is the need for activity, as the patients are encouraged to work at handicrafts or other hobbies. This involvement seems to offer them their only relief from their illness.

I only wish I could bury myself in my work as I did as a young man. Now so little holds my attention for any time that I have to content myself with a variety of small projects. I tend my own small corner of England as best I can.

Finally, I want to say that I will honour your decision to remain in London. I want you here with me, but I realize that I long ago gave up any right to compel you. I have found too that these letters are too fragile a link, and far, far too painful.

I've decided to take your advice and get out into the world more. Your suggestion that I find a local girl, a "milkmaid," is probably your idea of a joke. Why you want me to limit myself to milkmaids with hazel eyes is to me a mystery. Your own are brown . . . or are they green?

I hope to be in London next month. Will you see me?

Yours,
John Seward

But the great black anti-suns, wells of truth in the essential conspiracy, in
the grey veil of the hump-backed sky, come and go and suck one another
in, and men call them ABSENCES.
                                    — Rene Daumal

26

Letter, John Seward to Mina Murray

20th June 1889

My Dearest Mina,

I'm glad to hear that you are working again at the Lyceum Theatre this summer. I imagine it is quite a change from your regular employment as an assistant school-mistress.

Your big Irish friend, Mr. Stoker, came to visit me at the asylum last month. He, too, has been stricken by our common complaint and I have agreed to treat him, as he feels he is too well known in the play-going crowd to visit a London doctor. He is more afraid for Henry Irving's reputation than his own, though how Bram spends his time is his own business. Yet these actors are very sensitive about any hint of scandal, like Caesar's wife.

Bram went with me on my rounds and showed a great deal of interest in the patients. I loaned him a book on insanity by Dr. Pritchard and, as he showed some interest in the subject of monomania, I took him to see a patient who was thus afflicted, a Mr. Renfield.

When he first laid eyes on Mr. Renfield, Bram's mouth fell open and all the colour drained from his face. He positively dropped into the cane chair in the hall and was a terrible ashen grey for several minutes.

—Who did you say he is? he finally blurted out.

—Why, Mr. John Renfield, I said.

—It can't be, he said. That man is Sir William G_____, a highly respected physician. I've talked with him several times when he came to Sir Henry's for dinner.

—Nonsense, I said; this man is Mr. Renfield. He has spent most of his adult life in asylums. I have his records in my office that span the last two years.

—It can't be. I saw him just last October. He was in good spirits, normal, as sane as you or I.

I talked with him for quite some time before he regained his composure. I'm afraid I broke a confidence, giving him the name of the asylum in Islington where Mr. Renfield resided until this year and the name of his physician. Since then I have received this rather strange letter from Dr. Jonas Kelly of St. Mary's Asylum near London. The letter is very mysterious. I really don't quite know what to make of it. Please pass it on to Bram. It may have some meaning to him, but what? I hope you will speak to him about this.

Yours,
John Seward

[enclosure]

15th June 1889

Mr. Bram Stoker
in care of: John Seward, M.D.
Purfleet Sanitorium
Purfleet-on-the-Thames, Essex

Dear Mr. Stoker,
    I am sorry that it has taken so long for me to reply to your inquiry of 27th May, but I was puzzled by your request for information about a former patient of St. Mary's, for in your letter

you state that you are merely an aquaintance, rather than a close friend or a relation, of the patient. For this reason I am sending this reply to you by way of Dr. Seward who, I trust, will exercise his discretion in deciding how much of this information he can reveal to you under the oath we share as physicians.

First of all, I was a bit confused by your request for information about a patient named Renfield. According to our records, no patient by that name has been at St. Mary's Asylum at any time during the last two years. We have, however, a patient #124, a Mr. Thomas F. Mason, whose dates of admittance and release correspond to those of your "Mr. Renfield." I can only assume that your secretary erred in copying your letter, writing "Renfield" for "Mason."

When Mr. Mason first arrived, Dr. Ackland, his physician, explained that he had recently suffered a major stroke which resulted in paralysis in his left side and a partial loss of memory. He has since then completely recovered from the paralysis, except for a numbness and loss of feeling in places on his skin; that is, certain well-defined "spots" or patches of his skin do not respond to heat or cold, or to the application of a sharp surgical probe.

When he first arrived, Mr. Mason was subject to long bouts of melancholia, with only a few lucid moments. As time passed, however, his bouts of melancholy became fewer and of a shorter duration, while his periods of lucidity and absolute cheerfulness became more frequent and lasting. And yet, his is a cheefulness I do not trust. His is a dark and morbid humour. It is not healthy.

On one occasion I came to Mr. Mason's room shortly after supper and found him kneeling before his small table. At first I assumed that he was praying, for I could see his lips moving fitfully. Although I said his name in a clearly audible voice, he did not seem to be aware of my presence. After a few minutes, I noted that he was rubbing his palms together; and, after a while, he began to wring his hands as if he were washing them. Soon he was rubbing his hands all over his face and forehead, and with his fingertips on the center of his forehead, as if he had a very sharp pain there and was trying to rub or force it out. This whole process had gone on for nearly an hour when suddenly he heaved a great sigh and fell forward against the table.

I called an attendant and we carried him to his bed, where he cried out and began moaning as if in horrible pain. I gave him a strong sedative, and after a few minutes he fell asleep. When I asked him the next morning what had happened, at first he was evasive. Then he smiled at me with his frightful smile and said, "I am a worshipper of Beelzebub, the Lord of Flies!" and began to laugh. But later, as I thought about it, I realized that, indeed, his gestures that night had resembled nothing if not those of some gigantic fly.

Some time later, in late January, a still stranger incident took place that may have some connection with the patient. One night, at about ten o'clock, a woman was found by an attendant just within the courtyard of the asylum. She was crying and very disoriented. She would look up to the wall above the front entrance and then bury her head in her hands and then look again, & etc. Then all at once she shrieked, "Monster, give me back my child!" and then sobbed in a most pitiful and heart-rending way.

I tried to comfort her, but her anguish was beyond all help. She refused to go into the building, instead insisting against all arguments that we let her stay in the courtyard. All at once & again she shouted, "Give me back my child! What have you done with my child!" I let her stay in that kneeling position for nigh onto an hour, while an attendant went to fetch the police. I tried to give her a mild sedative, but she refused it.

Soon the attendant returned with a policeman and two men from St. Giles Workhouse in London. They told me that the woman was an inmate there who had run away several days before. There was something odd in the manner of these two men. And as they were leaving they looked up to the place where the woman was looking and suddenly both men cringed like whipped dogs.

I turned in time to see the patient, Mr. Mason, standing at the window of his room & glaring at them with a look of pure hate. The two men hurried the woman away to a waiting carriage and departed. Less than a week later, I received a letter from his solicitor, Mr. Hawkins, ordering that Mr. Mason be transferred to the care of Dr. Seward at Purfleet Sanitorium.

I hope this letter has answered your question adequately.

Sincerely,
Jonas Kelly, M.D., St. Mary's Asylum, Islington

The self, according to its powers, takes shape; but what if these powers
should increase, if they should afford a wider scope, what if . . . ?
— *The Immoralist*, Andre Gide

27

Letter, Mina Murray to John Seward

1st June 1889

Dear John,

Your latest letter explains Bram's depression after his return from Purfleet. When I asked him about the telegram he sent you, he told me that Sir William had a major stroke last November that has left him paralyzed on his left side. His family has cared for him at home (his son-in-law is also a doctor) until a few months ago when his condition worsened and he was admitted to Guy's Hospital.

Bram did not hear of his illness because he was very busy rearranging Sir Henry's bookings last November after an American producer canceled his production of "Dr. Jekyll and Mr. Hyde" at the Lyceum. It had played only ten weeks, but I think it was probably more "realism" than the play-going crowd could stand just then. And the papers, too, were all full of the ripper murders, not to mention the Lord Mayor's Procession and the coronation of the "Right Honourable James Whitehead, the Lord-Mayor Elect."

Sir Henry escorted me to the Inaugural Banquet at the Guildhall to see the triumph of "Labour and Merchantile Success," though Mr. Harie says it is the victory of "waste, dirt, misery and disease." The march from Handel's "Dream of Scipio" filled the banquet hall with properly dulcet and regal tones as Britannia's Elect quaffed 440 bottles of wine and consumed 250 chickens, 100 turkeys, 50 geese and untold quantities of beef, venison, pork, and vegetables by the cartload. Meanwhile London's poor ate pork pies and bread, with a glass of gin for each one, at a safe distance away from the hall. This "feast" was provided by the city in the hopes it would prevent an anarchist uprising.

Finally, I want to let you know that I have heard about your fiancee, Miss Lucy Westenra. She sounds like a nice girl, with pretty blue eyes and blonde hair. She is probably a nice protestant girl, or at least a virgin, although I suppose if there was one left in all of Britain you would find her. But you need not worry about how I am taking the news; for I have my own friend now—since I saw you last winter—an up-and-coming young law clerk named Jonathan Harker. In fact he is probably the long-lost identical twin brother of your Miss Westenra—blue eyes, blonde hair, and bawls like a calf when the spirit moves.

Oh yes, best wishes to you both.

Mina

He was born one gray November day . . .
—A Biography of Dracula, Ludlam

28

From the papers & personal effects
of Mr. John Renfield

D r. Seward says you are good therapy so he write you brown leather bound milky colored vanilla smelling paper that cuts already the hand that writes it with blood & finger makes his mark

—John Andrew Renfield, m.d.

oops mistake forgot must cross out md you didn't see it did you Good now he is only Mr. Renfield nice better this way make them forget something he forgot the blood filled eye is come

"Oh, the great march has sounded!"

this he knows little ones for

"I've seen an unscrewed Spider spin a Thought
And walk away upon the Wings of Angels."

he sees miss Lucy in the yard below the window

"So like a bat, thou shalt her eyes survey
And in death's deepest darkness dive away."

she turns and looks her hair God's golden feminine at him who sees her and the blood of nameless women on his hands spouts in a gory flood and/but with black caked blood upon his hands her hot virginity may wash them white again forget forget forget peace peace be still heart loins breasts kidneys in a pie with twenty not four is his weakness

"Immortal as thou art, I bring thy doom."

so sleep so forget so forget

———————————

*His face was strong—very strong—aquiline, with high bridge
of the thin nose and peculiarly arched nostrils; with lofty domed forehead,
and hair growing scantily round the temples but profusely elsewhere. His
eyebrows were very massive, almost meeting over the nose, and with
bushy hair that seemed to curl in its own profusion. The mouth, so far as
I could see it under the heavy moustache, was fixed and rather cruel-
looking, with peculiarly sharp white teeth; these protruded over the lips,
whose remarkable ruddiness showed astonishing vitality in a man of his
years. . . . The general effect was one of extraordinary pallor.*
—*Dracula*, Bram Stoker

29

Letter, John Seward to Mina Murray

10th June 1889

My Dearest Mina,

I suppose it is just as well that you learned about Miss Westenra in the way you did, but your feelings of anger are wasted, as is your desire to avenge yourself on me, for I have been hurt in that spot already. And, as the saying goes, old wounds must needs give way to new. It is true that I have asked Miss Westenra for her hand in marriage, just as Bram told you. But what he could not know is that Miss Westenra has rejected my offer of marriage. In fact, she is now betrothed to another man.

I hope you can bring forth the kindness and courage to forgive me for being drawn to a young woman of Miss L. Westenra's obvious charm, but I feel that you must bear some of the blame for what has happened. After all, it was you who first brought forth in my nature the quiet stirrings of manhood; and, after all, "natura est fatum." It was without hope or design that I was drawn to her by my grosser appetites, though I know that she was only a pale substitute for one who combines the perfection of desire and of tenderness, of courage and forgiveness.

Although my offer of marriage was disappointed of success, I realize now that my feelings were more sentiment than substance, more froth than sediment. The personal attractions of Miss Lucy Westenra were graced by virtue—and a modest accomplishment on the piano. As you have guessed, she is certainly a nice girl, with pretty blue eyes and blonde hair. And you may be right in supposing she is "a nice protestant girl, or at least a virgin," although this last I can not vouch for personally.

I wish you could meet Miss Westenra socially, for I am sure
that under different circumstances you could have become friends.
We met while I was spending a weekend in Whitby. She was
staying there with her cousin who runs a boarding house that
overlooks the harbour. Lucy's personal fortune is modest and her
family is respectable. Her family has lived in London for some
years, Lucy visiting her cousin in the summer months.

I do know that her main study is the Bible, and that she also
assiduously reads "Lives of the Saints" and "Foxe's Book of
Martyrs." She lately gave me a copy of Law's "A Serious Call to a
Devout and Holy Life." She prays often and believes implicitly in
salvation and election. She frowns upon drinking and dancing,
though she plays a variety of hymns on the piano and sings. She
has a low opinion of the theatre, considering it to be a pagan ritual
frequented by misguided sinners and a worldly temptation to all
Christian folk.

You will be glad to know that "mother" is showing some improvement in his condition. He is quite disturbed by what has
happened, but as I told him: "amor omnibus idem"—love is the
same for everyone—a sentiment that does not set well with
romantics like Bram. In my own case I have taken to heart the
words of Gibbon, "The warm desires, the long expectations of
youth, are founded on the ignorance of themselves and of the
world. They are gradually damped by time and experience, by
disappointment or possession."

I look forward to seeing you.

Yours,
John Seward

Most Pluto people have powerful physiques. The features are noticeably
heavy or sharp, and clearly drawn, and the nose is quite prominent,
sometimes beak-shaped. Ordinarily, the complexion is very pale, almost
translucent, and the brows are heavy and knit together over the bridge of
the nose. There's a crackling electric vitality about the very presence of a
Scorpio that gives him away. As quiet as he tries to be,
such a vital force can't be hidden completely.
—*Sun Signs*, Linda Goodman

30

From the papers & personal effects
of Mr. John Renfield

Little ones sit peeping on the cell door dreaming dreams of
Serpents on the sills of HEL the jaws that bite that catch them
unawares and crush them wings/legs over the lips look out
"Death's nothing; nothing after death will fall;
Time, and dark Chaos, will devour us all."
life feeds on death that feeds on sin that eats and eats and Eats so
why then love
"O Appetite of Angels! such with awe
Thou didst appear when first thy form I saw."
but in the western-rays immortal love inspires and respires in thy
breast of adamantine pureness where even a wren may sleep and
dream of the Ellysian fields for in thy voice the power lies
"Speak but the word; the dead, the dead shall rise."
birdlike from the flame where joined our souls may be for souls
fly winged between the bars of HEL
"Bind me in dungeons, yet I will not stay."
but to her bosom fly lie surging dreams the setting of the day
"Catch the bare soul just plunging into bliss,
And give it back with this fast deathless kiss."

so soon the master comes with breath to give so soon we joined
be beyond both sin and death.

---

*Scorpios will find many ways to keep your attention riveted on them
alone, until you are exhausted and drained. They are the vampires of the
zodiac. They feed on people and transform this sponged-up energy into
success and power at the expense of their victims.*
—*Sun Sign Revelations*, M.E. Crummere

31

Letter, John Seward to Mina Murray

20th June 1889

Dear Mina,

Since Bram's first visit here, I have taken a special interest in
the patient, Mr. Renfield. In June I noticed that Renfield was
catching flies to keep as pets. He would lure them to his window
sill with a mixture of sugar & milk, and them catch them between
his fingers. When I first saw him doing this, I expressed surprise
that he could catch them in this way without killing them. Renfield
explained that he caught them by clapping his hands together a
few inches from where they alight so that the sound vibrations
render them unconscious for a few seconds, long enough for him
to catch them and twist their wings so they cannot fly away.

Later that afternoon I tried this experiment several times, but
without success. I placed some of the sugar & milk on a stone
bench and tried several times to catch flies by knocking them out

with sound waves. But each time I clapped my hands over them, they simply flew away unharmed.

I went to Mr. Renfield's room and observed him for some time. He had no difficulty catching flies in this manner. When I told him of my difficulty, he laughed and said it took a great deal of practise in cupping the hands to achieve just the exact pitch to be effective; he says it also helps to say "abracadabra" just before clapping your hands.

Some time after this, Renfield began to keep spiders, feeding his flies to them to reduce their numbers. However, soon the spiders were so numerous that I had to tell him to get rid of them. He was quite annoyed, but finally agreed. It was just then that a huge horse-fly flew through his window and Renfield caught it in his fist. Before my eyes he took the hairy, emerald-green insect between his fingers and put it in his mouth.

I scolded him, but he insisted that they were quite healthful, like raisins, and that the fly was a strong life that gave life to him. I began then to suspect how he intends to get rid of his spiders.

A few days later, Renfield caught and tamed a sparrow and began feeding his spiders to it. Soon he had a small colony of sparrows and his supply of spiders was almost exhausted. He came to me then and said, exulting, "Dr. Seward, could I please have a small, a very small kitten, a nice little, sleek, playful kitten, that I can play with, and teach, and feed—and feed—and feed!"

When I denied this request he gave me a murderous look that I will never forget—a look which meant killing. Renfield is an undeveloped homocidal maniac. He bears watching.

The next day I found Renfield happily catching flies again—the business of the cat forgotten. I asked him about his birds, but he said they all "flew the couperet," while making a cutting gesture with the edge of his hand. I looked at him with surprise, while noting a pile of feathers near the foot of his bed and a few spots of blood. Later in the day, an attendant came to me and said, "My belief is, Dr. Seward, that he has eaten his birds . . . that he just took and ate them raw!" Renfield had disgorged a pile of feathers and raw flesh.

I have decided to describe Mr. Renfield's obsession as "zoophagia" or "life-eating." He has somehow come to the conclusion that he can live off of the life-energies of lower forms of life. The source of this delusion is not clear, nor is there any easy way to counter this belief. There is nothing in his file, or in the letter I received from Dr. Kelly, to explain this development or why it would manifest itself at this particular time. Though his request for a cat reminded me of a story I heard years ago about a medical student who, under the influence of hashish, ate a small kitten—as he later explained his act to his colleagues, "The better to experience it, my dear!"

A few days ago I gave Renfield a journal in which he can record his thoughts. I have encouraged him to write whatever he wishes. So far all that he has allowed me to see of his writing is a list of names and a phrase he has allowed me to copy—

"wings/legs over the lips look out"

The list of names includes a "Benjamin D'Israel" which had been heavily marked through so as to be almost illegible and also the name of Dr. Kelly, along with the names of Dr. Arthur Doyle, Professor J.H. von Helsing and several other physicians. Also prominent on the list were Sir Charles Warren, Sir Robert Anderson, and Lord Salisbury, along with Rev. Robt. James Lees and a few others I did not recognize. I don't understand the significance of these names, but I am sure they hold some hidden meaning for Renfield, a meaning that might provide the key to his illness. He still possesses some of the trappings of sanity; and yet, Poor Renfield, since the Light of Reason failed him, with what does he Illuminate his mind?

Please say nothing about this to Bram.

Yours,
John Seward

Scorpio . . . this sign is identified with Serpentarius as also with the dragon against whom St. George (Geo-Urgon) waged war.
—*New Dictionary of Astrology*, Sepharial

32

From the papers & personal effects
of Mr. John Renfield

He sits on the window sill as hands poised to catch the little
wings/legs rubs paws together searches the dark empyrean with
compound eyes and buzzes wings and fly angel fly shoots into the
hand cupped air and joy and life buzz against his palms and in his
mouth buzzes wet/dry
"And laugh'd and clapp'd her wings and blest the day."
he climbs down from the sill as wings/legs grows inside and fills
him till he feels himself a little one and joy brims his mouth and
peace and peace and joy and wings/legs tells him that the Prince
is coming here to this place to redeem with blood of his the flies
and friends of flies and all who live on the blessed isle of flies who
love him and serve him
"He like some rowling whale, who as he laves,
 With his bright Armory gilds all the waves;
 Dashes the frightened Nations from his side,
 That pale and foaming fury far off ride"
the Prince rolls the tide of history and shoulders the race of
spiders from the page of fame
"No power on earth could their lost empire save."
he sings the song of joy and many little wings/legs fly into his
room and he cuts his wrist and rich red wine flows on the stone
sill and wings/legs alight and drink their fill
"And with rich Wine drank their cold Spirits warm."
they drink and sing their Prince's name
drakulya
and he sings too and pledges his oath
". . . My soul receive,
Which thus infus'd shall a new being give,
Breathe with my breath, and with my being live."
and the little ones fly from the sill and sing the Master's name and

fly free and tell his oath of blood to all their kind of him of
wrenfield
"Who when his long toss'd loaded Vessel hits
Against some Rock, and with loud horrour splits;
First grasps one Casket which does all contain,
Then fearless, shoots himself into the Main."

---

*Stoker's Dracula can be identified without a shadow of a doubt with Vlad
V, called the Impaler, though it was . . . Vlad III who was the first
Wallachian ruler to be called "Dracul." Vlad III bore a cross with a
dragon on his escutcheon, and it was this dragon, rather than the
Rumanian homonym for devil, that was the source of the family
nickname "Dracul."*
—*The Truth About Dracula*, G. Ronay

33

Letter, John Seward to Mina Murray

June 27, 1889

Dear Mina,
     A terrible thing has occurred. I've just heard that Dr. Jonas
Kelly who governs the St. Mary's Asylum in Islington has died in
a terrible fire at the sanitorium on the 28th last. The conflagration
broke out, as I understand, when a patient went berserk and
overturned an oil lamp in Dr. Kelly's office. Attendants were finally
able to contain the blaze, but Dr. Kelly succumbed to the smoke
and heat.

A board member from St. Mary's has contacted me about the possibility of my accepting the position of head of St. Mary's. This is a very tempting offer, and I may eventually accept, especially as the proximity to London would make this professionally an astute move. What do you think? . . .

Yours,
John

_____

The order, founded in 1418, entailed many obligations, which included wearing a dark costume as a sign of penance every Friday and wearing the insignia of the dragon at all times. The insignia consisted of a prostrate dragon, wings expanded, hanging on a cross, with its tail curled around the head and its breast cleft in two. The green cross worn by the knights had an emblem that bore the motto of the society: "O quam misericors est Deus, justus et pius." The symbolism was designed to recall that Christ conquered the prince of hell by his death and resurrection.
—*Dracula, a Biography,* Florescu & McNally

34

Letter, Mina Murray to John Seward

3rd July 1889

Dear John,
    Life goes on in London-towne in a sort of endless Bartholomew Fair full of noise and laughter, parties, pranks and punch bowls. Just last night I attended a party at Mr. Wilde's house—you remember, no. 16 Tite street—and found the Irish Club in session:

Messrs. Wilde, Shaw, and Stoker (and a few others) arguing about the Cleveland Street goings on.

The police are doing their best, I've heard, to ignore the presence of a boy-brothel because of the patronage of Victoria's grandson. Bram was quite indignant, remarking that Sir Richard Burton's career was destroyed some years ago by simply writing a report on Egyptian boy-brothels for the military governor.

Burton's career has never fully recovered, especially after the African scandal and Speke's death. And now I've heard that Dr. Edwards is near death, or already there. Edwards was a close friend of Sir Richard and even accompanied Burton and Speke on an expedition to Africa, their first failed attempt to find the source waters of the Nile. It was Edwards who treated Burton—if you've seen the twin pair of crescent-shaped scars that Burton carries on each cheek—after Burton was attacked by African tribesmen. Burton had the bad luck to catch a native spear in his teeth "the hard way" as he would say. Since then he's had the matching scars and a rather gaunt, hollow-cheeked look, as several of his wisdom teeth were shattered.

Bram and Sir Richard were good friends, along with Dr. Edwards and Chas. Swinburne and Dr. Arbuthnot, though Bram hesitated about joining the Kama Sutra Society. That would be all too risque for poor Bram. It was quite a blow to Bram when Burton took a consular post in Trieste, and now that word has come from there that Burton is ill . . . well, Bram is even more troubled to know how to send word of Dr. Edwards' death.

I've also told Bram about Dr. Kelly's death by the fire at St. Mary's Asylum. He was, of course, glad for you, if this would indeed further your career, but he also seemed by his manner to be hiding something from me, as his face grew quite pale when I first told him about the fire.

If something has passed between you and Bram that I should not know, I hope you will be able some day to tell me as I will respect this confidence until then.

Love,
Mina

P.S. I've written a short note to your friend Miss Lucy Westenra and she was kind enough to invite me to visit her in Whitby. We intend to have a nice, long conversation about new friends and old suitors.

Apart from being the patron saint of England, St. George was also the patron saint of wolves, etc., and is most important as a protector of the peasantry. Because of this protection St. George was the sworn enemy of the vampire hordes.
—The Natural History of the Vampire, A. Masters

35

From the papers & personal effects of Mr. John Renfield

The street of the hawk, hawkings, hawkins, yes Mister Peter Hawkins esquire limited is his name and this his number of the beast on printed card, on printed sign, on printed metal plate, he is mine the betrayer and the betrayed his door, his desk, his life is mine:

1ST SEPT 1889
PROFESSOR JH VON HELSING, WALLENBERG INSTITUTE, DANTZIG
HOFFET AND MULGRAVE TODAY NOTIFIED VESSEL READY FOR HARVEST (STOP) NAPOLEON AND BOXES IN PURFLEET STORAGE (STOP) VESSEL MOVED LONDON (STOP) WALLENBERG EXPERIMENT READY (STOP) EXPECT CALL FROM FRIEND
PETER HAWKINS

Thus the proof of his lies and deceit are plain for all to see on this pretty paper, his turning to Von Helsing and denying me, and the three times denying as I lay in that stinking prison. . . .

THEY came for me. The police and the minister—a famous psychic, they said. They came for me, right up to the door of my home, because they said, he saw the spirit blood on my hands which does not wash, the stain of the women, their blood still burning on my hands. They put me in prison and then they passed judgement on me. Twelve physicians passed their sentence. They placed me in the insane asylum. But I escaped. I tricked them. Hawkins and his forged papers; he took me to Purfleet and the private hospital. No one would think to search for me there—not even Von Helsing.

Hawkins came to me. He told me of Von Helsing's plan. He told me of the Drakulya, hiding, like me, in his castle. We forged the plan. I escaped. I reached the port and my ship. I was free again. I went by train across europe to Varna and found the ship. Hawkins told me which one. It was the Demeter.

I became a sailor. I carried the boxes aboard the ship. I slept among the other sailors. I waited. So long I waited. And in the dark night I went to the hold to see my prize. Boxes of earth they said. I opened the boxes. I found them.

The next night I took a friend with me, to show him the treasure in the boxes I said. He hung a lantern on the beam nail over the box. Pushed back the lid—too late! I grabbed him by the hair and slit his throat over the box. Drink! Drink! I said to my friend. Blood poured over the earth. Life's blood to feed the dead.

I threw the empty carcass over the side. No one saw.

They searched for his body the next day. Lost overboard they finally said. I think they were sad.

I think my friends are thirsty again.

At night I brought another to the hold. He wanted to see the treasure too. Again the hanging of the lantern, the prying loose of the lid. The profane gaze that must be paid in blood.

I cast his empty corpse into the sea and returned to the hold. I placed my hand on the breast of the dead one. "Thank you," he said, "I was very thirsty." I nodded.

"Can I have another?" he said, smiling.

"Of course," I said, "tomorrow."

My friends were thirsty. They were very thirsty. In the darkness I could hear them calling out to me, crying. What could I do? Soon I began to run out of sailors. We had reached the English channel. Only a handful were left, but we needed them to sail the ship.

There was a terrible storm. I went down into the hold. I carried one of the boxes up to the deck and tied myself to it. The ship was going to run aground. I cast myself and the box into the sea.

The sea was very wet. It tossed us about. It pushed us toward the shore. I struggled. I wanted to live.

The beach. I dragged the box up onto the beach and slept. Soon the morning light woke me and I carried the box until I found a road. I got a ride on a cart. I made my way back to Purfleet. I hid the box in the old ruined abbey. I was safe.

My friend thanked me for saving him.

"You're very welcome," I said.

Akin to the Adventure of Perseus and Andromeda—indeed, by some supposed to be indirectly derived from it—is that famous story of St. George and the Dragon, which Dragon I maintain to have been a whale; for in many old chronicles whales and dragons are strangely jumbled together, and often stand for each other. . . . Bearing all this in mind, it will not appear altogether incompatible with the sacred legend and the ancientest draughts of the scene, to hold this so-called dragon no other than the great leviathan himself.
—*Moby Dick*, Herman Melville

36

Letter, John Seward to Mina Murray

12th September 1889

Dear Mina,

As you have guessed from the tone of my letter, there is no end
to the problems I have faced during the last few months. My own
special problem has been Mr. Renfield. He has manifested the
strangest behavior, beginning on 23rd June, when he suffered a
violent paralytic attack. He lay for several hours in a coma-like
trance, until sunrise when he became suddenly violent & had to
be subdued by three attendants. Then again he became quiet at
sunset and was just so until dawn. And then violent again until
sunset, and again, etc. for four days.

Finally one night after midnight, about 2 a.m. I think, I was
awakened by the night-watchman who said that Renfield had
wrenched the window loose from its casing and escaped by
jumping to the ground—some eight feet below his window.

We quickly raised the alarm and began a search of the whole
countryside, but Renfield was nowhere to be found! At dawn we
were met by the local constabulary who assisted us in a house-to-
house search, but with no luck.

Finally, four weeks ago, Renfield was discovered at an old house
near the sanitorium. One of the attendants had been walking past
the house—Carfax Abbey—and saw a group of men unloading
some long pine boxes from wagons that had been brought there
that morning.

As he watched, he happened to recognize one of the men as
Renfield himself! The attendant quickly ran to fetch help from the
sanitorium, and they were soon able to beard the lion in his den,
bringing him back bound with a straight-waistcoat.

I assume that Renfield had been hiding all this time at the old
ruined abbey and that he had been employed at odd jobs for local
people, including the new owner of Carfax Abbey, who was
unaware that Renfield was an escaped lunatic.

Indeed his disguise is a good one, for Renfield can feign lucidity
& reason, more easily than I could feign madness.

The final straw came today, when Renfield broke free from the
attendants and attacked me with a knife. I defended myself as best

I could, but he still managed to cut me deeply on the left wrist. His attendants burst in and seized him, but not before he fell to the floor and began licking up my blood that had spilled on the carpet.

To add to this morbid and confused state of affairs, as I wrote you a few weeks ago, apparently Miss Lucy Westenra has taken ill with some mysterious malady, like unto anemia, that I have endeavored to treat. I had hoped to have a complete recovery effected before her fiance, Arthur Holmwood, returned from visiting his father, Lord Godalming. But she has taken a serious turn for the worse and I have contacted my old teacher, Professor Joachim Von Helsing of Dantzig for consultation.

Lucy's blood seems to be draining away mysteriously, through some invisible haemorrhage, and I have been unable to discover the cause. Von Helsing seems to suspect some particular cause, but his treatment has been a bit unorthodox—folk remedies, in fact—like the garlic blossoms he's placed all over Lucy's room. Von Helsing has brought so much garlic into the house that the smell is oppressive. His only medical treatment for the blood loss has been hypnosis and blood transfusions from me and from himself, too. After so much blood you would think Lucy could have made a complete recovery. But so far her rallies have been only temporary, followed by rapid collapse and a dangerous death-like pallor and loss of vitality.

Von Helsing uses the Amanuist method in transfusing blood, involving a simple rubber tube with fixed hypodermic needles at each end and the manual "milking" of the tube. But after giving so much blood and after Renfield's attack, I've had to rest and try to recover as much strength as I can. I've had to rely on my good friend, Dr. Hennessey, to help out with the patients.

Please write to me as soon as you can. I would very much like to hear from you.

Yours,
John Seward

*In art St. George appears armed as a knight, mounted
on a horse, transfixing the dragon with his lance.*
—*Lives of the Saints,* Sabine Baring-Gould

37

From the papers & personal effects
of Mr. John Renfield

John Seward, John Seward, John Seward, John Seward, Dr. John
Seward, Dr. John Seward, Dr. John Seward, John Seward, MD.,
John Seward, MD., John Seward, MD., John Seward, MD. John
Seward, MD.

That certain death is past,
And I upon the blessed shore am cast.
Still my uncertain soul each tempest blinds
Like a dark vessel driven by polar winds.
I tracked a fiend I thought by furies driven,
I sought for Hell, but stumbled upon Heaven.

Love is all taste, relish, and vital good,
Spirits it gives that over life's channel brood,
And like wine-sparks dance through the brimming blood.
Each smile of thine drives from my age a day,
One balmy kiss would take a year away;
But oh the rest would give me youth again.
Dare like the foolish fly, whose vexing wings
Urge the slow flame to burn her as she sings.
From beds of flames where thou didst lie and roar,
Whirlwinds shall bear thee hot and reeking o're,
And sweating drops of blood, and round thee blow,
Then plunge thee in the abyss of ice and snow.

Bow ye bright dwellers, bow your heavens down
Impale his brows with an immortal crown.
Not as thy slave before thee now I stand
But as the lord, and one that will command.
As master of the world, I'll be
Spight of thy scorn, the master too of thee.

There is a bower, the mystic seat of Love.
Where death stands sentinel before the grove.

God, having set forth the great power of the Leviathan, calls him King of
the Proud. There is nothing, says he, on earth to be compared with him.
He is made so as not to be afraid. He seeth every high thing below him,
and is king of all the children of pride. But because he is mortal and
subject to decay, as all other earthly creatures are, and because there is
that in heaven, though not on earth, that he should stand in fear of, and
whose laws he ought to obey, I shall in the next following chapters speak
of his diseases and the causes of his mortality and of what laws of nature
he is bound to obey.
—*The Leviathan*, Thomas Hobbes

38

Letter, Dr. Henri Jarquelle, Buda-Pesth, to Dr. Seward

8th August 1889

Dr. Seward, Purfleet Sanitorium, Purfleet, Essex

My Dear Doctor Seward,
    I am by this letter placing in your hands the case of a young
Englishman who fell ill in our city not long ago and has been in

our care for nearly two months. He arrived here by train from Klausenberg and was taken into the custody of authorities for his own protection, as he was rushing violently around the station and demanding a train for London. When he arrived here at the hospital, he was quite calm and I soon recognized that his spirits were depressed to a dangerous degree. At first I thought that his actions were the result of a toxic concentration in his blood of some opiate, as his symptoms were like nervous waste. I asked him who he was, but he could only utter muted cries of "poison" and "the ravening wolf." Soon even these cries of anguish ceased and he became completely dumb.

During the second week of his stay, he became thoroughly listless, suggesting a debasement of the mental functions and a degeneration of the physical energies—until one day, as his nurse placed her hand on his arm, he sank into a coma-like sleep that lasted two days.

I was awakened the following night by cries of "fire" coming from the wing where the patient was confined. Attendants and nurses rushed to the ward and found the patient struggling to free himself from his bonds and screaming that "they" were burning him. He fainted when an attendant threw a bucket of water on him and then slept soundly until morning. The next morning, the patient awakened normally, as if unaware of his outburst of the previous night, and conducted himself in a perfectly sane and rational way—at least until a few days later when a priest came to visit him and asked him to accept the Holy Sacrament and the Sacrifice of the Sacred Blood of Jesus Christ for the Healing of the Spirit. The patient became quite angry and uttered the foulest blasphemies and soon had to be placed in his restraints. And yet, it was only after this incident that the patient was able to give us his name—Jonathan Harker—and the name of his fiancee, a Miss Mina Murray.

During the past two weeks there has been a noticeable improvement in Mr. Harker's condition, with his becoming in the last few days at least physically healthy. But there still remains a spiritual illness that eludes treatment. Mr. Harker sleeps long and deeply, but is still troubled by horrific dreams of being buried alive. He also claims to have awakened to the smell of burning flesh. He has told Sister Agatha, his nurse, that he is now one of the damned. This last is the most troublesome of all. Oddly, he has asked that the polished metal pier-glass in his ward be removed.

A few day ago I went on a long walk with Mr. Harker in the children's gardens on the hillside below the hospital. He told me of his terrible melancholy, describing it as a great pressure on his heart. I did all that I could to dispell the gloom, but with little success. Mr. Harker stated then that he had committed acts for which there can be no forgiveness, and that he had looked upon the Secrets of God which had been hidden from mankind at the foundation of the world.

At first I little comprehended his meaning, but as he talked I soon began to see that Mr. Harker had, during his business trip, taken carnal knowledge of a woman, and that there was a terrible darkness thrown over his relationship with his fiancee. At this time I led him back to his room, telling him as we went that there was nothing that was more powerful than love and that his young fiancee would surely forgive him, if she did truly love him.

In this moment, I threw open the door of his room to reveal the beautiful visage of Miss Mina Murray, the patient's fiancee, who had traveled here from England after receiving a letter from Sister Agatha. The patient fell on his knees as Mina embraced him and soon she was cradling his head on her lap, so that I left them alone, knowing that there was nothing else to do.

A short time later, thanks to the kind offices of the Sisters of Ste. Beatrice, Jonathan and Mina were married in a private service in the hospital's chapel; and they are soon to return to England as Mr. and Mrs. Harker.

Mrs. Harker asked that I contact you, as you have been a good friend of hers for some time. I recommend that you contact them shortly after they return home next month. I suggest then that you call upon them as soon as possible to determine if Mr. Harker's psychic health is fully restored.

Yours,
Dr. Henri Jarquelle
Hospital of St. Joseph and the Virgin of Buda-Pesth

*There, however, our dragon does not fail us, both Carpaccio and Tinoret
having the deepest convictions on that subject. . . . That it is an
indisputably living and venomous creature, materially, has been the
marvel of the world, innocent and guilty, not knowing what to think of
the terrible worm, nor whether to worship it, as the Rod of their lawgiver,
or to abhor it as the visible symbol of the everlasting Disobedience.*
— John Ruskin

39

From Jonathan Harker's Journal.

How I escaped from the dreadful castle is still a mass of
confusion in my mind. I count myself doubly blessed that I have
escaped to see the light of day once more, to look upon the night
sky without a feeling of overwhelming dread and despair. Setting
into the woods, I must have wandered down that cursed
mountain—down into the valley where I eventually stumbled into
the hut of a peasant family. Seeing the disorder of my clothes and
the bloody wound on my forehead, they took me by cart to the
nearest village. The villagers, in turn, saw the terrible condition
into which my mind and body had fallen, and took up a collection
to buy a carriage ticket for me and send me to a doctor in the
nearest town.

Upon arriving at the town, the doctor examined me carefully,
asking a lot of questions about my condition. My answers must
have seemed to him mostly incoherent gibberish, or so I thought.
But the doctor quickly caught on to my meaning upon hearing the
name "Drakulya" spoken in something other than the usual
whispers and hushed voices. Further, when I claimed to have slain
the Monster, the doctor raised his eyebrows and displayed a
curious astonishment, as if I had claimed to have had tea with the

devil himself. Needless to say, after a few days wild rumours began to spread around the town of my mishap; and soon a city official appeared with a train ticket and the request that I leave town as soon as humanly possible.

The local constabulary considered me a public nuisance and were anxious to have me leave. I insisted that a group of men go to the castle to investigate what had happened, but the police were not interested in exploring the old ruins of Castle Drakulya. Their main interest seemed to be getting me to leave town as soon as I could travel—and that was all.

I found myself soon enough in the city of Clausenberg, where I was taken to a hospital and placed under the care of Dr. Jacquelle. This doctor's manner seemed quite different from that of the country doctor who had examined me earlier. His concern for my welfare was evident, and he did not even flinch when I said the name "Drakulya" loudly in his offices. No one, in fact, seemed to have even heard of this Drakulya, or at least they pretended not to. The whole experience was quite maddening.

After several weeks I felt myself pretty well restored and quite ready to leave this awful country behind and continue on my trip to London. Dr. Jacquelle, however, insisted that I be fully re-covered before setting out again on the long and tiring trip that would bring me back home. Indeed, the doctor was so very kind to me that I came to welcome his visits and look forward to having dinner with him on those days when he spent the evening at the hospital.

The nurses were also very kind, with the exception of one elderly woman who persisted in staring at me and gesturing with the sign to ward off the evil eye—the gesture I had first seen in Bistritz on the way to Castle Drakulya. I came to wish that I had never seen that monstrous place. It has only brought me pain and sorrow. The memory of it nags at my mind like an old puzzle that cannot be solved—as the tongue always turns toward the sore tooth.

Finally, after about a month, Mina arrived from London—at the request it seems of Dr. Jacquelle—and at Mina's insistence we were married in a short ceremony at the hospital. I was surprised by the way both Mina and the nurses watched over me, but I could not complain that they were annoying, as they tried in every way to please me. Mina rented a small apartment near the hospital, and I was allowed to share these small rooms with her while returning to the hospital each day for a short interview with my doctor.

The all too brief days I shared there with my new bride Mina were indeed the happiest I have ever enjoyed in my life. Truly, I could not really appreciate life until I nearly lost it. Mina could barely conceal her love and concern, and it was only because of pressing concerns in London that she could be convinced to leave my side in order to return home.

Soon, as I was really quite recovered, I put Mina on the train back to London, promising I would follow as quickly as I could after clearing up a few last details. However, I had other quite specific plans in mind as I gathered up my few belongings and what little cash I had. Thus I planned to return to Bistritz, and, if at all possible, retrace my route to Castle Drakulya. If possible, I would prove my story—at least to myself—and hopefully I would prove to the world that I was not completely mad!

Some strange urgings moved me. An inexplicable power drew me to that horrid and god-forsaken castle. I told myself I could not leave this country without proving to myself if it were all true or not. But in fact some thing, some strange, dark "otherness" in my soul, something quite alien, was drawing me back to Drakulya's castle.

In the dawn of the language, the word "worm" had a somewhat different meaning from that in use to-day. It was an adaptation of the Anglo-Saxon "wyrm," meaning primarily a dragon or snake; or from the Gothic "waurms," a serpent; or the Icelandic "ormur," or the German "wurm."
—*The Lair of the White Worm*, Bram Stoker

40

From Jonathan Harker's Journal

I arrived in Bistritz shortly after dark and made my way to the inn where I had spent my last visit. Both the old woman and her husband were shocked—I looked to them as something that had come back from the dead, and they generally avoided being alone with me in any room of the inn. Even the main room was not safe enough, in their view, to risk contamination by a too close association with the young Herr. When I ordered a meal of beef and potatoes, they stood over me and watched with a mixture of fear and astonishment as I consumed the food hungrily. Later, when I asked about the carriage to Borgo Pass, it only served to confirm their fears.

When morning came, I learned that the carriage driver had refused to give me passage. I was forced to hire an old one-horse rig to take me into the mountains. I decided to begin the journey immediately—thinking of what I was about to do would only weaken my already shaky resolve.

By luck, along the way I found an old fellow, a gypsy, who knew the area quite well and for the promise of hard cash—half in advance—agreed to show me the way to Borgo Pass. He seemed to me a bit rough and even agreed to go with me to look at the castle, as long as we did so in the daylight. For he would not approach the area after dark for any price.

By noon we were well on our way, climbing the rough road into the mountains. We often had to get out and walk part of the way when the road was too steep for our horse. The way seemed quite different in the broad light of day, and I often had to ask my guide to make sure that we were indeed on the right road.

As the sun began to decline in the West, my courage seemed to decline with it, until it was very nearly gone. I had escaped this horrible place once. Why then did I tempt fate a second time? In contrast, the coming darkness seemed to strengthen the resolve of my gypsy companion. He seemed anxious, as if he wanted to jump from the rig and push it forward. Even as I related my story of my escape from the castle, he seemed more determined than ever to reach the castle. Strange! It seemed as though the possibility of Drakulya's death had emboldened him to see it for himself. Or perhaps he hoped to search the castle for any signs of gold or treasure. He was the sort of man ready to do anything if the promise of easy gold lay just ahead.

As the ground leveled off, we made good speed and quite literally seemed to fly across the ground that lay between the pass and the castle. The road was much different than it was that first night I traveled this way in Drakulya's coach. I was impressed by the lush foliage of the trees and grass, and even the few animals I saw along the way were reassuring in their serene beauty. I truly believed that with Drakulya's death a terrible evil had been destroyed and a dreadful curse lifted from this land.

The sun descended and touched the horizon as we finally pulled into the courtyard of the castle. I was concerned about our rig, as a wheel had been cracked in the last mile of the trip and it seemed unlikely that we could return without repairing the wheel struts. How were we to accomplish this without help?

The old gypsy scrambled from his seat and rushed up to the door where, by throwing his full weight against it, he literally pushed the great door in on itself. I followed him as quickly as I could, grabbing the lantern that we would almost certainly need before our work was done.

The old gypsy began a quick room by room search, tossing through the papers, books, and articles of clothing that were quickly strewn about the floor in his mad haste. I followed patiently, and in the moment when he seemed to tire—uncertain of where to search next—I suggested we go to the old chapel where Drakulya's coffin lay, so that he could see for himself that the monster was finally destroyed.

To this suggestion he readily agreed, as perhaps the thought of gold rings or a silver chain moved him to inspect the corpse. I led him quietly to the stairway and down into the crypt. As the door empty! The dozens of boxes were gone; all that was left was the coffin of Count Drakulya. I sat down at the foot of the stairs to think. Drakulya had arranged for the transport of the boxes to England. This was certainly the project the Szygny were carrying out for him when I escaped the castle. Could they have taken the boxes to a port? This seemed the only possible explanation.

As I sat there, trying to puzzle out what had happened, the old gypsy shuffled over to the coffin. He stood silent for some minutes, and then, falling to his knees, he crossed himself and placed both hands on the lid of the coffin. He raised the lid slowly and looked inside. A low moan rose from his throat as he began striking himself and pulling his hair. His plaintive cries became louder still as he lowered the coffin lid and lay down on the cold stone floor.

I moved over to the coffin and raised the lid. There lay the corpse of Count Drakulya, as I had left it, the throat severed by the rough edge of the spade. I took a heavy canvas bag I had brought with me from the wagon and reached into the coffin to remove the head of the Count. I placed the head into the bag. I was determined this time to bring back proof of the monster's destruction. I climbed the stairs back to the main living quarters of the castle.

A solid darkness had settled on the countryside, and with a sudden fear I realized that the three monster women I had seen before might return. I did not know if I had the strength to do battle with them. I was wearing my crucifix, but the gypsy was unarmed. The crucifix was our only protection. As I turned up the lamp to its full brightness, I saw that the gypsy had brought up from the chapel the spade I had used to sever Drakulya's throat. As I took it in my hand, I once again felt the old determination to struggle against hell itself, if necessary, to escape this cursed spot.

The old gypsy had given up his search and was quite willing to return to the courtyard. It was an open question whether we would be safer on the road where the wolves were no doubt still prowling or if it was better to stay here in the courtyard and face whatever supernatural dangers might await us.

As we stood in the courtyard, fate took a determining hand in the decision. The night sky, which had been full and clear, was suddenly filled with rolling dark clouds that came over the mountains from the East. In a few short minutes it suddenly became so dark that our small lamp seemed a tiny spark in a vast expanse of darkness. Lightning and thunder filled the sky. The old gypsy looked at me, wild eyed, and said that we had wakened some great evil, and only blood could answer for this.

I clutched the shovel in one hand and the lamp in the other, wishing that I had come prepared for a confrontation. The cold metal of the barrel of a scattergun would comfort me a great deal more than this wooden-handled shovel. A dozen more men with guns, dogs, and torches would have been especially welcome just then. A heavy rain washed down on us and we were forced to return to the castle for shelter.

My companion lost all courage and, grabbing a bottle of wine from the table in the main hall, ran into the darkness, looking for a crawlspace to hide in and drink himself into oblivion. I let him go; indeed I was tempted to do the same myself.

Carrying the lamp into Drakulya's private chambers, I searched for the bottle of rusty coloured absinthe that I once saw him drink from. After a search, I found the flask I remembered. I lay on the bed and drank it down in deep draughts as quickly as I could. Soon my head was spinning and I felt my eyes close, much against my will, as exhaustion seized me. Sleep took me, followed by a strangely vivid dream:

I was standing in a peaceful vale, before an orchard of apple trees. There was a beautiful woman standing by the trunk of a tree, one arm embracing the trunk and the other around the neck of a huge reptilian beast. In one hand she held an apple and in the other two large keys made of copper. She seemed to offer me the apple, but before I could accept it a horrible sight appeared—the body of a man, still living, his skin flayed from his body. He walked toward me and offered me what he held in his hands—the knife and the bloodied skin, delicate and of the color and texture of porcelain except for where it was spattered with blood in thin spider-web patterns.

He, too, disappeared and was replaced by a bearded figure who was being crucified on a huge X-shaped cross, like the spokes of a wheel. He began to turn, slowly at first, and then gaining in

He, too, disappeared and was replaced by a bearded figure who was being crucified on a huge X-shaped cross, like the spokes of a wheel. He began to turn, slowly at first, and then gaining in speed until he abruptly burst into flame, becoming a huge wheeling disc of fire that flew over the trees, scorching their uppermost leaves, and then suddenly exploding in fragments that scattered in every direction.

Finally there appeared a knight riding a black horse. His round shield was bright yellow, and inscribed on its surface were the words, "REX MUNDI." He rode to the place where I stood and placed the point of his lance against my chest. When he withdrew the point, my chest began to glow with a clear white light that spread through my body, displacing the darkness and the decay of the flesh with purifying rays. I felt as if I were being torn to pieces by wolves . . . or like a body dropped from the tower into a bottomless chasm . . .

I suddenly realized that I was no longer alone. I heard a voice say, "He is young and strong, there is enough here for us all!" I felt a great weight bearing down on me, and my senses reeling from the feeling of primitive sensual ecstasy that shot through me like lightning. In a fraction of a moment the thunder and lightning suddenly stopped. I was thrown clear of the dream, as if a giant hand had seized me and hurled me from the bed with great force.

In that instant I saw the light of the moon fall upon the bedroom floor and a swirl of dust suddenly rise up and seem to form itself into the very figure and self of the Count. His eyes blazed with fury and then a fierce grimace covered his face, as if to say, "It is not so easy to kill a being like myself." And just as quickly the horror faded in the waning light and the dust motes blew into a dozen directions. He was gone.

I rushed to the window. In the distance I saw bright lights in the sky, brighter than the stars, far brighter than any full moon I had ever seen. I was filled with strange desires, and a sense of impending doom lay on my soul. Like a convict walking to the gallows, I slowly made my way out of Drakulya's chambers and down through the long hallway to where my room had been. I pushed open the door and saw a man, very much like myself, lying on the bed.

I stood over him for a few seconds, which dragged on into minutes or even hours. I took great pleasure in listening to the rhythm of his breathing, the sound and rush of his heart beating and the blood pumping through his body. I placed my hand on his chest, to better sense this living thing . . . this thing that persisted in living, against the very touch of death. His life became a great source of comfort to me . . . I was not the only human being in the castle.

A dark cloud passed over us, and in the shadow of that darkness I wrapped him in a cloak and lifted him in my arms and carried him out of the castle and into the courtyard. When next the moon emerged from the clouds, I could see that my burden was actually the old gypsy. He had suffered several serious wounds, like rat bites, and was bleeding profusely.

I threw my jacket over him and dragged him up over to the back of the rig. It was clearly not fit for use, so I freed the horse and walked him back to where I remembered the carriage house should be. There I found the coach and worked the horse into the harness. Climbing onto the seat I easily guided the horse into the courtyard. I carried the gypsy to the coach and made him as easy as possible. I placed the bag containing the severed head and several other items under the seat. Into the seat again, I lashed the horse and we shot out of the courtyard and onto the road back to Borgo Pass. I did not slow down or look back.

Once we reached the pass, I stopped the rig and went to examine the old man's wounds. As I pulled back the blanket I saw a patch of discolored skin on his throat and in the center were two wounds, about two inches apart and at least a quarter-inch deep. I could see that he was cold and covered him with the blanket and my jacket. In the moonlight I could see that he was deathly pale, perhaps near death. As we descended the mountain road as quickly as we could, I searched the side roads for signs of a cottage or any place where we could rest; but it wasn't until I reached the valley that I saw a small cottage, just off the road.

An elderly couple and their son lived there. And they were quite happy to take in the old man. They did not, however, offer me a bed, and they soon made it clear that I could leave him in their where of his accident, but I did not wish to stay for that. The old man placed his hand over the crucifix that hung around his neck and asked, in broken German, "Who are you?" This question spun about in my head, and, looking him straight in the eye, I responded, "I am Drakulya."

Soon I returned to the carriage, after leaving enough money to pay for his care. I climbed up to the seat. A heavy, blinding rain had started. I took the Count's head from the place under the coachman's seat. I unwrapped it and held it in my hands. The coldness of the flesh penetrated what was left of the warmth in my hands. The dead lips spoke to me:

"You are the means by which I will escape . . . to London."

I wrapped the head again in the folds of my cloak. I turned the coach toward the port of Trieste.

As oxen breed bees, putrefying horses breed hornets, and beetles rise from the carcasses of dead asses, so the humours and juices of the marrow of a man's body coagulating, produce serpents.
—Cleomenes, Plutarch

41

Letter, Sir William G____. to Prof. J.H. von Helsing

30 March 1888

My Dear Prof. Von Helsing,

I have followed your experiment notes, as we agreed in our meeting. The tissue samples arrived in good order, and the additional samples you have provided since then have been most helpful in maintaining the quality of my work. The fluids were easily injected directly into the blood stream and the diseased tissue samples were ground up, placed in a carrier fluid and injected directly into a muscle. According to your theory, the infected tissues and fluids should carry the "vampire" disease into the new host, and the host should then experience a catatonic state during which metamorphosis to the new "undead" state takes place, followed by a rapid recovery. There have, unfortunately, been several setbacks in the experiment.

So far, three test animals have died as the direct result of contact with the contaminated samples. In each case the subject was rapidly overtaken by wasting illness, followed by madness, and finally a sudden and violent death. I have performed autopsies on the bodies and brains of each subject, but so far have been unable to determine the nature of the illness.

To make matters even worse, most recently one of my test subjects escaped from confinement, and I was forced to search for him. Luckily, your Mr. Peter Hawkins has proved quite useful in tracking down the subject and dealing him a fatal blow. The subject escaped through a basement window, but the knife blow to the abdomen proved fatal. In fact, the test subject actually died in the arms of a local physician, but gave up the ghost without seriously compromising our project. As a result, I have continued my experiments using only female subjects, as they have proven more docile and manageable.

I will, of course, continue my experiments along the lines you have set out for me. However, I seriously believe that we will have to acquire a "living" tissue donor—one that has already demonstrated a developed immunity to the disease, rather than continue trying to work with tissue specimens from dead bodies.

I think in this case Mr. Hawkins can be put to good use. I will, of course, rely on your inventiveness in locating a suitable subject.

Yours,

Sir William G____.
London

P.S. I find my work has taken on a life of its own. The patients have proven more than I can handle, perhaps more than any man could stand to work with. I have had half-a-dozen attendants quit me in the last year. Only those who have no other opportunities are willing to stay with the work any length of time. I do my autopsies alone. No witnesses are needed, but there is no assistance either. Mr. Hawkins has his own business to run and cannot help me with the day-to-day labour. Who could keep his humanity in the face of such a disease—the slow wasting away of a human life. My autopsies prove nothing—they are fruitless exercises in futility . . . and the blood, my god, the blood everywhere till i don't know where to turn or even who i am or what i am becoming . . . i am now infected with my own creation . . . from handling the tainted blood and tissues . . . god help me man . . . the corpses piled in a basement corner and the stench of blood filling nostrils . . . dust and dirt and the many rats who watch me . . . the flies, the flies . . . they talk to me, do you know that, yes, they talk to me about blood and that's not all . . . they watch me when I kill . . .

Thus behind the Greek notion that women may conceive by a serpent-god seems to lie the belief that they can conceive by the dead in the form of serpents. If such a belief was ever held, it would be natural that barren women should resort to graves in order to have their wombs quickened, and this may explain why they visited the shrine of the serpent-god Aesculapius for that purpose; the shrine was perhaps first a grave. It is significant that in Syria the shrines of St. George, to which childless women go to get offspring, always include a tomb or the likeness of one.
—*The Golden Bough*, Sir J.G. Fraser

42

Letter from R.F. Burton to Arminius Vambery

4 Sept. 1889
Arminius Vambery
Claridge's Hotel, Brook Street, London

Dear Arminius,
Last evening I was having a late supper at the home of the French consul when he told me a story that might be of interest to you. It has to do with a mysterious foreigner, a Comte de Saint-Germain, who knew his grandmother during the time of the French Revolution. The consul developed an interest in Count Saint-G. and has been studying the history of this enigmatic character. Indeed, he has requested a post in Vienna in order to further investigate the origins of this Comte de S.-G.

The Count was, according to the consul, a figure shrouded in mystery. It is known that he came to France from Vienna in 1740 or 41, where he quickly began to move among the French aristocracy and, in a short time, became an agent for the King of France, often acting in the King's behalf in "diplomatic missions" to other European countries.

The Count was an accomplished linguist, having a strong command of French, English, Italian, Spanish, Latin, Swedish, Greek, Polish, Czech, Russian, Turkish, and a half-dozen minor Balkan dialects. This gift for languages was equalled only by his fondness for aliases.

This Count was a brilliant conversationalist who visited countless dinner parties given by the French aristocracy. But in all that time he is said never to have been seen eating in public. In addition, he is said to have had an almost encyclopedic memory for historical events, often chatting for hours on end about events that occurred during the reigns of Charles V, Charlemagne, and the Merovingian kings, and he often related conversations that took place centuries ago.

The Count's gifts were, of course, greatly exaggerated by the Parisians who thrive on court gossip. When he told Marie Antoinette that he was "very much older" than he appeared, it was soon widely rumoured in Paris that he had discovered the Elixir of Life and that he was over five-hundred years old! The Count often played on the credulity of his listeners, once describing the Marriage at Cana and the "great secret" and "wondrous events" that took place. Some time later when the famous Casanova asked about these rumors, the Count replied, "These Frenchmen believe me to be five hundred years old, and I do not bother to disillusion them. Though, indeed, I am much older than I look." When Casanova, who was not entirely satisfied with this answer, pressed him further, he merely smiled and said, "My friend, I am only a little less than three hundred, but after the first few centuries it becomes quite difficult to keep track and I may be a bit older."

More amazing still are the stories about the Count's fabulous jewel collection. Indeed, it is this jewel collection that first drew the consul to the story of the mysterious Count. On one occasion the Count displayed to his friends a jewel box with an enormous yellow topaz inlaid on the cover. During the time they observed the box, the jewel actually changed color from yellow to a deep red. The Count claimed that the heat from the fireplace had affected the color. He poured water from his glass onto the stone and it changed back to its original yellow!

On another occasion, the Count was showing his jewels to the Queen, with Mme. du Hausset in attendance. According to the story, Mme. du Hausset greatly admired a cross of red and white stones in the collection, fashioned in the shape of a dragon. The Count insisted that she keep it, and the Queen—believing the stones to be mere paste immitations—indicated that she could accept the gift. Later, when the stones were examined, they were discovered to be rubies and pearls of immense value. The pin was, of course, returned.

In addition to his other talents, the Count was an accomplished musician, playing the harpsichord, violin, and guitar with great skill and even composing a number of pieces for the violin. On one occasion, when some friends began discussing music, he asked that they change the subject, declaring, "I have already said all that can be said on this." The Count also knew the young Anton Mesmer and is believed to be the source for his theories of animal magnetism.

The Count was also a chemist of great ability, pioneering the use of pesticides and developing a number of dyes and bleaches, including the development of an inexpensive carmine dye which eventually helped to make him quite wealthy.

Eventually, however, history caught up with him, as powerful nobles became envious of his relationship with the King and Queen. While on an important mission to England, his position was cleverly sabotaged and he was forced to flee the country. No one is quite sure what his mission was or how he was compromised, but there are rumors that while he was in London, St. Germain met the young Wolfgang Mozart and initiated him into his own "masonic" order.

After the passage of several years, the Count returned to Paris and tried to see the King. All his attempts failed, and instead soldiers were sent to arrest him. But when they reached his home, he had already disappeared. It is rumored that his friends placed him on a ship bound for the New England colonies and that he took part in the American Revolution, adopting the identity of a Polish aristocrat.

The Count was both a brilliant strategist and an accomplished cavalry officer, having fought in the Russian Revolution of 1762. But after fighting in the Colonial army for several years, he was wounded by a stray shot from one of his own sentinels, while returning from a reconnaissance mission. This brush with death appears to have dampened his enthusiasm for fighting, as he then faked his own death—including a burial at sea—in order to travel to Canada unhindered.

At this point the Count disappears from history—until his death was reported in 1786. However, this seems to be simply another of his subterfuges, as he is believed to have returned to Paris in 1789 and for a time found common cause with the revolutionaries. His opposition to the use of the guillotine led to his own imprisonment, but once again he escaped.

In 1793 he was reported to be helping aristocrats escape the guillotine, conveying them by secret routes to England. One source claims that the Count was captured by French agents and spent his last days in a prison cell. Still others report seeing him in Egypt in 1815, and still others in Tibet in 1818. Eventually, the reports dwindle to a mere trickle.

The greatest mystery of the Comte de Saint-G. is his origin. During his lifetime he often claimed to be "the last of the Rakoczy" and heir to the throne of Transylvania. Little truth is set by this claim, but certainly he has his origins in eastern Europe, perhaps as the son of a wealthy Jewish merchant—his refusal to eat in public stemming from the observance of dietary law.

Still others believe that he was a kabbalist who had in fact discovered the "elixir vitale" through an ancient alchemical process. If this is true, then perhaps he has some connection with the story you told me.

But what really brought home this story is the fact that a few weeks ago a young man took ship here for England. This man had in his possession a jeweled brooch of red and white stones in the form of a dragon, not unlike the one described by the French consul as having once belonged to the Count Saint-G. He was brought to me because his papers showed him to be an Englishman named Jonathan Harker, but his manner and East European accent suggested something else. Indeed, although he has never before visited the Continent, I was able to detect that he knew at least five local dialects fluently enough to follow my questioning of other travelers. But as his passport and papers were in perfect order, I could not legally detain him.

This story strikes me as having the promise of one of those fabulous "Mysteries of the Orient" that you appreciate so much. You may find a place for it in one of your literary collections. Who knows?

R.F.B.,
London and Trieste

Mr. and Mrs. Etheridge began to fondle, and after struggling a little
together on the bed, Mamma was pulled onto her husband,
and they commenced a most luscious St. George.
—*The Power of Mesmerism*, Anon.

43

"What are you? And on what account have you come aboard my ship?" Thus I was confronted by the Captain of the Niobe as I came up the gangway of the passenger steamer. I handed him my ticket and my papers. He looked them over with one eye and carefully took my measure, too, as my new wardrobe did not suit me well.

"Please come aboard, Mister . . . Harker; your bags have already been taken to your stateroom." I pushed past him aloofly, without speaking. There would be plenty of time for the social amenities once we left port.

"Mr. Harker! Mr. Harker!" I responded a bit too slowly and turned to face a young seaman. "Your chest was taken to a forward hold, like you asked, sir, and here are the papers." He handed me the documents as I slipped him a modest tip for his trouble.

I went to my stateroom and opened the leather pouch. It contained the bill of lading for the old sea chest. This, of course, was the first time I had smuggled human remains onto a ship. But I managed the chest safely through customs, despite the noisy interference of the English Consul and was now safely launched on my journey to England.

Going up to the deck, I moved silently to the prow enveloped in the growing darkness—a lone figure on a tossing, violent sea. The smell of the salt brine brought with it a much stronger sensation—a sudden belief that I, who had for so many years been dead to life, was now truly alive, was now at last to taste life; it was years since I have felt such health, such hunger.

That evening I drank a toast to the sea.

Later that night, I watched the distant lights as we left the harbour. My first voyage on a large sea-going ship makes me uneasy somehow. The port of Trieste may not be much different now than it was a century ago, but one can sense that the old fears—the dangers of sea-travel—have faded and the spirits of Mercantile Success have replaced the old gods. St. Christopher is no longer venerated and St. Nicholas with his glass grail is forgotten—fire is not now a threat but a friend-servant to the sailors.

At the same time I set out on the passenger ship Niobe from Trieste, I knew that the 49 boxes of earth were aboard an old relic—a hulking wooden sailing ship called the Demeter. It was only right that this cargo be carried aboard a ship dedicated to one of the old goddesses. I could not imagine these boxes being carried in the cavernous belly of one of these iron leviathans. The question of safety bothered me, but I knew too that in case of shipwreck they could perhaps break free of a wooden vessel, float to shore, and receive a true burial. But in an iron ship they could only sit at the bottom of the sea in a rusting iron vault—with not a hope of release and an earthly burial.

And I will arrive in London, where I will soon begin my search for a hiding place for the lot of them. The boxes are by now well on their way through the Atlantic, lodged safely in the hold of the Demeter. Their importance cannot be overestimated, for they are as life itself to me, the very proof of my new existence. Through these relics I have the strength of all the dead ones who live in me. I now carry them within me—their souls, their lives, their memories—all that they were has found its preservation through me, as my soul will find its salvation through them.

I will arrive in London a few days ahead of the boxes—long enough to arrange for a safe hiding place for them when they arrive. It is in this transaction that my enemies' plans and papers have been most helpful. Although they planned that the boxes would go to Carfax Abbey, I can now easily divert them to a different destination—one of my own choosing—to some small town in Wales or Scotland. I have to accomplish this before Mr. Hawkins and the others discover my betrayal.

Now I am much less an enigma than a man. Granted that I have
cheated death over and over, played life like a card game, using
each of my victims to cheat death one more time. Granted that I
have forced Harker to become the vessel, the grail of this eternal
soul, the carrier of this selfhood. And what did he gain? Eternal
life. And what did he lose? His soul. This is the legacy of the
Drakulya.

---

*Nor is the Phallic cultus in any respect a cultus of the full-grown and
branching tree. In its earliest form the symbol is everywhere a mere
stauros, or pole; and although this stock or rod budded in the shape of the
thyrsus and the shepherd's staff, yet, even in its latest developments, the
worship is confined to small bushes and shrubs and diminutive plants of
a particular kind. Nor is it possible again to dispute the fact that every
nation, at some stage or other of its history, has attached to this cultus
precisely that meaning which the Brahman now attaches to the Linga
and the Yoni. That the Jews clung to it in this special sense with
vehement tenacity is the bitter complaint of the prophets; and the
crucified serpent adored for its healing powers stood untouched in the
Temple until it was removed and destroyed by Hezekiah.*
—Ophiolatreia, or Serpent Worship, H. Jennings

44

I found myself at last in London. I made my way up from the
docks to the very center of the city. Quite near were the wide
streets, brightly lit and inviting us to join the crowded throngs of
people. Carriages rolled past, carrying revelers to the opera, to the
theater, or perhaps a party or a ball. I had never before seen the
city in quite this way. I had never seen the real London; and even
though I now so much wished to see it, mine was the anticipation
of one who—more than just to look on a new and different thing—

wished it near me so that I could reach out and take it. This was a yearning to attain, a hunger to taste, a desire to be bathed with its being.

Safe, I passed down the avenues—safely I mixed with the crowd where it was deepest. To be still was not in my power. I was helpless to resist. I could not quietly observe. I reveled in the scene! I drank in the cold night air like wine!

I knew my route to my hotel, yet it seemed as if I was hindered from pursuing it directly. A sight or a sound drew me aside. Voices called to me, luring me down this alley and then down that street. As the great god Thor once tried to drink up the sea, I now tried to quench the passionate thirst for new life. Amidst the glare and hurry, the throng and noise, I still secretly hoped to find one who, knowing the nature of my thirst, could explore the uttermost center of my being.

To those who love darkness and cold night, the daylight is a harsh and painful mistress. But we creatures of the night do not fear the light of lamps; rather they draw us near to them so that we can drink their light, their warmth. But there is one light that we search for endlessly. It is the light of Truth. Unlike the fire that lives and dies, it is like the sun that lives forever shining in perpetual rhythms of strength and weakness, light and darkness.

I turned then toward my hotel. I hoped to find Mina there, waiting for me. I knew, as only I could know, that it was here that I was to find her, the true Mina, it was here that she would give herself into my hands—of her own free will—as her true husband. Or so I thought.

But it was not to be, not tonight. The hand of fate had intervened.

The sun had begun to rise, and I turned quickly toward my hotel. For blood that does not hide itself in the earth before the dawn is soon drunk up by the sun. Only a madman enjoys the ability to move smoothly from a nocturnal to a daylight existence without confusing his day-dreams and his nightmares.

I reached the hotel where our bags had already arrived. The night porter handed me my key and I turned toward the stairs. "Mr. Harker." I turned to the porter, clearly annoyed to be hindered from going straight to my room.

"Mr. Harker . . . a telegram." He handed me the envelope.
I tore it open as I shut the door to my room. A slip of paper
inside said only,

SHIP DEMETER OFFICIALLY DECLARED OVERDUE.

I knew in an instant that the boxes were gone. But taken by
whom? Peter Hawkins? Or perhaps his employer? Or some
other, still hidden in the shadows. I could only wait now and
hope that the evening papers could tell me where they had
been taken.

And as Moses lifted up the serpent in the wilderness, even so must the
Son of Man be lifted up; that whosoever believeth in him should not
perish, but have everlasting life.
—John 3:14-15

45

In what region, amongst what strange beings was I waking?
Two days have passed, and there has been no news of the
Demeter. One ship claims to have sighted her in the North Sea,
but it was during a heavy storm and there has been no further
confirmation of this from other ships.

I have gone out again tonight among the people of London, and
as I pass among them I see again the strange mix of expressions
on their faces, the faces of men and women who are long dead,
victims of a living death. It is strange, as the years pass, to see the
same expressions so exactly reproduced by their children and
their grandchildren, so that every crowd seems to contain many
copies of the same mix of pain and fear.

I have followed them into the main arteries of the town. They seem to ignore me as they pass into the lighted rooms. I go up to them, smile, even buy them a drink. But they do not recognize what I have become, which is just as well.

I pass into another party, and then another, and another. I watch them all as they eat and drink, oblivious to my presence here among them. The wine swirls down their throats to quench their inexhaustible thirsts, and champagne spouts from countless bottles into long-stemmed glasses. I watch them descend into drunkenness and stupor, their human natures debased and slowly annihilated. And in those moments I see immortality rendered, if not irrelevant, at least impossibly wrong. They are the shadows of men, enslaved by mortality and judged by fate to be unworthy of eternal life. And so here they try to drown this judgement in drink and laughter. But I have no right to judge them, except in so far as I am drawn into contact with them and forced to breathe the odour of excrement, decay and death.

I am . . . alone. I speak and no one hears. They are the shadows of men. They possess only their human existence, severed long ago from the knowledge that I would awaken in them. The mud of the river begets them of the slime. They grow warm in the morning light and thrive, nurtured in mud, until the sunset. They grow without thought, without will, without the knowledge even of their own existence. But now . . . I feel as if my own life is being appropriated by some hidden force. I can not wait much longer.

He was the same as Osiris, the Sun; and hence was often called Ob-El, or Pytho-Sol; and there were pillars sacred to him, with curious heiroglyphical inscriptions, which had the same name. they were very lofty, and narrow in comparison to their length; hence among the Greeks, who copied from the Egyptians, everything gradually tapering to a point was styled Obelos, and Obeliscus. Ophel (Oph-El) was a name of the same purport, and many sacred mounds, or Tapha, were thus denominated from the serpent Deity, to whom they were sacred.
—*Ophiolatreia, or Serpent Worship*, H. Jennings

46

I reached Whitby by train two days after the newspapers reported that the Demeter had run aground during a storm in this small harbor town in the north of England. I hoped to make inquiries with the local authorities. I could easily claim the boxes—written up as a shipment of Transylvanian soil. But I knew also that by now the boxes would in all likelihood be on their way to some new destination—But where?

Arriving at Whitby shortly after sunset, I soon made my way to the harbor and inspected the ruptured hull of the Demeter. It lay aground on a sand bar like a beached whale, and people were crawling over its form like an army of ants. The cargo holds had already been emptied. I asked about the boxes, and the old shipping agent scratched his head and puzzled, "Boxes of earth?" He moved slowly, looking through a sheaf of papers in his metal clip.

"The name on the shipping manifest is Count Drakulya."

"Yes . . . Mr. Drakulya . . . they were taken yesterday by wagon to . . . yes . . . sent to a warehouse and then they go next week, I guess, to . . . yes . . . Purfleet, Essex." He added, "Some place called Carfax Abbey. Must be some relics or such. Holy dirt. Beats me why people ship common dirt around the world. What's wrong with good old English dirt, eh???"

I moved away, uncertain then whether I was the victim of some ruthless British efficiency or an actual conspiracy. I started up the long stairs to the Crescent Hotel, where my bags had gone earlier. Stopping on the first landing, I looked out over the quiet harbor. The moon had risen in the north, over the sea, and shadows of the clouds fell across the opposite bluff. And there, on the bluff's edge, was a graveyard and a lone figure waiting there, dressed all in white, with her hair shining in the bright moonlight.

I descended the sea stairs slowly and deliberately, and quickly crossed the wooden walkway to the opposite embankment. Climbing the hillside by a winding, roundabout path, I lost sight of her for several minutes. Soon, however, I passed through the iron gateway, moving among the blank stones to the place where she had stood.

I turned toward the sea, and then I saw her seated on a stone bench facing the sea. She seemed a vision to me, a link to the past. There was something familiar in her poise, the way she held her head.

I rushed to join her. She did not notice, but looked out over the sea. She seemed old, ancient, though in earthly years a mere twenty-five or six. But she was more beautiful than I can describe. And I knew that my trip to Whitby had been set by fate attuned to a higher law than I could comprehend.

Standing behind her, I placed my hands on her shoulders. She was cold, terribly cold, like marble, and for a moment I thought she was a statue placed here to overlook the harbour. As I bent over her, I felt the cold magnetic power drawing me to her. A barrier that had separated us before, but suddenly it fell away. And never again would we fear to be apart from each other, as I pressed my lips to her shoulder and then to the white moonlit spot on her throat.

As if with surprise, she cried out a muffled cry and then was silent. An eternity passed. The void! The void! I stood on the edge of the maelstrom that was her soul, sucking me in. I pulled back from the abyss. Struggling against the void, I pushed her away from me.

She was sleeping as I lay her body across the stone bench. It was then I heard the sound of steps on the path below warning me of the approach of a young woman. "Lucy! Lucy!" I heard her call, "Wake up, please, wake up!" as I stepped back into the shadows of an enormous oak. The intruder passed a cloak around her shoulders and led her, silent, down the path toward the walkway. I watched as they started their descent of the slope. Her name came readily to my lips. "Lucy, Lucy," I repeated. How can this be? I had believed this woman to be Mina, but instead it was her friend Lucy Westenra. Then, the horror of this mistake pressed into my soul; I followed the two of them down the hill.

I reached Mina before she could take her first step on the stair. "Mina!" I called. I saw her turn and look at me, seemingly for the first time. And then she said, "Jonathan" and, leaving Lucy to rest on a wooden seat, she turned and ascended the hill to where I stood. The look in her eyes troubled me deeply, for I saw that she did truly love this Jonathan Harker whose body I had appropriated. She rushed to me and her hand brushed my cheek. A tear formed in my eye . . . the first tear I had shed for myself in many years. I held her as if I had both lost and then found her again, for truly I had found and lost her in the same moment.

"Do you then love Jonathan that much?" I said. Her face revealed shock as she pushed away from me. "Who? . . . What are you?"

"Do you not recognize me, my love? Indeed, we had very little time together when you visited my homeland last summer. Then, too, we met in a graveyard, just outside Buda-Pesth. You were seated at my shrine, The Widow's Seat. Just as Lucy sat at the Widow's Seat here tonight in this English graveyard."

"Drakulya!"

"Yes. You do know me. Good. For I am now your husband Jonathan. Or at least his bitter half. Do you know that Jonathan tried to kill me. Not that I don't deserve death, but I am not that easy to destroy . . . You do love him, don't you?"

"Yes, I love him more than life."

"Very well, I may return him to you, after I have finished my mission here. But you must not interfere with me. Not if you wish you husband back."

"Jonathan, let me take you to see Dr. Seward. I'm sure he can help you."

"You are wasting time. Jonathan cannot hear you. I cannot let him hear you. I need his identity for a few short weeks. Then I will move on to a new body and give up this one. Remember, if you want him as a whole man, then do not search for me. Do not interfere in my movements. Do not go to the police."

I walked over to where she stood, near the sleeping Lucy. I took her arms and looked into her dark eyes. These were the eyes I saw in my vision, my vision of England.

"I love you Mina, more than you can know. Your love for Jonathan only makes me want you more. Do you really love him so much that you would deny me. Say that you do not love me."

She did not answer.

"Could you love us both? If I keep his body, eventually in time we would mix our souls. This new being would be both the man Jonathan and the undead Drakulya. Could I hope that one day we would both love you together, then I would stay with you as your husband for as long as this body would permit. I might even die a mortal death, to be with you. If you could love both men, like the rise and fall of the tides are the same sea. Is there a hope that you could love us both?"

She did not answer, but placed her hand on my cheek. I placed my hand on her arm and she fell into a deep sleep. The power of my spell was still there. "Take Lucy to the hotel. I will be along soon to claim my baggage. But you will not see me again as Drakulya until after I have finished my mission here in England. When you wake from this sleep in a few moments, you will not remember seeing me here in Whitby."

I sat Mina on the bench next to Lucy and moved back into the trees to wait for their departure.

The "stipes crucis." In ordinary language, the trunk of the cross, for stipes can mean a trunk (of a tree or plant), a stake and even a pale. This was what in early times was meant by the word cross. "Crux," like "stauros" in Greek, meant no more than a stake fixed vertically in the ground, much the same as "skolops" which means a pale; indeed the words "stauros" and "skolops" could be interchanged, so that certain authors have used the word "anaskolopisein" (to empale) in regard to the crucifixion of St. Peter and that of Our Lord Jesus Christ.
—A Doctor at Calvary, Pierre Barbet

47

After some careful questioning of the hotel manager, I managed to confirm that the woman in the graveyard had been Mina's friend, Miss Lucy Westenra of Brook Street, London. Lucy had clearly been under a mesmeric suggestion, to have wandered so far from the hotel in her nightdress. But it was not a spell of my making. Yet even with these facts, I could not grasp the motive for what had been done. And yet, my meeting with Mina had given me a new purpose.

Then the next morning in the papers, I read about the murder of nearly the entire crew of the Demeter, the ship that had carried my boxes. This horrible butchery! Lost and confused, I set out the following evening for Carfax Abbey in Purfleet.

What would happen there was impossible to tell. Could Hawkins be there? Or perhaps his employer? Someone knew what was being carried aboard the Demeter, and, from the stories in the paper, that someone was careful, ruthless, and fully capable of using horrific butchery to instill fear.

The murders of the Demeter's crewmen, and finally of the Captain—his throat torn out by some half-human beast—this fact alone showed me that someone had entered the hold and had opened the boxes. And that person was completely insane.

The knowledge of these relics could, in a mind already unstable, result in homicidal mania. But whoever he was and no matter where he had gone, he was no longer here. The boxes, delivered to Purfleet, would lure him out of hiding. And I would be waiting there too.

I arrived at Purfleet and made my way to the Abbey. It was well after dark. Standing near the gateway to Carfax Abbey, I could easily look to the west and see the glow of London in the distance. It is there in London that Mina waits for me, like a ripe pomegranate. But she must wait, for my great enemy is near.

I entered the grounds, and strangely no watch was set against my coming—am I then an intruder? Or am I just an insect flying past a web set for another?

The outer doors were not locked, and I soon found my way into the innermost recesses of the Abbey, using a set of keys left on a hall table. And in the pitch-dark vault I found them, set out in rows, as I would have set them. How did they know to set the boxes out this way?

My confusion grew, but before I could further inspect the boxes, I heard several loud voices coming from outside . . .

"Mr. Renfield . . . John . . . please don't run."

"Stay back!"

"Resistance is useless. Please don't struggle. We don't really want to hurt you . . ."

"You needn't tie me; I shall go with you quietly."

I went to the front window and looking out saw three men escorting a fourth away from the house and toward the asylum beyond the old wall. There was something in this fourth man's manner that struck me as rather odd. He was past middle-age and heavy-set, yet strong and thickly built, with an odd gait when he walked that reminded me of the Emperor Napoleon. That fact would, of course, explain why he was now a resident of an asylum. Such places are filled to brimming with Napoleons. This one had attempted his escape tonight by going across the abbey grounds, but his attendants had caught him.

Once they were out of sight, I returned to the vault and opened the boxes, one by one. Everything was in order, with one exception. The body of my brother Vlad was missing from the group. The rest were none the worse for their sea adventure. I closed the boxes again and screwed the lids shut.

Do I dare to wait? I could not leave them here long, for others, besides Hawkins, could know of their presence in the Abbey. I decided to move them, a few at a time, to other locations. My existence was insignificant compared with theirs. Or is it something else? Was I simply grasping a naked blade, repeating King Arthur's mistake by confusing the blade and the pommel?

Two weeks passed, during which I made arrangements for moving the boxes. I could not use the name Harker nor that of Mr. Hawkins. They were too obvious and too well known to my enemies. I needed a real name to borrow—one not easily traced.

I made the arrangements. The carter took my gold coin and my written instructions. In the morning he would return to transport a half-dozen boxes to a house I had rented in the London suburbs.

"Thank you, Mr. Renfield, I shall return o' the morrow to move and 'carry out' your instructions—to the letter sir."

I sent him off with the keys, and they would return tomorrow to move the last of the boxes. The boxes had been moved only a few at a time, using different movers and being routed to separate locations. The slow process had taken two full weeks, as I remained in hiding at the old Abbey, not even daring to light a candle. Not until they were all safely distributed could I move to the next step—confronting Mr. Hawkins and his employer.

That evening I made my way to Mr. Hawkins' place of business. A tiny bell rang as I entered from the street entrance. I waited. No answer, just quiet stillness. I let myself in with my key and walked back to the office. There I found Hawkins at his desk, slumped over a stack of papers. His eyes bulged from their sockets and his flesh was quite cold. I picked up his cup of tea—half full—and detected the faint odour of almonds.

He was dead, poisoned by . . . whom? I went through the papers on his desk, one by one, until I came across a familiar name: Prof. Joachim Heinrich Von Helsing, Wallenberg Institute, Dantzig.

I then read Mr. Hawkins unsent letter mentioning Prof. Von Helsing's work on human mental evolution and hypnotic suggestion. Hawkins bragged about how he, a simple solicitor, was doing some special work for Prof. Von Helsing that could advance human knowledge to an enormous degree. He failed to go into any detail of what kind of work he was doing for the Professor.

I left Mr. Hawkin's corpse where it was and returned to the house I had rented in the west end of London. I brought with me the papers from Hawkins' office relating to the purchase of Carfax Abbey and the transportation of the boxes to Purfleet. I found, too, several letters and notes from Mina to her step-father.

Going through the papers, I found references to a Lord Godalming. Somehow it was no surprise when the next day I read about Lord Godalming's death in the evening papers. And there were other incriminating papers too, including copies of commitment letters for the alleged lunatic, John Renfield.

The subtle thread connecting it all together still eluded me. Why would they go to such trouble to take the boxes and then allow me to take them back again without a struggle? Who is this John Renfield—the so-called lunatic? And what is his connection to Carfax Abbey? Could he have taken the body of Vlad Drakulya?

Christ hath redeemed us from the curse of the law, being made a curse for us; for it is written, "Cursed is every one that hangeth on a tree."
—*Galatians 3:13*

48

From Jonathan Harker's papers

Ebb tide in appetite to-day. Cannot eat, cannot rest, so write instead. Since my return from Buda-Pesth I have a sort of empty feeling; nothing in the world seems to be worth the doing. Strange gaps have formed in my memory of recent events. I seem divided in my very soul, and a strange lethargy has claimed possession of me . . . As Dr. Seward says that the only cure for this sort of thing is looking at it in a more violently deranged mental state, I went down amongst his regular patients. Dr. Seward suggested I meet Mr. Renfield, a lunatic who had escaped the asylum two months ago and was only recently recaptured near the Abbey. No one seems able to discover where he was during those missing weeks. Today I seemed to get near to the heart of his mystery.

I questioned Renfield fully, with a view to making myself master of the facts of the case. In his manner, I now see something of the cruelty of his nature. Indeed, I have come to suspect that Renfield may himself have been somehow responsible for the deaths of the crew of the Demeter. This seems impossible, yet Renfield is, I believe, fully capable of murdering a dozen men in order to achieve his ends. If there be anything behind this suspicion it will be valuable to trace it afterwards accurately for the authorities, so I had better commence to do so, therefore—

Mr. Renfield, age 59. Hard temperament; great strength; morbid, excitable, gloomy, obsessive, ending in some fixed idea which I cannot make out. I presume that the personality itself and the disturbing influence end at the grip of his fingers. A dangerous man, probably even more dangerous if religious.

"In centrum sensibus." That I think of this on the metaphorical point of a compass is shown thusly: When my self is the fixed point, the driving force is my love for Mina. It is that force which bounds my passions and holds my insanity in check.

My love for Mina is my religion, so that when she asked that I place myself in Dr. Seward's care as a patient "in residence," I could not resist her request. Indeed, I may here continue my quest for sanity by testing myself against the insanity of the inmates here.

Jesus was called "John" because it was believed that he "had," that is possessed, and was possessed by, the spirit of the Baptist. . . . It was generally believed that the spirit of any human being who had come to an unjust, violent, or otherwise untimely end was of enormous power.
—*Jesus the Magician*, Morton Smith

49

From Jonathan Harker's papers

Renfield grows more interesting the more I know the man. He is selfish and secretive. I wish I could get at his secret. He seems to have some scheme of his own, but what it is I do not yet know. His mind seems focused on his pets; indeed, he has such curious turns in his thinking that I imagine he is only cruel.

When a horrid blow-fly, bloated with some carrion food, buzzed into the room, he caught it, held it exultantly for a few moments between his finger and thumb, and, before I knew what he was going to do, put it in his mouth and ate it. The attendants scolded him for it, but he argued quietly that it was very good and very wholesome; that it was life, strong life, and gave life to him.

He has some deep problem in his mind, for he keeps a little book in which he is always jotting down something. Whole pages of it are filled with masses of figures, generally single numbers added up in batches, and then the totals added in batches again, as though he were trying to sort out some experimental calculation.

There is a method in his madness, and an idea of what he is up to is growing in my mind. I kept away from him for a few days, so that I might notice if there were any change. Things happened so that, several days later, I mistakenly said something that angered him. His face fell, and I could see a warning of danger in it, for there was a sudden fierce, sidelong look which meant killing. The man is a homicidal maniac. I shall test him with his present craving and see how it will work out; then I shall know more.

11 p.m. Renfield was given a strong opiate to-night, enough to make even him sleep, and I took away his pocket-book to look at it. The thought that has been buzzing about my brain lately is complete, and the theory proved. This homicidal maniac is working out some plan in his head, the results of which could have dire consequences, if he were given freedom to carry it out. What would be his later steps? It would almost be worth while to complete the experiment. It might be done if there were only a sufficient cause.

Mina has arrived to take dinner with Dr. Seward and myself. She has been absent a great deal of late, as her friend, Miss Lucy Westenra, has taken ill. Mina has been very busy trying to nurse her back to health. She seems very tired, almost exhausted, but keeps up a good front in my presence.

We are both weary tonight and low in spirits. I cannot but think of Mina, and how different things might have been if I hadn't gone on that terrible journey . . . No, I shall not think of those creatures tonight! I have thought of Mina, and I shall not dishonour her by mixing the two. I hope tonight shall be dreamless . . . At the stroke of midnight I felt a strange compulsion seize me. Mina was asleep; I did not wake her. Not tonight. Instead, I wandered out into the darkness and across the lawn to the wall that separates the asylum from Carfax Abbey. Moving along the wall, I soon arrived at the gate and entered the graveyard of the old deserted Abbey. It all seemed like a dream. Soon I found myself in the Abbey itself.

Oddly enough, the Abbey was apparently being used for storage as a great many wooden boxes were stacked together in the main room. A weird force seized me, and I began to open the boxes, one by one. Strange, each box was filled with a layer of earth, plain dirt. Why were they here? And who brought them here? I grew very puzzled and tired. But soon I was struck by an even stranger sight. I saw Mr. Renfield enter the room by a far door. He seemed unaware of my presence, snuffling at the boxes and then moving on to a place just before the altar. Here he seized hold of a block the size of a gravestone and lifted it out of the way with his bare hands.

This left a hole in the floor about four feet square, and I move forward to see what he was about. As my eyes adjusted to the greater darkness, I saw that Renfield had a coffin hidden in the crawlspace below the altar. As he raised the lid, I saw a corpse—what was left of a corpse, anyway. And then Renfield . . . I cursed my eyes that I would ever witness such a horrible sight . . . Renfield laid hands on the corpse and began to eat.

I was sickened and terrified at the same time, and in an instant I found myself back in my room at the asylum. Was this a dream? God forgive me for such thoughts.

———————————

Again, in Rhodes the fair Helen was worshipped under the title Helen of the Tree, because the queen of the island had caused her handmaids, disguised as Furies, to string her up to a bough.
—The Golden Bough, Sir J.G. Fraser

50

From Jonathan Harker's papers

The case of Renfield grows even more strange. He has now so far quieted down that there are long spells of calm. For the first week after his most recent attack, he was perpetually violent. Then one night, just as the moon rose, he grew quiet, and kept murmuring to himself: "Now I can wait; now I can wait." The attendant told me of this, so I went down at once to have a look at him. He was still in the strait-waistcoat and in the padded room, but the manic look had gone from his face, and his eyes had something of their old pleading—I might almost say, "cringing" softness. The patient had sense enough to see my distrust, for, coming close to me, he said in a whisper, all the while looking furtively:

"You think I could hurt you! Fancy me hurting you! You are my brother in blood."

Am I to take it that I have anything in common with him, so that we are, as it were, to stand together; or has he gained from me some good that my well-being is needful to him? I must find out later on. Tonight he will not speak further.

After a while I left him. The attendant tells me that he was quiet until just before dawn, and that then he began to get uneasy, and at length violent, until at last he fell into a paroxysm which exhausted him so that he swooned into a sort of coma.

Next day. Renfield had only one outburst and that was yesterday at an unusual time. Just before the stroke of noon he began to grow restless. The attendant knew the symptoms, and at once summoned aid. Fortunately the men came at a run, and were just in time, for at the stroke of noon he became so violent that it took all their strength to hold him. In about five minutes, however, he began to get more and more quiet, and finally sank into sort of melancholy, in which state he has remained up to now.

The attendant tells me that his screams whilst in the paroxysm were really appalling; they soon found their hands full attending to some of the other patients who were frightened by him. Indeed, I can quite understand the effect, for the sounds disturbed even me, though I was some distance away. It is now after the dinner-hour of the asylum, and as yet the patient sits in a corner brooding, with a dull, sullen, woe-begone look in his face, which seems rather to indicate than to show something directly. I cannot quite understand it.

Another change. At five o'clock I looked in on him, and found him seemingly as happy and contented as he used to be. He was catching flies and eating them, and was keeping note of his capture by making nail-marks on the edge of the door between the ridges of padding. When he saw me, he came over and apologized for his bad conduct, and asked me in a very humble, cringing way to be led back to his own room and to have his ledger-book again.

Midnight. Another change in him. I was standing at our own gate looking at the sunset, when once more I heard him yelling. As his room is on this side of the house I could hear it better than in the morning. It was a shock to me to turn from the wonderful smoky beauty of an English sunset with its lurid lights and inky shadows and to realize all the grimness that streams from this cold stone building, with its wealth of breathing misery, and my own desolate soul to endure it all.

I reached him just as the sun was going down, and from his window saw the red disc sink. As it sank he became less frenzied; and just as it dipped he slid from the hands that held him, an inert mass, to the floor. It is wonderful, however, what recuperative power lunatics have, for within a few minutes he stood up quite calmly and looked around him.

Then, Dr. Seward called me to his office and sent me to London, cat-quick, in order to hand deliver a letter for him to Arthur Holmwood:

6 September.

My dear Art,

My news to-day is not so good. Lucy until this morning had gotten a bit better—but then a sudden collapse. There is, however, one good thing which has arisen from it; Mrs. Westenra was naturally anxious concerning Lucy, and has consulted me professionally about her. I took advantage of the opportunity, and told her that Dr. Von Helsing is in London and has heard of Miss Lucy's case. He has asked that I put Lucy in his charge; so now Von Helsing can come and go in her mother's house—and this without alarming Mrs. Westenra unduly, for a shock to her would mean sudden death, and, in Lucy's weak condition, this might be disastrous to her too.

I have also sent Jonathan Harker to help Mina with Lucy and Mrs. Westenra. Jonathan has been here several weeks recovering from the difficulties of a recent trip. But I am sure the change of scene will do him good. And he will fit in with the household, as the husband of Lucy's dear friend Mina, without upsetting their routine. We are hedged in with difficulties, all of us, my poor old fellow; but, please God, we shall come through them all right. If any need arises I shall write, so that, if you do not hear from me, take it for granted that I am simply waiting for news. In haste,

Yours ever,

Seward

Was this the face that launched a thousand ships,
And burnt the topless towers of Ilium?
Sweet Helen, make me immortal with a kiss;
Her lips suck forth my soul, see where it flies.
Come, Helen, come, give me my soul again.
Here I will dwell, for heaven is in these lips,
And all is dross that is not Helena.
—Doctor Faustus, Christoper Marlowe

51

From Jonathan Harker's papers

We sat late, and talked it over. Mina was dressing, and I called at the hotel after a few minutes to bring Von Helsing over . . . . Professor Von Helsing was, I think, surprised to see me. When I came into the room where he was, and introduced myself, he took me by the shoulder, and turned my face round to the light, and said, after a sharp scrutiny: "Madame Mina told me you were ill, that you had a shock." It was so strange to hear my wife called "Madame Mina" by this foreign, strong-faced old man. I smiled, and said: "I was ill, I have had a shock; but you have cured me already." "And how?" "By your letter to Mina." I reached into my pocket and produced the envelope.

"Professor Von Helsing," I said. "I was in doubt about what had happened to me, and then everything took a hue of unreality, and I did not know what to trust, even the evidence of my own senses. Not knowing what to trust, I did not know what to do; and so had only to keep on working in what had hitherto been the grooves of my life. These ceased to avail me, and I mistrusted myself; you don't know what it is to doubt everything, even yourself."

"And you, young Herr—I have read the letter from Dr. Seward about poor Miss Lucy, and he speaks well of you; I also have a letter from Dr. Jaquelle of Buda-Pesth, so I know of you for some days from the descriptions of others; but I see your true self now. You will give me your hand, will you not? And let we be friends for all our sakes." We shook hands, and he was so earnest and so kind that it made me quite sad.

"And now," he said, "may I ask your help? I have a great task to do, and you can help me here. Mein Herr, can you tell me what were your experiences on your going to Transylvania? Later on I may ask more help, and of a different kind; but at first this will do." "Look here, sir," I said, "does what you have to do concern my illness and what happened to me in Transylvania?" "It may; indeed, I believe it does," he said solemnly. "Then Professor, I am with you heart and soul. As you go by the 10:30 train, you will not have time to read it; but I shall ask Mina to get my old Journal for you. It has been locked up in my father-in-law's desk since my return. But Mina can fetch it, and you can take it with you and read a part of it on the train."

After breakfast I saw him to the station. When we were parting he said, "Perhaps you will come to town to visit me if I send to you, and take Madame Mina too." "We shall both come when you wish," I said.

I didn't have long to wait, as the very the next day Von Helsing sent for me to assist Mina and himself with Lucy's case.

As Mina and I came in the door of the Westenra home, Von Helsing, who was waiting in the hall, addressed me: "Has Dr. Seward said any of this to Arthur Holmwood?"

"No," I said. "He waited till I had set out, as he said in his telegram to you. Seward wrote him a letter simply telling him that you were coming, as Miss Westenra was not so well, and that he should let him know if need be."

"Right, my young friend," Von Helsing said, "quite right! It is better that he know not as yet; perhaps he shall not ever know. I pray so; but if it be needed, then he shall know all. And, my good friend John, let me caution you. All men are mad in some way or the other; and inasmuch as you deal discreetly with your enemies, so deal with God's enemies, too. You and I shall keep as yet what we know here." He touched me on the forehead, and then touched himself the same way. "I have for myself . . . thoughts at the present. Later I shall unfold to you."

Last is the fire; which, though it live for ever,
  Ne can be quenched quite; yet, every day,
  We see his parts, so soone as they do sever,
  To lose their heat, and shortly to decay;
  So, makes himself his owne consuming prey.
  Ne any living creatures doth he breed;
  But all, that are of others bredd, doth slay;
  And, with their death, his cruell life dooth feed
Nought leaving but their barren ashes, without seede.
—*The Faerie Queene,* Spencer

52

From Mina Harker's diary

While Jonathan rested in the front room, Von Helsing and I were shown up to Lucy's room. He was "concerned" when he saw her yesterday; I was horrified when I saw her today. She was ghastly, the bones of her face stood out prominently; her breathing was painful to see or hear. Von Helsing's face grew set as marble, and his eyebrows converged till they almost touched over his nose. Lucy lay motionless, and did not seem to have strength to speak, so for a while we were all silent. Then Von Helsing beckoned to me, and we went gently out of the room. The instant we had closed the door he stepped quickly along the passage to the next door, which was open. Then he pulled me quickly in with him and closed the door. "Mein Gott!" he said, "There is no time to be lost. She will die from want of blood to keep the heart's action as it should be. There must be transfusion of blood at once. Is it I, or should I ask your Jonathan?"

"He is very ill, Professor."

"Then I ready myself at once. I will bring up my bag. I am prepared."

Then with swiftness, but methodically, Von Helsing performed the operation. As the transfusion went on, something like life seemed to come back to poor Lucy's cheeks, and through Von Helsing's growing pallor the joy of his face seemed to absolutely shine. After a bit I began to grow anxious, for the loss of blood was telling on him, strong man as he was. It gave me an idea of what a terrible strain Lucy's system must have undergone that what weakened the Professor only partially restored her. The Professor's face was set, and he stood with watch in hand and with his eyes fixed now on the patient and now on me. I could hear my own heart beat. Presently he said in a soft voice: "It is enough." When all was over I could see how much he was weakened; I dressed the wound.

Von Helsing spoke without turning round—the man seems to have eyes in the back of his head. "The brave young Miss Lucy, I think, deserves some rest, which she shall have presently." And as he had now finished his operation, he adjusted the pillow to the patient's head. As he did so the black velvet band which she seems always to wear round her throat, fastened with an old diamond buckle which her lover had given her, was dragged a little up, and showed a red mark on her throat. This was the strange wound Lucy had gotten during our visit to Whitby a few weeks ago. I could hear the deep hiss of indrawn breath which betrayed Von Helsing's emotion.

Lucy's eyes fluttered shut and soon she was sleeping gently. Her breathing was stronger; I could see the outer blanket move as her breast heaved. By the bedside Von Helsing sat, looking at her intently. I asked the Professor in a whisper: "What do you make of that mark on her throat?"

"What, young Miss, do you make of it?" He then and there proceeded to touch her throat; just over the jugular vein there were two punctures, not very large. There was no sign of disease, but the edges were white and worn-looking. "This is the strange wound Lucy received that night in the graveyard at Whitby."

It at once occurred to me that this wound, or whatever it was, might be the means of that loss of blood; but I abandoned the idea as soon as formed, for such a thing could not be. The whole bed would have been drenched to a scarlet with the blood which she must have lost to leave such a pallor as she had before the transfusion. A terrible presentment welled up in the back of my mind.

"Well?" said Von Helsing.

"Well," said I, "I can make nothing of it."

"No? Most strange that you of all people would not gather the meaning of this mark. Did you not receive a similar mark last year during your trip to Transylvania?"

"Yes, there is a similarity."

The Professor stopped and looked at me curiously. "Mrs. Harker, have you read from your husband's journal with his descriptions of the events that occurred there?"

"No, I have not. Jonathan did not wish me to."

The Professor stood up. "I must go to Purfleet tonight," he said. "There are books and things that are there which I want. You must remain here all the night, and you must not let your sight pass from her."

"Shall I have a nurse?" I asked.

"We are the best nurses, you and I. Call Jonathan if you wish some moments to yourself, but you must keep watch all night; see that she is well fed, and that nothing disturb her. You must not sleep all the night. Later on you may sleep. I shall be back as soon as permitted. And then we may begin."

"May begin?" I said. "What on earth do you mean?"

"We shall see," he answered, as he hurried out. He came back a moment later and said with a warning finger held up: "Remember, she is your charge. If you leave her, and harm befalls her, you shall not sleep easy hereafter!"

For that which guides them, the fire, will give them an illusion of truth, and will shine on them with a perishable beauty, and it will imprison them in a dark sweetness and captivate them with fragrant pleasure. And it will blind them with an insatiable lust and burn their souls and become for them like a stake stuck in their heart which they can never dislodge.
—The Book of Thomas the Contender.

53

From Mina Harker's diary

Jonathan returned home, while I sat up all night with Lucy. The drug worked itself off towards dusk, and she woke easily; she looked a different being from what she had been before the operation. Her spirits were good, and she was full of happiness, but I could see evidences of the former weakness which she had been laboring under. When I told Mrs. Westenra that Dr. Von Helsing had directed that I should sit up with her, she dismissed the idea, pointing out her daughter's renewed strength and excellent spirits. I was firm, however, and made preparations for my long vigil. When her maid had prepared her for the night I came in, having in the meantime had supper, and took a seat by the bedside and held her hand. She did not in any way make an objection, but looked at me gratefully whenever I caught her eye.

I read to her from a book she kept on her night table for about an hour. After a long spell she seemed sinking off to sleep, but with an effort seemed to pull herself together and shook it off. This was repeated several times, with greater effort and with shorter pauses as the time moved on. It was apparent that she did not want to sleep, so I said, "You do not want to go to sleep?"

"No; I am afraid."

"Afraid to go to sleep! Why?"

"Ah, not if sleep was to you a doorway to horror!"

"A doorway to horror! What on earth do you mean?"

"I don't know. And that is what is so terrible. All this weakness comes to me in sleep; until I dread the darkness."

"But, you may sleep tonight! I am here watching you, and I can promise that nothing will happen."

"Ah, I can trust you!" I seized the opportunity, and said, "I promise you that if I see any evidence of bad dreams I will wake you at once."

"You will? Oh, will you really? How good you are to me. Then I will sleep!" And almost at the word she gave a deep sigh of relief, and sank back, asleep.

All night long I watched her. She never stirred, but slept on and on in a deep, tranquil slumber. Her lips were slightly parted, and her breast rose and fell with the regularity of a pendulum. There was a smile on her face, and it was clear that no bad dreams had come to disturb her.

Something about Lucy's terrible mental state reminded me of the poem by John Keats:

This living hand, now warm and capable
Of earnest grasping, would, if it were cold
And in the icy silence of the tomb,
So haunt thy days and chill thy dreaming nights
That thou wouldst wish thine own heart dry of blood
So in my veins red life might stream again,
And thou be conscience-calm'd—see here it is—
I hold it towards you.

In the early morning her maid came, and I left Lucy in her care and took myself back home, for I was anxious about Jonathan and many other things.

Jonathan sent a short wire to Von Helsing and to Arthur, telling them of the excellent result of the operation. A telegram came from Von Helsing at Purfleet whilst we were at dinner, suggesting that I should be with Lucy in Hillingham tonight, as it might be well to be at hand, and stating that he was leaving by the night train and would join me early in the morning.

I was tired and worn out when I got to Hillingham. For two nights I had hardly had a wink of sleep, and my brain was beginning to feel the exhaustion. Lucy was up and in cheerful spirits. When she shook hands with me she looked sharply in my face and said, "No sitting up tonight for you. You are worn out. I am quite well again; indeed, I am; and if there is to be any sitting up, it is I who will sit up with you." I would not argue the point, but went and had my supper. Lucy came with me, and we had an excellent meal and a couple of glasses of wine. Then Lucy took me upstairs, and make room for me on the trundle bed next to her own. "Now," she said, "you must stay here with me. You can lie on the bed to rest for I know that nothing would induce you to go to sleep. If I want anything I shall call out." I could not but acquiesce, for I was terribly tired and could not have sat up in a chair had I tried. So, on her renewing her promise to call me if she should want anything, I lay on the narrow bed and forgot about everything.

HEPHAESTUS: This arm is rivet beyond release.
KRATOS: Then chain the other fast; so he may learn
*   That all his cleverness falls short of Zeus.*
HEPHAESTUS: In this none but himself can blame my work.
KRATOS: Now thrust the biting wedge of adamant
*   Straight through his heart and drive it bravely home.*
HEPHAESTUS: Alas, Prometheus, for thy woes I groan.
—*Prometheus Bound*, Aeschylus

54

From Mina Harker's diary

I felt the Professor's hand on my head, and started awake all of a sudden.

"And how is the little patient?"

I remembered that Lucy had gotten up already, just at sunrise, and I was thoroughly ashamed to admit I had fallen asleep. "Well, when I left her, or rather when she left me," I answered.

"Come, let us see ourselves," he said. And together we went into the dressing room. The blind was down, and I went over to raise it gently, whilst Von Helsing stepped, with his soft, cat-like tread, over to the sofa where Lucy lay resting.

As I raised the blind, and the morning sunlight flooded the room, I heard the Professor's low hiss of inspiration, and knowing its rarity, a deadly fear shot through my heart. As I passed over he moved back, and his exclamation of horror, "Gott in Himmel!," was reflected in his agonized face. He raised his hand and pointed to the sofa, and his iron face was drawn and ashen white. I felt my knees begin to tremble.

There on the sofa, seemingly in a swoon, lay poor Lucy, more horribly pale than ever. Even the lips were white, and the gums seemed to have shrunken back from the teeth. Von Helsing stamped his foot in anger. "Quick!" he said, "bring the brandy." I flew to the dining-room, and returned with the decanter. He wetted the poor white lips with it, and together we rubbed palm and wrist and heart. He felt her heart, and after a few moments of agonizing suspense said:

"It is not too late. It beats, though but feebly. All our work is undone; we must begin again. There is no one else here now; I have to call on you yourself this time Miss Mina." As he spoke, he was dipping into his bag and producing the instruments for transfusion; I had rolled up my blouse-sleeve. And so, without a moment's delay, we began the operation. After a time I began to feel the progressing weakness; it did not seem a short time either, for the draining away of one's blood, no matter how willingly it be given, is a terrible feeling.

Von Helsing held up a warning finger, "Do not stir," he said, "but I fear that with growing strength she may wake; and that would make danger, oh, so much danger. But I shall give a hypodermic injection of morphia." He proceeded then, swiftly and deftly, to carry out his intent.

The effect on Lucy was not bad, for the faint seemed to merge subtly into the narcotic sleep. It was with a feeling of hope that I could see a faint tinge of color steal back into the pallid cheeks and lips. No one knows, until they experience it, what it is to feel your own life-blood drawn away through a needle and a rubber tube.

The Professor watched me critically. "Enough," he said. "Already?" I cried. "You took a great deal more from yourself." To which he smiled a sad sort of smile as he replied, "You have work,

much work, to do for her and for others; and the present will
suffice."

When he stopped the operation, he attended to Lucy whilst I
applied a bandage to my own arm. I lay down, while I waited his
leisure to attend to me, for I felt faint and a little sick. By-and-by
Von Helsing bound up my wound, and sent me downstairs to get
a glass of wine for myself. As I was leaving the room, be came
after me, and half whispered:

"Mina, nothing must be said of this. If Jonathan should turn up
unexpected, as before, no word to him. It would frighten him. So!"

When I came back he looked at me carefully, and then said:
"You are not much the worse. Go into the room, and lie on your
bed, and rest awhile; then have some breakfast, and come here to
me."

I followed out his orders, for I knew how right and wise they
were. I had done my part, and now my next duty was to keep up
my strength. I felt very weak, and in the weakness lost something
of the amazement at what had occurred. I fell asleep on the small
bed, however, wondering over and over again how Lucy could
have been drained of so much blood that morning with no sign
anywhere to show where it had gone.

I think I must have continued my wonder in my dreams, for,
sleeping and waking, my thoughts always came back to the little
punctures in her throat and the ragged, exhausted appearance of
their edges—tiny though they were. The dream seemed to touch
some memory that I struggled to control. My mind turned over
and over again, working at some frightening speed, turning in on
itself like a snake swallowing its tail. Something lingered at the
back of my mind. But soon I slept, though fitfully, while dreaming
of blood.

Lucy slept well into the day, and when she woke she was fairly
well and strong, though not nearly so much so as the day before.
When Von Helsing had seen her, he went out for a walk, leaving
me in charge, with strict injunctions that I was not to leave her for
a moment. I could hear his voice in the hall, asking the way to the
nearest telegraph office.

Lucy and I chatted freely, and she seemed quite unconscious
that anything had happened to her during those few minutes

between her rising and Von Helsing's arrival. When her mother came up to see her, she did not seem to notice any change whatever, but said to me gratefully:

"We owe you so much, Mrs. Harker, for all you have done, but you really must now take care not to overwork yourself. You are looking pale. You require some nursing and looking after yourself!"

As she spoke, Lucy's visage became excessively pale as she turned imploring eyes to me. I smiled and nodded, and laid my finger on my lips; with a sigh, she sank back amid her pillows.

Von Helsing returned in a couple of hours, and presently said to me: "Now you go home, and eat much and drink. Make yourself strong. I will stay here tonight, and I shall sit up with Miss Lucy myself. You and I must watch the case, and we must let none other know. I have grave reasons. No, do not ask them; think what you will. Do not fear to think even the most impossible. Good-night." I got back here in time for a late dinner with Jonathan; and I set this down while waiting for sleep. . . .

This afternoon I went over to Hillingham and found Von Helsing in excellent spirits, and Lucy much better. Shortly after I arrived, a big parcel from abroad came for the Professor. He opened it with much flourish, assumed, of course, and showed a great bundle of books. He carried these into the drawing room and placed them with two other boxes of books that had arrived earlier. He had begun setting up a library and a laboratory in the drawing room. Returning to Lucy's bedroom, he went up to her and placed a silver crucifix round her neck. The last words he said to her were: "Take care you do not disturb it; and even if the room feels close, do not tonight open the window or the door."

"I promise," said Lucy," and thank you both a thousand times for all your kindness to me! Oh, what have I done to be blessed with such friends?" As she spoke, I saw next to her bed on the night table a copy of the complete edition of Coleridge's poetical works and it was open to "The Virgin's Cradle-Hymn":

Sleep, sweet babe! my care beguiling:
Mother sits beside thee smiling:
Sleep, my darling, tenderly!

If thou sleep not, mother mourneth,
Singing as her wheel she turneth:
Come, soft slumber, balmily!

The irony of this verse in comparison with poor Lucy's situation
was too much for me to bear. I went downstairs to collect my
baggage and prepare to leave.

As we left the house, Von Helsing said, "Tonight I can sleep in
peace, and sleep I want—much of travel, much reading in the day
between, and much anxiety on the day to follow, and a night to sit
up, without a wink. Tomorrow in the morning early you can call
for me, and we will come together to see the pretty miss."

He seemed so confident that I, remembering my own confidence two nights before and with the baneful result, felt awe and
vague terror. It must have been some weakness that made me
hesitate to tell him about my fearful premonitions, but I felt it all
the more, like unshed tears.

---

*He then told me a story which I would hear from every gypsy I met. Some
of the details varied, but the punchline was always the same. In Steve's
version the Roman soldiers crucifying Jesus intended to use four nails, but
a gypsy stole the fourth nail, the one meant for His heart, and in
gratitude Christ, on the cross, declared that gypsies could go on stealing
forever.*
—King of the Gypsies, Peter Maas

55

From Mina Harker's diary

I called and found Von Helsing, as usual, up on time. The
carriage ordered from the hotel was waiting. The Professor took
his bag, which he always brought with him.

Let all be put down exactly. Von Helsing and I arrived at Hillingham at eight o'clock. It was a lovely morning; the bright sunshine and all the fresh feeling of early autumn seemed like the completion of nature's annual work. The leaves were turning to all kinds of beautiful colors, but had not yet begun to drop from the trees. When we entered we met Mrs. Westenra coming out of the morning room. She is always an early riser. She greeted us warily and said:

"You will be glad to know that Lucy is better. The dear child is still asleep." The Professor smiled and looked quite jubilant. He rubbed his hands together, and said, "I think my treatment is working," to which she answered:

"You must not take all the credit. Lucy's state this morning is due in part to me."

"What do you mean, madame?" asked the Professor.

"Well, I was anxious about the dear child in the night, and went into her room. She was sleeping soundly—so soundly that even my coming did not wake her. But the room was awfully stuffy. So I opened a bit of the window to let in a little fresh air. You will be pleased with her, I am sure."

She moved off into her boudoir, where she usually breakfasted early. As she had spoken, I watched the Professor's face, and saw it turn ashen grey. He had been able to retain his self-command while the poor lady was present, for he knew her state and how dangerous a shock would be; he actually smiled on her as he held open the door for her to pass into her room. But the instant she had disappeared he pulled me, suddenly and forcibly, into the drawing room and closed the door.

Then for the first time I saw Von Helsing break down. He raised his hands over his head in a sort of mute despair, and then beat his palms together in a helpless way; finally he sat down on a chair, and putting his hands before his face, began to sob, with loud, dry sobs that seemed to come from the very racking of his heart.

Then he raised his arms again, as though appealing to the whole universe. "God! God! God!" he said. "What have we done, what has this poor thing done, that we are so sore beset? Why must such things still be? In such a way this poor mother, all unknowing, and all for the best as she thinks, does such a thing as lose her daughter body and soul; and we must not tell her, we must not even warn her, or she die, and then both die. Oh, how we are beset! How all the powers of the devils are against us!" Suddenly he jumped to his feet. "Come," he said, "come, we must see and act. Devils or no devils, or all the devils at once, it matters not; we fight him all the same."

He went to the hall for his bag; and together we went up to Lucy's room. Once again I drew up the blind, while Von Helsing went toward the bed. This time he did not start as he looked on the poor face with the same awful, wan pallor as before.

"As I expected," he murmured, with that hissing inspiration of his which meant so much. Without a word he went and locked the door, and then began to set out on the little table the instruments for yet another operation for the transfusion of blood. I had long ago recognized the necessity, and begun to take off my sweater, but he stopped me with a warning hand. "No!" he said. "Today you must operate the equipment. I shall provide. You are weakened already." As he spoke he took off his coat and rolled up his shirt-sleeve.

Again the operation; again the narcotic; again some return of color to the ashy cheeks, and the regular breathing of healthy sleep. This time I watched while Von Helsing packed away his apparatus and rested himself on the day-bed.

Then he said that he would watch this night and the next and would send me word when to come. After another hour Lucy woke from her sleep, fresh and bright and seemingly not much the worse for her terrible ordeal. What does it all mean?

*The conception of the serpent as the emblem of evil is not nearly so
widespread as the idea that it is the appropriate symbol of Deity, but it
may be found early, as in the case of Apep, Apopi, or Apophis, the
serpent of the Egyptian Hades, which is represented on mummy cases . . .
Typhon, who is mentioned by Plutarch as having made war against Jove,
killed Osiris, and was himself attacked by Osiris' son, Horus. The last
named deity is often represented as standing upon Typhon, who lies
prostrate in the serpent form of Apep, nailed to the earth by the spear of
the god which pierces his head. But though apparently conquered
he survives to work evil.*
—The Encircled Serpent, M.O. Howey

56

From Mina Harker's diary

Just off for a train to London. The arrival of Von Helsing's
telegram filled me with dismay. A whole night lost, and I know by
bitter experience what may happen in a night. Of course it is
possible that all may be well, but what may have happened? Surely
there is some horrible doom hanging over us that every possible
accident should thwart us in all we try to do. I shall take this
journal with me, and then I can complete my entry at Lucy's side.

Jonathan and I drove at once to Hillingham and arrived early.
Leaving the cab at the gate, we went up the avenue together. I
knocked gently and rang as quietly as possible, for I feared to
disturb Lucy or her mother, and hoped to only bring a servant to
the door. After a while, finding no response, I knocked and rang
again; still no answer. I rang again, but still without response.
Hitherto I had blamed only the servants, but now a terrible fear
began to assail me. Was the desolation but another link in the
chain of doom which seemed drawing tight around us? Was it
indeed a house of death to which I had come, too late? I knew
that minutes, even seconds of delay, might mean hours of danger

to Lucy, if she had again one of those frightful relapses; and I sent Jonathan round the house to try if he could find by chance an entry anywhere. But he could find no means of ingress. Every window and door was fastened and locked, and he returned baffled to the porch.

As he did so, I heard the rapid pit-pat of a swiftly driven horse's feet. They stopped at the gate, and a few seconds later we met Von Helsing running up the avenue. When he saw us, he gasped out: "Then it was you, and just arrived. How is she? Are we too late? Did you not get my telegram?" I answered as quickly and coherently as I could that we had only got his telegram early in the morning, and had not lost a minute in coming here, and that we could not rouse any one in the house. He paused, took a set of keys from his coat, and proceeded to open the door.

The Professor went in, and we followed him. There was no one in the kitchen or in the servants' rooms, which were close at hand. We tried all the rooms as we went along and in the dining-room, dimly lit by rays of light through the shutters, found four servant-women lying on the floor. There was no need to think them dead, for their heavy breathing and the strange fruity smell of the room left no doubt as to their condition. Von Helsing and I looked at each other, and as we moved away he said: "We can attend to them later." Then we ascended to Lucy's room. For an instant or two we paused at the door to listen, but there was no sound that we could hear. With trembling hands, we opened the door gently, and entered the room.

How shall I describe what we saw? On the bed lay two women, Lucy and her mother. The latter lay farthest in, and she was covered with a white sheet, the edge of which had been blown back by the draught through the broken window, showing the drawn, white face, with a look of terror fixed upon it. By her side lay Lucy, with face white and still more drawn. Her throat was bare, showing the two little wounds which we had noticed before, but looking horribly white and mangled. Without a word the Professor bent over the bed, his head resting on poor Lucy's breast; then he gave a quick turn of his head, as of one who listens, and leaping to his feet, he cried out to me: "It is not yet too late! Quick! quick! Bring the brandy!"

I flew downstairs and returned with it, taking care to smell and taste it, lest it, too, were drugged like the decanter of sherry which I found on the table. The maids were still breathing, but more restlessly, and I fancied that the narcotic was wearing off. I did not stay to make sure, but returned to Von Helsing. He rubbed the brandy, as on another occasion, on her lips and gums and on her wrists and the palms of her hands. He said to me: "I can do this, all that can be at the present. You go wake those maids. Make them get heat and fire and warm towels. This poor soul is nearly as cold as that beside her. She will need be heated before we can do anything more."

I went at once, and found little difficulty in waking three of the women. The fourth was only a young girl, and the drug had evidently affected her more strongly, so we lifted her on the sofa and let her sleep. The others were dazed at first, but as it came back to them what happened, they cried and sobbed in a terrified manner. I was stern with them, however, and would not let them cry. I told them that one life was bad enough to lose, and that if they delayed they would lose Miss Lucy. So, sobbing and crying, they went about their way, half clad, and prepared the fire. Fortunately, the kitchen fire was still alive, and there was no lack of hot towels.

Whilst we were busy warming her limbs there was a knock at the hall door. One of the maids ran off, hurried on some more clothes, and opened it. Then she returned and whispered to us that there was a gentleman who had come with a message from Mr. Holmwood. I bade her simply tell him that he must wait, for we could see no one now. She went away with the message, and, engrossed with our work, I forgot all about him, preoccupied with the task at hand.

Once again I went through that ghastly operation. I have not the heart to again describe the details. Lucy had got a terrible shock and it told on her more than before, for though plenty of my blood went into her veins, her body did not respond to the treatment as well as on the other occasions. Her struggle back into life was something frightful to see and hear. However, the action of both heart and lungs improved, and Von Helsing made an injection, as before, and with good effect. Her faint became a profound slumber. Then Von Helsing saw to the bandage on my arm as I was then too weak to deal with it.

I never saw in all my experience anyone work in such deadly earnest as the Professor. I knew—as he knew—that it was a fight with death, and in a pause I told him so. He answered me with the sternest look that his face could wear: "If that were all, I would stop here where we are now, and let her fade away into peace, for I see no hope for her." Presently we both began to be conscious that the heat was beginning to be of some effect. Lucy's heart beat a trifle more audibly, and her lungs had a perceptible movement.

I noticed that Van Helsing tied a soft silk handkerchief round her throat. She was still unconscious, and was quite as bad as, if not worse than, we had ever seen her. Von Helsing called in one of the women, and told her to stay with her and not to take her eyes off her till we returned, and he beckoned me out of the room. "We must discuss what is to be done," he said as we descended the stairs.

In the hall he opened the dining-room door, and we passed in, he closing the door carefully behind him. The shutters had been opened, but the blinds were already down, with that obedience to the etiquette of death which the British women of the lower classes always rigidly observe. The room was, therefore, dimly dark. It was, however, light enough for our purposes. Von Helsing's sternness was somewhat relieved by a look of perplexity. He was evidently torturing his mind about something, so I waited for an instant, and he spoke: "What are we to do now? Where are we to turn for help? We must of the certain have another transfusion of blood, and that soon. You are exhausted already; I am exhausted too. I fear to trust those women to keep secret what we are doing, even if they would have courage to submit. And Jonathan has been too ill. What are we to do for some one who will open his veins for her?"

"What's the matter with me, anyhow?" The voice came from the sofa across the room, and its tones brought relief and joy to my heart, for they were those of Quincy Morris. Von Helsing started angrily at the first sound, but his face softened and a glad look came into his eyes as I cried out: "Quincy Morris!" and rushed towards him with outstretched arms. "What brought you here?" I cried as we embraced. "I guess Art is the cause." He handed me a telegram:

> Have not heard from Harker or Seward for three days, and am terribly anxious. Cannot leave. Father still in same condition. Send me word how Lucy is. Do not delay.
> —HOLMWOOD.

"I think I came just in the nick of time. You know you have only to tell me what to do." Von Helsing strode forward, and took his hand, looking him straight in the eyes as he said: "A brave man's blood is the best thing on this earth when a woman is in trouble. You're a man and no mistake. Well, the devil may work against us for all he's worth, but God sends us men when we want them."

Another French version is evidently of Egyptian origin, and an adaptation of the legend of Horus and Set. It is embodied in a bas-relief in the Louvre, in which a hawk-headed St. George garbed in Roman military uniform and mounted on a horse, is killing a dragon in the form of Set's crocodile.
—The Encircled Serpent, M.O. Howey

57

From Mina Harker's diary

The Professor watched whilst I went downstairs with Quincy Morris and sent Jonathan to pay off one of the cabmen who were waiting. I left Quincy after having a glass of wine, and told the cook to get ready a good breakfast. Then a thought struck me, and I went back to the room where Lucy was. When I came softly in, I found Von Helsing with a sheet or two of note-paper in his hand. He had evidently read it, and was thinking over its contents as he sat with his hand to his brow. There was a look of grim satisfaction in his face, as of one who has had a doubt solved. He handed me the paper saying only: "It dropped from Lucy's breast."

I opened the sheets and found written, in a frail and weakened hand:

"Oh my dear god. It is him. He has come back and means to take my life. Oh my poor Mina, he will most certainly destroy you, too, for I can see it in his face, in this new face that he wears in the darkness. Oh God, can this be happening? Can he really be this thing of darkness? Can he mean to bring me into the darkness with him?"

When I had read it, I stood looking at the Professor, and after a pause asked him: "In God's name, what does it all mean? Was she, or is she, mad; or what sort of horrible danger is it?" I was so bewildered and so afraid for Lucy that I did not know what more to say. Von Helsing put out his hand and took the paper, saying: "Young Miss Mina, do not trouble yourself about it now. Forget it for the present. You shall know and understand it, and in good time; but it will be later."

In the hall I met Quincy Morris with a telegram for Arthur telling him that Mrs. Westenra was dead, that Lucy also had been ill, but was now a little better, and that Von Helsing and I were with her. I told him where I was going, and he hurried me out, but as I was going said: "When you come back, Mina, may I have two words with you all to ourselves?" I nodded in reply and went out.

When I got back Quincy was waiting for me. I told him I would see him as soon as I knew about Lucy, and went up to her room. She was still sleeping, and the Professor seemingly had not moved from his seat at her side. From his putting his finger to his lips, I gathered that he expected her to wake before long and wanted to be there when she woke. So I went down to Quincy and took him into the breakfast-room, where the blinds were not drawn down, and which was a little more cheerful, or rather less cheerless, than the other rooms. When we were alone, he said to me, "Mina, I don't want to shove myself in anywhere where I've no right to be; but this is no ordinary case. You know I loved that girl and wanted to marry her; but, although that's past and gone, I can't help feeling anxious about her all the same. What can it be that's wrong with her? The German is an odd fellow he is; I can see that–he said, that time you two came into the room, that she must soon have another transfusion of blood, and that both you and he were exhausted. Now I know well that a man must not expect an explanation of what his friends' thoughts are. But this is no common matter, and, whatever it is, I shall do my part."

"I believe you will," I said. And he went on: "I take it that both you and Von Helsing have given your blood already. Is this so?" "That's true also." "And I guess Seward was in it too. When I saw him four days ago he looked queer. I have not seen anything pulled down so quick since I was on the Pampas and had a mare that I was fond of go to grass all in a night. One of those big bats that they call vampires had got at her in the night, and what with the vein left open, there wasn't enough blood in her to let her stand up, and I had to put a bullet through her as she lay. Mina, if you may tell me without betraying a confidence, John was the first, is not that so?"

As he spoke the poor fellow looked terribly anxious. He was in a torture of suspense regarding the woman he loved, and his utter ignorance of the terrible mystery which seemed to surround him intensified his pain. His very heart was bleeding, and it took great faith for him to keep from breaking down. I paused before answering, for I felt that I must not betray anything which the Professor wished kept secret; but already he knew so much, and guessed so much that there could be no reason for not answering, so I answered in the same phrase: "That's true also." "And how long has this been going on?" "About ten days." "Ten days! Then I guess, Mrs. Harker, that that poor pretty creature that we all love has had put into her veins within that time the blood of three strong people. Man alive, her whole body wouldn't hold it." Then, coming close to me, he spoke in a fierce half-whisper: "What took it out?"

I shook my head. "That," I said, "is the mystery. Von Helsing is simply frantic about it, and I am at my wits' end. Von Helsing has a whole room full of books and a small laboratory set up in the next room. There were a series of miscalculations as to Lucy being properly watched. But these shall not occur again. Here we stay until all be well—or no."

Quincy held out his hand. "Count me in," he said. "You and the German can tell me what to do, and I'll do it."

"Yes. God help us." I said.

"I just hope Von Helsing runs out of books before we run out of blood."

He told the Oberstdorf judges that eight years before on his way to the forest to cut down fir trees, the drover Jakob Walch, a townsman of his who had died eight days before, suddenly appeared before him. . . . After a year the dead cowherd appeared before him again, dressed all in white, with a red cross on his chest, and invited him to follow.
—Night Battles, Carlo Ginzberg

58

From Mina Harker's diary

When she woke late in the afternoon, Lucy's first movement was to look around the room; and, seeing where she was, she shuddered and gave a loud cry and put her thin hands before her pale face. We both understood what that meant—that she had realised to the full her mother's death—and what we could to comfort her was to little effect. Doubtless sympathy eased her somewhat, but she was very low in thought and spirit, and wept silently and weakly for a long time. We told her that either or both of us would now remain with her all the time, and that seemed to comfort her.

All night she slept fitfully, being always afraid to sleep, and somewhat weaker when she woke from it. The Professor and I took turns at watch, and we never left her for a moment unattended. Quincy Morris said nothing about his intention, but I knew that all night long he patrolled round and round the house with his rifle.

I lay down by her side to rest, and presently she moved uneasily, causing me to get up again. At the same moment there came a sort of noise at the window. It was about 4 a.m. I went over to the window sofly, and peeped out by the corner of the blind. There was a pale moon on the edge of the horizon, soon to be eclipsed by the morning sun, and I could see Quincy just outside on the lawn, pacing back and forth. When I came back to my seat, I found that Lucy had moved slightly. Von Helsing relieved me shortly after.

When the daylight came, I got up from my little bed for a moment to check on Lucy. The sun burst in through the windows and its searching light showed the ravages in poor Lucy's strength. There were, once again, the signs of terrible weakness. I was so horrified that I could not puzzle out what to do. Von Helsing had, apparently, stepped out of the room for a moment and left me alone with her.

I called quickly for Von Helsing, and he tried, one final time, a blood transfusion. A chemical test had revealed that Quincy's blood was unsuited to the purpose, and so this time we were forced to turn again to Dr. Seward, who had just arrived from Purfleet, for the donation of his life's-blood. But this time the transfusion gave little results. Lucy was hardly able to turn her head, and the little nourishment which she could take seemed to do her no good. Something about her expression when she slept filled me with terror; my hands shook as I sat near her bed. The game is up; we have lost her.

Later that morning Arthur arrived. It was nearly eight o'clock, and the sun was rising full and warm, and the red light streamed in through the window and gave more colour to the pale cheeks. When he saw her, Arthur was simply choking with emotion, and none of us could speak. She rallied a little, and spoke to him more brightly than she had done since we arrived. He too pulled himself together, and spoke as cheerily as he could, so that the best was made of everything.

Later. Only resolution and habit can let me make an entry tonight. Jonathan is asleep. I am too miserable, too low-spirited, too sick of this desperate battle. Except for Jonathan, I would not care if I heard this moment the flapping of the wings of the angel of death. And he has been flapping those grim wings to some strange purpose of late–Lucy's mother and Arthur's father, and now. . . . Let me get on with my worldly chores. . . .

Later this morning, as I entered her room, I saw that Lucy's face, which lay in her pillow, was almost whiter than the snow. She lay quite still, and I looked round the room to see that all was as it should be. Lucy was breathing somewhat heavily, and her face was at its worst, for the open mouth showed the pale gums. Her teeth, in the dim, uncertain light, seemed longer and sharper than they had been in the morning. The whiteness of her teeth filled me with some uncertain fear that was impossible to name.

Presently she woke, and I gave her food, as Von Helsing had prescribed. She took but a little, and that languidly. There did not seem to be within her now the struggle for life and strength that had before so marked her illness.

At noon Von Helsing came to relieve me. Arthur had fallen into a doze on the sofa. When Von Helsing saw Lucy's face I could hear the hissing indraw of his breath, and he said to me in a sharp whisper: "Draw up the blind; I want light!" Then he bent down, and, with his face almost touching Lucy's, examined her carefully. He lifted the silk handkerchief from her throat. As he did so he started back, and I could hear his ejaculation "Mein Gott!" as it was smothered in his throat. Her expression had hardened into a mask-like expression, as if a second personality was struggling to the surface and taking control of her sleep. For fully five minutes Von Helsing stood looking at her, with his face at its sternest. Then he turned to me and said calmly, "She is dying. It will not be long now. Wake that poor boy, and let him come and see the last; he trusts us, and we have promised him."

I went to the dressing-room and woke Arthur. He was dazed for a moment, but when he saw the sunlight streaming in through the edges of the shutters he realized where he was. I told him as gently as I could that Von Helsing feared that the end was near. He covered his face with his hands, as he fell back on the sofa, where he remained, perhaps a minute, with his head buried in a cushion, whilst his shoulders shook with grief. I took him by the hand and raised him up. "Come," I said, "summon all your strength: it will be best and easiest for her."

When we came into the room she opened her eyes, and seeing him, whispered softly: "Arthur! Oh, my love, I am so glad you have come!" Arthur took her hand and knelt beside her, and she looked her best, with all the soft lines matching the beauty of her eyes. Then gradually her eyes closed, and she sank to sleep. For a little bit her breast heaved softly, and her breath came and went like a tired child's. Then, insensibly, there came the strange change which I had noticed the night before. Her breathing grew heavy, the mouth opened, and the pale gums, drawn back, made the teeth look longer and sharper than ever.

I kept my eyes fixed on Lucy, as did Von Helsing, and we saw Lucy's breathing become soft again, and all at once it ceased. "It is all over," said Von Helsing. "She is dead!" I took Arthur by the arm, and led him away to the dressing room, where he sat down on the sofa, and covered his face with his hands, sobbing in a way that nearly broke me down to see. I went back to the room, and found Von Helsing looking at poor Lucy, and his face was more stern and solemn than ever. Some change had come over her body. Death had given back part of her beauty, for her brow and cheek had recovered some of their flowing lines; even the lips had lost their deadly pallor. It was as if the blood, no longer needed for the working of the heart had gone to make the harshness of death as little rude as it might. I stood beside Von Helsing, and said—"Ah, there is peace for her at last." It is then he turned to me, and said with grave solemnity—"Not so; alas! not so. It is only the beginning!" When I asked him what he meant, he only shook his head and answered—"We shall wait and see."

*At the battle of Antioch, St. George and his celestial companions saved
the Crusaders from ignominius defeat. . . . A similar army of angels
appeared when the Crusaders were attacking Jerusalem, and under the
generalship of St. George, who wore white armour with a red cross upon
it, they scaled the walls successfully and captured the city on
15th July, 1099.*
—George of Lydda, Sir E.A. Wallis Budge

59

From Mina Harker's diary

The funeral was arranged for the next day, so that Lucy and her
mother might be buried together. I attended to all the ghastly
formalities, and the urbane undertaker's staff were all affectedly
blessed with something of his own obsequious suavity.

I noticed that Von Helsing never kept far away. This was
possible due to the disordered state of things in the household.
There were no relatives at hand; and, as Arthur had to be back
the next day to attend his father's funeral, we were unable to
notify any one who should have been bidden. Under the
circumstances, Von Helsing took it upon himself to examine
Lucy's papers by himself. I asked him why, for as a solicitor's wife
I feared that Von Helsing, being a foreigner, might not be aware
of English legal requirements, and so might in ignorance make
some unnecessary mistake, and I suggested that Jonathan could
easily assist him. He answered me, "I know; I know. But this is
not altogether for the law. We knew that, when we avoided the
coroner. I have more than him to avoid. There may be papers
more such as this." As he spoke he took from his pocket-book the
memorandum which had been in Lucy's breast.

"When you find the name of the solicitor for the late Mrs.
Westenra, seal all her papers, and write him tonight. For me, I

was here in the room and in Miss Lucy's old room all night, and
I myself searched for what may be found. It is not well that her
every thought goes into the hands of strangers." I went on with
my part of the work in Mrs. Westenra's papers, and in another
half hour had found the name and address of Mrs. Westenra's
solicitor and had written to him. All the poor lady's papers were
in order; explicit directions regarding the place of burial were
given.

I had hardly sealed the letter when, to my surprise, Von
Helsing walked into the room, saying: "Can I help you, Mrs.
Harker? I am free, and if I may, my service is to you." "Have you
got what you looked for?" I asked, to which he replied: "I did not
look for any specific thing. I only hoped to find, and find I have,
all that there was—only some letters and a few memoranda, and
a diary. But I have them here, and we shall for the present say
nothing of them. I shall see that poor lad tomorrow evening, and,
with his sanction, I shall use some of them."

When we had finished the work in hand, he said to me: "And
now, friend Mina, I think we may go to bed. We want sleep, both
you and I, and rest to recuperate. Tomorrow we shall have much
to do, but for the tonight there is no need of us. Alas!" Before
turning in we went to look at poor Lucy. The undertaker had
certainly done his work well, for the room was turned into a small
shrine. There was a wilderness of beautiful white flowers, and
death was made as little repulsive as might be. The end of the
winding-sheet was laid over the face; when the Professor bent over
and turned it gently back, we both started at the beauty before us,
the tall wax candles created sufficient light to show it well. All
Lucy's loveliness had come back to her in death, and the hours
that had passed, instead of leaving traces of "decay's effacing
fingers," had but restored the beauty of life, till positively I could
not believe my eyes that I was looking at a corpse.

The Professor looked grave, but he had not loved her as I had,
and there was no need for tears in his eyes. He said to me,
"Remain till I return," and left the room. He came back with a
handful of wild garlic from the box waiting in the hall and placed
the flowers amongst the others on and around the bed. Later on,
I was starting to undress in my own room, near the servants

quarters, when, with a premonitory tap at the door, he entered, and at once began to speak: "Tomorrow I want you to send for Dr. Seward, before night, and ask that he bring a set of post-mortem knives from the hospital." "Must you make an autopsy?" I asked. "Yes and no. I want to operate, but not as you think. Let me tell you now but not a word to another. I have good reason now for all I intend to do. You have to trust me; you have to believe me, as in weeks past, when there be things so strange that you might have well doubt. Believe me yet a little."

He paused a moment and went on solemnly: "Friend Mina, there are strange and terrible days before us. Let us not be two, but one, that we work to a good end. Will you not have faith in me?" I took his hand and promised him that I would. I held my door open as he left. Now I have a new mystery to think on, a new puzzle to grapple with.

Thence she thee brought into this Faerie lond,
  And in an heaped furrow did thee hyde,
  Where thee a Ploughman all unweeting found,
  As he his toylesome teeme that way did guyde,
  And brought thee up in ploughmans state to byde,
  Whereof Georgos he thee gave to name;
  Till prickt with courage, and thy forces pryde,
  To Faery court thou cam'st to seeke for fame,
And prove thy pussaunt armes, as seemes thee best became.
—*The Faerie Queene,* Spenser

60

From Von Helsing's memo book
(in the original English)

I write this in case anything should happen to me. I go alone to watch in that churchyard. It pleases me that the un-dead, Miss Lucy, shall not leave tonight, that so on the morrow night she may be more eager. Therefore I shall fix some things she likes not—garlic and a crucifix—and so seal up the door of the tomb. She is young as un-dead, and will fear them. Moreover, these are only to prevent her coming out; they may not prevail on her wanting to get in—for even the un-dead are desperate, and must find the line of least resistance, whatsoever it may be. I shall be at hand all the night from sunset till after the sunrise, and if there be aught that may yet be learned I shall learn it. For Lucy or from her, I have no fear, but that other to whom she is un-dead, he has now the power to seek his tomb and find shelter. He is cunning, and now from Mr. Jonathan's Journal I learn how he fooled Jonathan into thinking him destroyed, and from the way that all along he has fooled us, when he played with us for Miss Lucy's life, and we lost; in many ways the un-dead are strong. He has always the strength in his hand of twenty men; even we four who gave our strength to Miss Lucy it also has all gone to him. Besides, he can summon his wolves and I know not what. So if it be that he comes thither on this night he shall find me; but none other shall find us until it be too late. But it may be that he will not attempt the place. There is no reason why he should; his hunting is more of a game than the churchyard where the un-dead woman sleeps, and the one old man watch. Therefore I write this in case . . . Take the papers that are with this memo book, the diary of Harker and the letters, and read them, and then find this great un-dead, and cut off his head and burn his heart or drive a stake through it, so that the world may rest from him. If it be so, farewell. — J. H. Von H.

As he stood there with the maiden her red mouth made haste to speak:
"In truth, your name is Parzival, which signifies 'right through the
middle.' Such a furrow did great love plow in your mother's heart with
the plow of her faithfulness."
—*Parzival*, Wolfram Von Eschenbach

61

Two weeks have passed, during which I was preoccupied with moving my boxes to different locations throughout London. During the last few days, I've gone by Lucy's home on Brook Street several times, I have seen various strange men, along with Mina and the servants coming, in and out. And then I saw the funeral.

My curiosity aroused, I followed them to the graveyard. Two funerals, two women. Mrs. Westenra and her daughter Lucy. I returned to Purfleet and waited. A few days later I returned to the graveyard and forced my way into the tomb. I opened the coffin and saw that Lucy's head had been cut off and removed from the grave. A wooden stake had been driven through her heart. I placed my hand on her breast and felt a slight give. After a few minutes of searching I found the hidden catch that lowered Lucy's corpse into the false bottom and released the fake lining that fell into place, hiding the corpse. An old magician's trick—clearly Von Helsing's work—using it to trick someone into believing that Lucy's corpse could enter and leave the tomb at will. What was he up to? And suddenly I was afraid.

I returned to the Westenra house and approached a servant-woman as she left in the evening. I said, "Can you tell me if Miss Mina has been here?" The old woman then began to cry profusely. She blew her nose on a rag and said, "Oh, dear Sir, our Miss Lucy is dead, dead and gone, and her poor mother too; and the poor young girl was to be married to the young lord. Oh no, no one has been here, except Miss Mina, since then. And most of us are merely kept on until Lord Godalming can sell the house."

I grabbed her hand, "Tell me quickly. Where is Mina?" The shock of my grip on her arm brought her very near to crying out, and she soon described Seward's Sanitorium in Purfleet. I quickly made may way there, arriving some time after midnight.

I would as soon be on the Indian seas, where your dreams send me rowing every night, or crashing through the ice near the Poles, or ploughing with my naked corpse through the billows of that ocean where I must one day plough forever and reap despair!
—*Melmoth the Wanderer*, Maturin

62

From "1889 field notes—Prof. Von Helsing"
(translated from the German)

On the evening of day #45, 4:35 pm. I went to Purfleet. The maid announced my arrival as, "Professor Helsing," and I was ushered into the dining room of the Purfleet Sanitorium. As I entered the room, I left my medical bag on a chair and tossed my coat over it. A young man, Dr. Hennessey, rose to shake my hand. "Professor Von Helsing, I am very pleased to meet you, Sir, as Dr. Seward speaks very highly of you."

"Yes, I am glad to meet you also Mr. Hennessey. But I must ask that you not mention this little visit to our friend Seward when he arrives later with Mrs. Harker."

"I understand your desire for discretion, Sir, although I admit to some curiosity about why you wish to meet and talk with one of Dr. Seward's patients in his absence."

"Mr. Hennessey, I do realize your concern—after all, Dr. Seward has left you in charge of the asylum in his absence, a very important responsibility. However, this is a very unusual situation."

"In what way?"

"I would like to speak with one of your patients . . . a Mr. Renfield."

"May I ask why?"

"I knew Mr. Renfield some years ago. He was once a medical student in London at the same time I was."

"I was not aware of that."

"Nor is Dr. Seward aware of that fact. It might adversely affect his treatment of Mr. Renfield. After all, it is one thing to treat an unfortunate lunatic—it is quite another to treat the former colleague of your old teacher."

"I see. But what happened to Mr. Renfield? I wonder how he came to be institutionalized."

"That is very difficult to explain . . . Some years ago when I was a student in London, I met Mr. Renfield. He was a gifted man, some would say brilliant. He knew a great deal about neurology and was probably the most promising experimental researcher in the school . . . until he was expelled."

"And how did that come about?"

"Mr. Renfield took his experiments too far. He began to use himself as a subject in his research . . . I imagine you've heard the story about the cat?"

"Was that Mr. Renfield? Amazing!"

"Yes, but it went even further than that. There were some unorthodox experiments . . . which resulted in several deaths."

"God in heaven!"

"Yes. Mr. Renfield was committed by his family to an institute for the insane. In reality, this step merely avoided more serious punishment—prison, in fact!"

"I see."

"Yes. Mr. Renfield's family is fairly prominent in London society. They wanted very much to avoid a scandal."

"I can certainly understand why you hesitated to mention this to Dr. Seward."

"Yes. But let me ask you this. I was led to believe that Mr. Renfield had been confined to an asylum in Islington. How did he come to be here instead?"

"Well, Professor, according to his file the transfer was arranged by a soliciter acting for his family . . . a Mr. Peter Hawkins."

"I see. That does clarify things." Von Helsing muttered.

"But . . . surely you knew that Mr. Renfield was transferred here."

"Oh, indeed I tried to contact the asylum in Islington. But their records are rather sketchy since the fire there . . . and with Dr.

Kelley's death, no one there could remember where Mr. Renfield had been transferred. Actually, it was something that Dr. Seward said to me in one of his letters that led me to believe that Renfield was here."

"Ah, well, let me take you to his room. He should be in a fairly reasonable state at this time of day."

I picked up my medical bag and proceeded down the hall to the stairway and then down to a small room on the first floor. I entered the room alone and confronted the sole occupant of the cell.

"Dr. Renfield, I presume! Or should I say, Sir William . . ."

Renfield moved toward me threateningly.

". . . Please, violence is not necessary. After all, I am not going to betray you."

"Why have you come here then with your lies and your spider's soul?"

"Not to bait you, certainly. But a certain curiosity compels me."

"Have you heard about curiosity and the cat?"

"No. But I'm sure you could tell me about it."

"What is it that you want, Von Helsing? Can't you just leave me alone, a poor lost soul. A maniac."

I said, "You are a great scientist, Sir William, probably the greatest experimental scientist in England . . . except, of course, for a single fault, a lack of concern for the subjects of your experiments; . . . not that this is a serious fault, mind you, but one that you were never able to mask with benevolence, or at least a funny foreign accent."

"No I haven't, although you have mastered it as an art."

"Truly as you are the greatest scientist, I am the greatest student of human nature. I have taken your plan, so carefully crafted, and adopted it as my own. It is a brilliant plan, getting Peter Hawkins to meet Drakulya in Bistritz and then to send the young Mr. Harker to Transylvania to complete the paper-work. Surely you knew that Harker was probably being sent to his death."

"It did not affect the outcome."

"True enough. And I should be able to use Harker's return to good effect. But why, once the vampire was on his way here, did you try to waylay his shipment of boxes, first by bribing the mate of the Demeter and then by murdering the crew?"

"The boxes were important to Drakulya, important enough for him to bring them with him all this way. The vampire, himself, is too unpredictable, too dangerous to control. But by seizing his boxes, I could keep him on a short leash."

"You've also managed to escape from your cell here, at least for a few hours, without being detected. How do you manage that?"

"I have convinced everyone that I am violent only during the day, so at night they do not bother to watch me closely."

"I see." I turned to face the door. "There is one more question . . . the experiment. What went wrong?"

Sitting on the bed, Renfield leaned over, placing his hands over his face. "The experiment. Of course, that is why you've come."

"Yes, the experiment. What happened? Tell me."

"The experiment failed."

"Failed how?"

"Whatever this is we are dealing with, I could not isolate it from the blood and tissue samples . . . Oh, the effects were there. I injected a patient with a small amount of the blood and within a few months she developed the symptoms you predicted—a slow anemia-like wasting, followed by a cataleptic paralysis and loss of life signs."

"I see . . . and there were no lasting effects, except death."

"I found the opportunity, Professor, to perform an autopsy . . . several autopsies . . . There were no permanent changes in the tissues . . . at least none that could be detected."

"Did you get the chance to examine the brain of the deceased for any signs of contiguous evolutionary development?"

"No. I hadn't the time. I was working with very restricted time constraints."

I looked toward the door. "I know that you have some feelings in this matter, but I have need of your surgical skills. I want you to perform an autopsy on the brain of the vampire's latest victim."

I carefully placed my large black medical bag on Renfield's lap and went to the door. Renfield glared at me. "Who?"

I stopped a moment and then said, closing the door behind me, "Why Miss Lucy Westenra, of course!"

I walked down the hall, toward Seward's office, ignoring the sharp cry of horror that came from the hall behind me.

_____

Are you that Beowulf who contended with Breca, competed in swimming on the broad sea? . . . There you clasped the sea-stream, measured the sea-ways, and with plowing shoulders parted the waves.
—Beowulf.

63

From "1889 field notes—Prof. Von Helsing"
(translated from the German)

That same evening, at about 9 pm, after Seward's return, we separated ourselves from the others and went to Seward's study. Seward said, "There is still a great deal that I don't understand."

"It is very easy to account for all of these phenomena, my friend. It is only necessary that we use Occam's scalpel to cut down to the core of these events. The reason why you have been unable to accept the possibility of these physical effects is because your concept of the vampire is basically materialistic. You see, the vampire's hold on his physical form is far more tenuous than our own."

I paused for a moment and then continued, "By studying certain books of arcane philosophy, I have discovered that living bodies possess, and are animated by, a vital force called 'animal spirits'— which the Chinese call the P'o, or the lower soul. During our lives, and for a short time after death, these animal spirits reside in the human body. As long as we live, our physical bodies feed these animal spirits. But after we die, they slowly diminish. Because the vampire, in contrast, is able to prevent these animal spirits from dissipating, he can maintain an un-dead existence. The vampire can use these spirits to preserve and animate his body, as I believe almost all recently created vampires do. Or he can do as I believe Drakulya has done and abandon his dead body. He can then mold his animal spirits into a human, though unsolid form, and make it visible, clothed as in life, by projecting its image into our minds. In this way the vampire can be seen in our mind's eye, but he will have no image in a mirror and cast no shadow. If the vampire wishes to solidify this spirit body, he can do so, because, according to St. Thomas Aquinas, animal spirits can be condensed into a physical body—as has been proven by the spiritualists, who can create physical plasmic objects from their own bodies. I believe that the vampire becomes solid by absorbing into his form the blood of his victims—for human blood contains a rich concentration of animal spirits—and in this way he can act as a physical body. As animal spirits can be either intangible or solid, according to their concentration, the vampire can adopt the form of 'mist' in order to pass unhindered through small openings, and can then reassume his physical form, becoming less transparent as his density increases."

I continued, "In addition, the vampire can mold this plasmic body into any shape he chooses, by an act of the will. In this way the vampire is able to adopt the form of a wolf or a bat, although the more unlike his own human form the shape is, or the less familiar the shape is, the more difficult it is for him to adopt and maintain that form. The vampire must, however, take on his solid human form in order to rest in his grave during the day-time, when his powers are weakest—and this is why he can be destroyed."

I pointed to a small vial of blood on Seward's desk and said, "Because animal spirits have a tendency to diminish with the passage of time, the vampire is forced to replenish his spirits with the blood of the living, in the same way we replenish our own animal spirits through the food we eat. All animal life is ultimately dependent on plant life for the nourishment it needs, and plant life is dependent on the sun, which is the ultimate source of animal spirits."

"And yet, this is all so . . . strange."

Taking his arm, "John, I realize that you might be bewildered
by all of these ideas, but you can adjust to them. Their novelty will
pass. I have told all of this because I felt that you, more than
anyone else, would give me a fair hearing." I paused for a
moment. "We are hot wax, and are different from our colleagues,
who are cold, yellow, crumbling, and smell with age. We can take
on the shape of reality, conforming ourselves to its shape, rather
than trying to force reality to demonstrate the ever-shifting
opinions of scientists and philosophers. We must be objective and,
simultaneously, reject the illusions of subjectivity."

"But Professor, I still have trouble believing what we saw
happening to Lucy . . . the slow wasting away . . . the loss of blood
so much that even with blood transfusions from all her friends—
Mina and myself, and even you—we could not prevent her death.
And then later seeing the thing she became . . . the walking dead.
And the small children she attacked. Even now I can't rid my
mind of the image of what she had become . . . and what we did
to her, as we all together drove the wooden stake through her
heart and then . . ."

"Cut off her head? It was all necessary, friend John, for her sake
so she could sleep as the true dead, the blessed dead. We can not
look back now. Too much is ahead of us."

"What more can there be? Have we not had horrors enough?"

"I fear my friend that a greater peril lies ahead of us. You see,
I believe that our friend Mina has, like Lucy, been infected with
the disease of vampirism. I do not yet know how she contracted
the disease, but I fear that the illness has already unhinged her
weak nerves."

"Good God, Professor! Not Mina!"

"Yes, I fear that some evil force has taken hold of her soul.
Several curious events during the illness of Miss Lucy led me to
suspect that she was not truly on our side in this battle. If we
cannot save her from this evil, we may be called upon to drive a
stake through her, just as we did Lucy."

*Keats commonly walked over to Enfield once a week to borrow my books.
He devoured rather than read, and he translated and copied an immense
quantity. So litle idea had I of his real love of poetry, that I imputed to a
  boyish ambition his asking the loan of Spenser's "Faery Queen": Keats
  ramped through the scenes of that purely poetical romance like a young
  horse turned into a Spring meadow. I shall never forget the expression of
  pleasure and surprise in his face while speaking of that poet's power. One
  of the instances most strongly in my recollection is where Spenser speaks
  of the "sea-shouldering whale." Keats hoisted himself up, looking burly
  and dominant as he said, "What an image that is—
    sea shouldering whales."*
—Charles Cowden Clarke

64

From Mina Harker's diary

I had come to Purfleet to stay with Jonathan for a few days. Dr.
Seward was kind enough to let me share the small room with
Jonathan, well away from the corridors where the violent patients
were kept. Lucy's death had caused a sudden relapse of the old
fears that haunted him.

I had got Jonathan the London papers of the previous night, and
while we were talking on the veranda, watching the sunset, he was
turning them over, each page carefully. His eyes suddenly seemed
to catch some word or phrase, and he said, "If this is His work! If
I only knew! If I only knew!" I feared to keep his thoughts on the
subject by asking him anything, and so I remained silent.

Eventually I was able to draw Jonathan away quietly out into the
yard, and he, holding my arm, came easily. We walked a little
further, and then went in and sat for a while in the cemetery of
the asylum. It was a cool evening, and there was a comfortable old
seat in the shade. After a few minutes' staring at nothing,
Jonathan's eyes closed, and he went quietly into a sleep, with his

head on my lap. I thought it was best for him, so did not disturb him. As the sun slipped behind the horizon, just beyond the old abbey, he woke up, and said to me quite cheerfully: "Why, Madame Mina! Oh, do forgive me for being so rude." His strange way of addressing me, and the peculiar way he intoned his words, made me think he was playing a game.

"Beautiful, isn't it." His eyes stroked the scene, like a man long imprisoned. "Do you not recognize me, from so long ago." He paused and cocked his head to one side. "I am called Drakulya."

A sudden chill went up my spine, and I realized that this spirit who had taken possession of my husband was indeed the Drakulya who I had met in Transylvania. As if a heavy veil fell from my mind, suddenly I was able to recall the details of my meeting with Drakulya in Whitby. My real father had been a spiritualist minister, and as a child I had seen many demonstrations of spirit possession and spirit-writing. I, myself, had served as a spirit-medium at many seances. But how had this Drakulya come to possess the body of my husband, Jonathan? Why had he possessed Jonathan? And by what power could he be forced to release him? I could not decide to run, or to stay.

I turned to face him in the darkness. "Good evening, Sir."

"Please, let us have no formalities between us. I am not very good at this kind of thing. Please, you must call me Mircea, if you don't mind my . . . forwardness. But habit compels me to speak to you."

"I believe I do know you, don't I?"

"If you remember your trip to Transylvania, it is possible."

"In fact, I believe you were in Whitby a few weeks ago."

"Yes, I was there, although I'm surprised you remember seeing me there."

"You knew my step-father too."

"Indeed, and who is he?"

"He was Mr. Peter Hawkins."

"Ah, yes. The late Mr. Hawkins. I did meet him during his visit to my country last year. He carries with him on his travels a very striking photo-engraving of you. I still recall the first time he showed it to me. Unfortunately, I did not get the chance to see him recently, not in life anyway."

"You saw him?"

"Yes, I went to ask him some questions. But when I arrived, he was already dead . . . poisoned."

"I thought as much. I knew from his manner when I saw Mr. Hawkins a few weeks before that something was wrong. But you had nothing to do with his death?"

"Madame Mina, poison has never been my way."

"And what about Miss Lucy?"

"I have come to ask you that same question."

"Remember that it was I who saw you with Lucy in the graveyard at Whitby."

"Yes, that is true. Which brings me to the question: What happened to her body?"

"Why she is in the grave, of course. Where else would she be?"

"Madame Mina, I would not dare to contradict you in this matter, except for the fact that I have been to her grave—her tomb has been opened and her corpse mutilated—her head is missing."

"Missing?"

"Yes, it is as I have said."

He was silent for a moment. I stepped onto the veranda beside him, and he said, "Von Helsing."

"Yes, you know him?"

"I met him some years ago . . . He wanted to buy a religious artifact from me. Would you believe that he thought I possessed the lost Ark of the Covenant?"

"Really? I suppose after what has happened I could believe anything." I looked at him directly. "Do you have the lost Ark of the Covenant?"

He smiled, "No more so than you or anyone else."

"A good answer, although not very forthcoming."

"I am all that you see here, there is little else."

"Still ambiguous." And then seriously, "But I am afraid for myself and my husband. I do not trust Von Helsing, but he has some terrible hold over the others. I feel that you, too, are in some danger. And you have endangered Jonathan."

"The story of my life, I'm afraid." Taking my hand he said, "Madame Mina, if you should ever need my protection, such as it is, you need only touch my arm, thus, at sunset or at sunrise.

Recently I have had some difficulty controlling Jonathan. It has come to the point that I can only exert myself through your husband at those times." He kissed my hand warmly.

"Wait," I said. "You should know that it was I that you were to meet when you came to Whitby. Poor Lucy was only there at my suggestion . . . because I was going there."

We stood there in the half-light and spoke quietly, like old friends. We each sensed the secret springs that drove the other, and this knowledge was for us a refuge, a place of safety. I felt secure in his presence, as if under the influence of a strange spell. I seemed to brighten in his presence, drawing on new feelings, sparking to life new senses. The darkness was not an enemy, but a friend, for in the darkness all the wisdom of the weary world was negated—and the "why" became "why not?"

We walked upstairs together to my bedroom. And this strange creature—part husband and part stranger—lay on the bed. In a moment his eyes closed. Jonathan slept soundly for a few minutes and then started, as if in a dream. His eyes flew open and he said, "What a strange dream, Mina. How strange. I dreamt of meeting Lucy on the bluff overlooking the sea. And I kissed her strangely." He blushed then as he saw how I stared at him.

"Jonathan, do not worry about dreams. Now go back to sleep." I closed his eyes with a kiss.

But he knew better, did the Christmas robin—
The murderous robin with his breast aglow
And legs apart, in a spade-handle perched:
He prophesied more snow, and worse than snow.
—*Food for Centaurs*, Robert Graves

65

From Mina Harker's journal

The following night I led Jonathan to the graveyard at sunset. Once again, he lay his head on my lap and fell asleep as the sun went below the horizon. The strange action repeated itself as Jonathan's body was possessed by the soul of Mircea Drakulya. His eyes opened, and he smiled as he gazed into mine.

"Mina, you've come."

"Yes, I said I would seek you out again when I needed you. Although you have not yet shown yourself to be sincere. After all, I am risking a great deal in summoning you, as is Jonathan in acting as your vehicle. But what are you risking?"

"Everything that I have is in jeopardy if Von Helsing succeeds."

"You know what it is that he wants?"

"I suspect."

"Do you know that he plans to break into Carfax Abbey to-night?"

"No, but there is nothing there for him to harm—not anymore."

"I think that either Renfield or Seward has told him that some of your boxes have been moved to other locations."

"Who is this Renfield?"

"I don't know, but I fear him. And my step-father feared him too. Once, under his breath, I heard him say that Renfield was the Napoleon of Evil. I think he had more to do with Lucy's death than he admits."

"Yes, I think so too. But it is important that I find out what happened to Lucy."

"Why?"

"It is possible that even though she is dead to human eyes, she may still be returned from death . . ."

"I think not."

"And why not?"

"Dr. Seward told me that they all together went to Lucy's grave. Von Helsing convinced them that Lucy was a vampire. There they drove a stake through her heart. And then they cut off her head, and then, just today, they sent her body to the crematorium. Lucy was cremated."

Suddenly he was filled with anger, "They will pay for this! All of them, Von Helsing, Renfield, Seward, all!"

I turned from him. "But what about Jonathan. What about our life together? How much longer are you going to use him?"

"Are you afraid of me."

"When my step-father, Mr. Hawkins, returned from Transylvania last year, he told me a great deal about you. He saw some good thing in you, a quality he admired a great deal. And I see that same quality. Whatever you are, I believe you will deal fairly with us." I paused, "Von Helsing and this Renfield had some terrible hold over my step-father. I think it had something to do with his youth—when he was in Ireland—but I don't know what."

"Don't you have any idea?"

"I do know that Professor Von Helsing carries a black medical bag around with him all the time. He never seems to put it down for more than a few moments at a time. He made a joke to Mr. Hawkins about delivering his medical bag to the Parnell Commission, but father looked very grim and didn't laugh. I got the chance to look in it once, but the only thing unusual in there is a case of dirty old surgical knives."

Drakulya scowled. "The bag has some connection, too, with Renfield."

"That may be. But there is one other thing that I must ask you before you go back." I paused. "I know that you would not have harmed Lucy, if it could be helped. I believe that you would not harm me." I put my hand on his arm, but he said nothing

After we exchanged a few inconsequential words, Drakulya left me in the graveyard and walked toward the sanitarium. "Go to your room," he said. "You shall have your Jonathan back tonight."

*I remember the first albatross I ever saw. It was during a prolonged gale,
in waters hard upon the Antarctic seas. From my forenoon watch below,
I ascended to the overclouded deck; and there, dashed upon the main
hatches, I saw a regal, feathery thing of unspotted whiteness, and with a
hooked, Roman bill sublime. At intervals, it arched forth its vast
archangel wings, as if to embrace some holy ark. Wondrous flutterings
and throbbings shook it. Though bodily unharmed it uttered cries, as
some king's ghost in supernatural distress.*
—Herman Melville

66

I determined to find Mr. Renfield and force him to confess what
he and Von Helsing had done to poor Lucy. I waited until the
others were occupied and then entered Renfield's small room. He
was turned away from me, writing in a small note-book.

"Renfield!"

He turned to face me and then turned away to finish writing,
saying, "Master, I knew you would come. I've covered my tracks
well, but it was always only a matter of time."

"Renfield, if that is your name . . . I want to know why you have
lured me here. And why did you kill Miss Lucy Westenra and
then desecrate her corpse?"

"I . . . I did not kill Lucy. I did the other things, yes, and would
gladly do them again, for the sake of the flies. But I would not
have harmed Lucy for the world, for all the lifetimes that you
possess."

"It was Von Helsing then?"

"Mine was the plan. But involving Lucy was his doing. His
doing! It was his evil that damned my little wren soul."

"But why?"

"It was an experiment . . . the experiments were illegal and
several women died . . . were killed. And the blood, the lovely

blood. It was too easy. I was caught and put in an asylum near London. I managed to get transferred here, with the help of my friend Mr. Hawkins. It was the obvious place to hide. After all, who would think of looking for a little lost wren in an asylum. I was safe here until Von Helsing found me. He spoiled it all. And now you've come too."

"The experiment—what was it?"

"I introduced tainted blood, the blood of one of your victims, into the body of one of my patients. I wanted to find out if I could create vampires, creatures like yourself. It was Von Helsing's plan. He is a fool!"

"Then why did you help him?"

"I wanted immortality . . . for my own reasons. And I knew that I could wrest the secret from your blood . . . before Von Helsing destroyed you. Yes, the blood is the life. The blood."

"And then?"

"When I . . . disappeared . . . Von Helsing became impatient. He wanted you here and in his control, to study your habits, to find out what makes you what you are. It was a dangerous step to take, of course. Especially when he decided to use Miss Lucy to trap you; to use Lucy's blood . . . I, too, drank the blood," he smiled, "from Seward, after I attacked him with a knife." An evil grin marched across his face. "You see, my friend, I am becoming a creature like you—powerful—immortal—a being to be feared. Von Helsing thinks that you are a product of environment, but he is wrong. You see, I discovered your secret. I have eaten the flesh and drunk the blood of the Children of the Night. I feel their strength flowing through me now. For I am a vampire like you."

I had anticipated this turn. Renfield had indeed discovered the secret of eternal life, with that native maniacal cunning that made him an enemy to be truly feared. I could see reflected in his face the struggle for control of the mind of this lunatic.

Renfield lunged at me, and I felt his fingers, like iron claws, sinking into my flesh. I grappled with him, but he was too powerful in his madness. He was able to hold me so that I could not escape him.

After a brief struggle, I said, "You've won, Renfield. I will tell you what you want to know." I felt his grip loosen. "You are the only one I've met who really deserves this secret, the only one I can trust." I met his eyes. "Are you ready for eternal life?"

"I am, Master . . . yes!"

"Then look at me. Look in my eyes and see the secret that lies hidden there. You must not resist the ultimate truth of what you want to become."

Renfield gazed deeply into my eyes for several minutes. His expression was childlike—trusting and submissive—as if waiting to hear his favorite bed-time story. His eyes were glassy, as though a powerful drug was working in his system. I took his hand in mine and spoke softly to him.

"Do you see it?"

"Yes, I see it. I feel it."

"Do you see it? Do you feel the strength, the youth and vitality flooding into your body?"

"Yes. I feel it. The tiredness, the exhaustion, it is gone."

"You feel it, the feeling of peace, of contentment?"

A faint smile appeared on his face.

"I am now going to tell you the two things you must know. These two things are the only true things in the world, and as long as you hold them within you, strength and power are yours forever."

"Yes. Please tell me."

"The first secret is . . . there is no past."

A smile spread over his face. A soul burdened with a lifetime of guilt was suddenly, in that instant, set free.

"Are you ready for the second secret?"

"Yes. Please. Please!"

"Good. And this is the second secret . . . there is no future."

The smile disappeared from his face. His whole expression went blank, lifeless . . . without will, without a reason to exist.

Renfield fell forward, dropping face first against the floor.

"Yes, Renfield. These are the two secrets. They are the only truths you can believe."

I forced the potion between his slacked jaws. I left him there on the floor, catatonic—a fair copy of the living death he so greatly deserved. I had not wanted to take this step, but it was clear that Von Helsing meant to destroy me if he could. Taking Renfield's

body was the only route open to me. Before morning, Renfield the
Injester of Flies, would be reborn as Drakulya "Lord of the
Undead" and would walk the earth one last time to do battle
against the forces of virtue.

----

*"Ah, young sir, the Szekelys—and the Dracula as their heart's blood, their
brains, and their swords—can boast a record that mushroom growths like
the Hapsburgs and the Romanoffs can never reach. The warlike days are
over. Blood is too precious a thing in these days of dishonorable peace;
and the glories of the great races are as a tale that is told."*
*It was by this time close on morning, and we went to bed. (Mem., this
diary seems horribly like the beginning of the "Arabian Nights," for
everything has to break off at cockcrow—or like the ghost of Hamlet's
father.)*
—*Dracula*, Bram Stoker

67

Mina's room was on an upper floor, but the hallways were
empty. I found her waiting for my return. I said, "They've located
the houses?"

"Yes." Mina paused. "You're not concerned, are you?"

"No. I've already substituted boxes of good English earth for
mine. An old gentleman in Whitby gave me the idea."

"So your own boxes are safe."

"They're being loaded on board a ship. They are on their way
home."

"Then you're leaving."

"I've come to say goodbye. And to give you something. If you
want it."

"I don't know . . ."

"Please. There is no reason why you could not live out your life
here. But some day this English life will not be enough for you.

And then, when you wake from the sleep of this living-death, I want you to come to me. I can wait for you as long as it takes. I will wait."

"But what will happen if you are killed . . . by the others?"

"I must make them think that they have succeeded in thwarting my plans, for your sake and mine. The vampire will confront them tomorrow here at Dr. Seward's sanitorium. I have found a way to save us both." Mina's face revealed her relief. "But if I fail. If they do destroy me, then even that will not be the end for us. For even then I can live in you as all the other Dead-Ones have lived through me."

"I don't understand."

I handed her a glass vial. "When the time comes, drink the contents of this vial. You can go then to my castle. There you must open the boxes. And when you do, you will find the Children of the Night waiting. And then the Children of the Night will teach you as they taught me. You will hold the knowledge of all the dark things I have protected these many years. You will understand everything."

She held me and then kissed me. She bit my lip so that it bled quite freely. And then she kissed me—for eternity!

I heard voices and footsteps in the hallway. I embraced Mina one last time and then kissed her again on her white shoulders and on her throat. There was some violence in this act, quick and deliberate, which I regret. But the taking of blood was all too necessary this time, for the sake of Mina. For she must be seen as my unwilling victim.

The door burst open and Von Helsing fell forward onto the floor, the others pressing in behind him. Von Helsing's face had the angry expression of someone who had been caught listening at a keyhole. Covering my face, I pushed the others aside, diving past the sudden rattlesnake strike of a Bowie knife, until I was half-running, half-sliding down the stairwell. I burst, laughing, into the night.

I laughed at their impotent plans. My own plans were deliberate, almost military in their execution. I ran around the short hedge, heading for Renfield's room.

It was no wonder the Kukulcan and Quetzacoatl were sometimes identified long afterwards, for the former means "serpent swimming in the water"; while Quetzacoatl means "serpent covered with the feathers of the Quetzal bird. . . ." Among the Teocallis in the enclosure was an altar consecrated to Quetzacoatl, circular in form, and having an entrance in imitation of a dragon's mouth, bristling with sharp fangs, and dripping with blood. . . . If depicted in human shape, he has a crown suspended over his head, shaped like a Quetzal bird pouncing, and a mask over his face from the coils of a turquoise snake.
—In Quest of the White God, Pierre Honore

68

The next day, shortly after sunrise, Renfield's body, animated solely by myself, rose from the floor of the cell. With my great physical strength, I forced the door of the cell and escaped, heading down the hall, past Seward's office.

I threw open the hall door and marched steadily toward the main room. Moving quickly, I opened the door and found myself, face to face, with Von Helsing, Dr. Seward, Quincy Morris, and Lord Godalming. These three—Quincy, Arthur, and Dr. Seward—had all, at one time, been lovers of the dead Lucy. And now Von Helsing had forged them into the instrument of my destruction. They were armed to the teeth with knives, a sword, and a few bits of holy bread. None of them had the foresight to carry a lance or spear, but even so the odds against my leaving were not good. The bloody foam on my lips left them no doubt as to the great evil they faced.

"Well, Dear Professor, I see that you have gathered together all our . . . friends."

"I am very sure," replied Von Helsing, "that by now you have come to realize that there is a deadly struggle taking place here."

"I am aware of no such thing, Professor. There may, perhaps, be a small disagreement between us, but I am sure that it can be resolved quite easily . . . after these gentlemen cease waving about their weapons."

"You don't quite understand. It is precisely these weapons that will resolve our 'disagreement.'"

"You are . . . determined?"

"Exactly."

"Then it shall be as you desire. But before we play the final scene in your comedy of morals, I must ask all of you to consider an important point. As you see me here, among my . . . friends, can you really bring yourselves to believe that I am the same Drakulya who was born four centuries ago? Can you really believe that Drakulya lives? Yet, nevertheless, I am here, speaking to you, battling you with all the power that I possess. As you fight me, risking the only life that you know, you may perhaps feel that this is all a grand joke devised by the Professor and myself. But do not be deceived. It is easier to believe that the dead continue to live than to believe that they do not. Do you think it ironic that the dead continue to live? You shouldn't . . . at least not here. Not in London."

Quincy chose that moment to lunge at me with his sword. But I easily sidestepped the blow, and grabbing a handful of money that had been left on the table, I shoved Quincy back. They all rushed at me at once, but I had already leaped for the window before they could decide who would strike first.

A few of them followed me to the street, but they were too late. Dr. Seward took Von Helsing by the arm, "My God! Renfield and Drakulya are one and the same. He was the vampire all along." Von Helsing answered, "He was possessed by the evil of Drakulya. We must track him down and destroy him, for Lucy and for Mina's sake."

Abraxas is generally represented with the body of a man, but his head is that of a cock or hawk to signify watchfulness and foresight. His legs are formed of twin serpents, symbolizing mystery, vitality and eternity; in one hand he grasps the scourge of power and authority, whilst with the other he holds a shield, the emblem of wisdom.
—*The Encircled Serpent*, M.O. Howey

69

Returning to Purfleet, I waited in the old abbey. The windows of the chapel were a good vantage point for watching the sanitorium. The hairs on the back of my neck stood up. I could feel Von Helsing and the others plotting.

On the floor below were two dozen boxes of earth. Von Helsing had "sterilized" them with his bits of holy wafer and his crucifixes. The sight of them irritated me, but I did not feel the old weakness, just the nausea and disgust.

"The holy crucifix will protect the dead and the quick!" Von Helsing had declared—the old hypocrite. He had no idea what they represent—the cross, the empty tomb, the resurrection and the life.

But here that was all forgotten, like a dead language. Here the worshippers crowd in like sheep, their pale faces all in a row, waiting for the butcher. This then was the secret that I had purchased with my death: When the worshippers come into the temple and join the communion to drink the blood of their god, it is they who are drunk. Indeed, they are drunken with his love. He gives his love and they give their blood. I do no less; then why am I condemned? I flee the shadow of the cathedral, for it would swallow my shadow in its own greater darkness. I am but a small maggot in the shadow of the Great White Worm of the Church.

We parasites recognize each other, and we hate each other.

At the precise hour, I left my perch in the old ruined abbey and made my way to the docks. Here then was the great Thames. This was the main artery of the city. The life of the city depends on this river, or so I thought.

But in the last few days I began to see the other face of London. I saw the life force of this city in the shops of Piccadilly, in the ships of the port, in the great houses of the money changers, in the exchange of currency. Buying and selling is the true life force of this city. The quiet of the weekends is only the repose after the feast.

These people with their swollen guts represent London itself. Their sin is the greatest of all sins: the sin of those who, to quench their thirst, drink each other's blood. London is a city of cannibals.

This is the thing for which they cannot be forgiven: they have accepted death. Instead of struggling against it, they have made it a part of them, simply another occasion for the exchange of money.

I am separated from them, not by time and space, but by the grave. I am Lazarus returned from the grave to speak of death, but no one listens. They reject me and the tale I would tell. But when I go among them as a man, there is the chance that I may lure them, one by one, into the catacombs, perhaps by the promise of a cask of wine four centuries old, and there teach them my tale.

It is a slow process. But even now my story spreads across the continent. Perhaps, some day, it may even reach London.

This stern, punitive aspect of God, one of his ten mystical attributes, has at its lowest manifestation some affinity with the realm of evil referred to as "the dregs of the wine," and it is out of this that Lilith emerged together with Samael. . . . She is slender, well-shaped, beautiful and nude, with wings and owl feet. . . . God was apprehensive lest they fill the world with their demonic brood, and to prevent this, he castrated Samael. This mythologem, found in several 17th century Kabbalistic books, is based on the identification of "Leviathan the Piercing Serpent and Leviathan the Tortuous Serpent" with Samael and Lilith, respectively. . . .
—*The Hebrew Goddess*, Raphael Patai

70

I hear the clanking of chain and the sails snapping in the wind, and by that sound I know that I have escaped. But I also sense that a volley of spears has been launched in pursuit, each to find its separate place in my heart.

The effect of my passing among them has been lost on them. The contrast between us is too great. They prefer to ignore me, to ignore even the possibility that I might be among them. Few of them even suspect that I exist. But that is my own fault. I have been the main actor in Von Helsing's comedy of morals, but the unfolding of the plot does not require my presence on the stage. I wait in the wings until the moment when I am required to walk on stage, say a few words, and then walk off again. And then the others go on without me. The performance is repeated again and again, but so far they have failed to pin me down. Perhaps some day my destruction will come—a lucky thrust of a lance, a well-aimed blow of a dagger, or even a slight misstep and a fall onto a sharpened pale—and then the rest of the acts can unfold, determined by my fortunate demise. The play itself would then disintegrate into a thousand lesser dramas—some better than others—until it becomes little more than a ritual mugging in the gas-light of some backwater Dublin theatre.

It is a cold morning, and the masts shudder in the wind. The fog in London had been thick and heavy for many days, with little intermission. None was present just now, however. The sky had partly cleared, but was very gloomy. In the northeast where the sun would rise in a few hours, there was pale dead light both beautiful and awful, touching the clouds with color. Toward London, however, a lurid glare overhung the whole dark waste; and the contrast between these two lights, and of the imaginary scene of thousands of people reflected in an unearthly fire, was too disturbing and too cruel to think of.

I had no thought that morning—none came to me then of what my fate was to be. I was at a loss and uncertain of myself. I have since connected that feeling with that place and time, and with everything associated with that vision of Hell, even the distant voices of the crew and the sound of creaking timbers. Transylvania. There I would be safe.

I went down into the hold, where my boxes were stacked against a damp and rotting wall. I won't try to sleep here, although I'm feeling horribly cold.

HERMES: And all that while
  The winged vulture-hound of Zeus shall tear
  Thy helpless body into mighty shreds,
  A guest unsummoned, feeding all day long
  With bloody jaws upon thy blackened heart.
  No end is thine to look for in such plight
  Till willingly there come another god
  To spell thee in thy misery, himself
  Choosing to make his voluntary way
  To gleamless Hades and black Tartarus.
  —Prometheus Bound, Aeschylus

71

The ship dropped anchor at the port of Varna, and I decided to make my way to shore as best I could. The weakness has returned again. Each day it seems a little worse. The old sailor rowed me across the water in a small rowboat. As he rowed, I looked over the boat's edge, at the lapping water. I saw myself there, my face in the shining surface. I had outlived my time.

In those hours I often reflected on the memory of the last time I saw Mina, there at Purfleet, before my departure from London. She was sitting at Seward's desk, typing up the infernal log of my destruction—the diaries, letters, and papers that pointed toward me as the Monster among them. Each key-stroke was another spear thrust finding its way into my heart.

She turned to look out the window, at the approaching darkness . . . or was it dawn? I don't remember. But I felt her eyes say to me, "Return to Transylvania. There they might destroy you, but they won't drain you of life and toss you aside like an empty jug. There at least you have a chance to escape. But here . . . here?"

Is it true? Is it better to die like a pig with its feet bound and its throat cut so that its blood spurts onto the earth, or like a butterfly suddenly impaled on a pin—its wings outstretched in the sensuous and trembling expectation of life?

I can feel them pursuing me; I hear the hoofbeats as they bear down their horses against me, daggers drawn.

And you Mina? And you?

When the others reached the kitchen they saw the table flung aside now
and Grimm stooping over the body. When they approached to see what he
was about, they saw that the man was not dead yet, and when they saw
what Grimm was doing one of the men gave a choked cry and stumbled
back into the hall and began to vomit. Then Grimm too sprang back,
flinging behind him the bloody butcher knife, "Now you'll let white women
alone, even in hell," he said.
—*Light in August,* William Faulkner

72

From an early manuscript of Bram Stoker's "Dracula"

Mina Harker's journal

The Professor and I had already reached the castle, and it was only waiting the arrival of our friends that held us back—the Professor having already entered the castle and found it empty. . . . From this place beside the great gate of Castle Drakulya, we could see the point where the tower cut the sky; we saw it in all its grandeur, perched a thousand feet on the summit of a sheer precipice, and with seemingly a great gap between it and the steep slopes of the adjacent mountain on every side. There was something wild and uncanny about the place. We could hear the distant howling of wolves. They were far off, but the sound, even though deadened by the falling snow, was full of terror. I knew from the way Von Helsing was searching about that he was seeking some strategic point where we would be less exposed in case of attack. The rough roadway still led downwards; we could trace it through the drifted snow.

In a little while the Professor signalled to me, so I got up and joined him. He had found a wonderful spot, a sort of natural hollow in the rock, with an entrance like a doorway between two boulders. He took me by the hand and drew me in: "See!" he said, "here you will be in shelter; and if the wolves do come I can meet them one by one." He brought in our furs and made a snug nest for me. He then got out some provisions and forced them upon me, but I could not eat; to even try to do so was repulsive to me, and, much as I would have liked to please him, I could not bring myself to do much more than chew on a piece of jerky-beef. He looked disturbed, but did not reproach me. Taking his field-glasses from the case, he stood on the top of one of the boulders and began to search the horizon. Suddenly he called out, "Look! Madame Mina. Look! Look!"

I sprang up and stood beside him on the rock; he handed me his glasses and pointed. The snow was now falling more heavily and swirled about fiercely, for a high wind was beginning to blow. However, there were times when there were pauses between the snow flurries. From the height where we were it was possible to see a great distance; and far off, beyond the white waste of snow, I could see the river lying like a black ribbon in kinks and curls. Straight in front of this and not far off—in fact so near that I wondered that we had not noticed before—came a group of mounted men hurrying madly. In the midst of them was a cart, a long leiter-wagon which swept from side to side, like a dog's tail wagging, with each rough spot in the road. It was obvious from their clothes that the men were peasants or gypsies of some kind.

The cart carried a great square chest. My heart leaped as I saw it, for I felt that the end was near. The evening was now drawing close, and well I knew that at sunset the Thing, which was till then imprisoned within his human form, would take new freedom and could in any of many forms elude all pursuit. In fear I turned to the Professor; to my consternation, however, he was not there. An instant later, I saw him climbing the sheer face of the rock wall. Above on the rock he was drawing a circle enclosing a cross. When he had completed it he stood beside me again saying, "At least you will be safe from *him!*"

"Professor, it is for you that I fear. There is no further harm that can be done to me. I am quite safe from whatever creatures Drakulya may choose to bring against us."

The Professor nodded as he looked at the deep red scar on my forehead. It was the mark of Drakulya. And as his bride I was safe from any supernatural harm that might befall us here. . . .

In those few precious moments the silence was broken by the call of angry men coming around the bend in the road below us. The wagon carrying Drakulya's coffin came into view, and with it the dozen or so gypsies who were his protectors. And only a short length behind were the horsemen, with Jonathan and Quincy at their head.

The wagon came to an abrupt, jolting stop before the great gate. Von Helsing had sealed it with a chain, and he had jammed great stones against it; so the gypsies were forced to fight in the open. Soon we saw the effect of the Remington repeating rifles, brought to bear with great efficiency against the single-cartridge rifles that the gypsies carried. In less than a minute, the leaders of the gypsy band lay dead, and the rest drew back from the bloody carnage, drawing cutlasses for a last-ditch stand around the wagon. It was to be hand-to-hand, gypsy knives and swords against Quincy's American-made pistols and Bowie knives. . . .

The dark was coming hard upon us as the sun edged below the horizon. In the mad rush of bodies and the scream of horses and the cursing of the men as they struggled, life against death, for the possession of my soul, I saw Jonathan leap to the wagon. He lifted the shovel high over his head and brought it down to smash the coffin. The coffin spintered and collapsed like a crate full of rocks. The men dived toward the coffin, and Quincy slashed at the now helpless form of Count Drakulya as he lay in the great box; but the blade passed through the monster's body without meeting resistance. Not until Jonathan, with a strength which seemed incredible, raised the body and flung it over the wheel to the ground, could the last perishing rays of sunlight avail them in their purpose.

Jonathan and Quincy leaped from the wagon, and on the instant came the sweep and flash of Jonathan's great Kuru knife. I shrieked as I saw the curved blade shear through the throat; whilst at the same moment Mr. Morris's Bowie knife was thrust lance-like into the monster's breast. . . . It was like magic; but before our very eyes and almost in the drawing of a breath, the whole body fell apart, as if eaten by spectral worms, and crumbled into dust, thus passing from our sight.

Jonathan had barely completed his horrible task as night-fall came over us; and Dr. Seward recovered from his faint as the Szygny fled from the scene in terror.

Despite our victory, tragedy had also fallen to our lot. For in the moment Quincy struck the fiend his death-blow, he also died from his wounds. We carried his body to Bistritz where we buried him the next morning. . . . Professor Von Helsing read the Lord's Prayer while the men all stood in a circle around the grave. I sat on a stone bench near the gate of the churchyard.

The morning sun was now right down upon the tree tops, and the red beams fell upon my face, so that it was bathed in a rosy light. With one impulse the men sank on their knees and a deep and earnest "Amen" broke from all as their eyes followed Jonathan's pointing finger to the place on my forehead where I wore the mark of Drakulya—the scarred flesh where Von Helsing had touched me with the Host. I stood.

"God be thanked that all has not been in vain. See! The mark is gone; the snow is not more stainless than her forehead. The curse has passed away!"

Both of them, Samael and Lilith, were born in a spiritual birth as androgynes, corresponding to Adam and Eve—below and above two twin figures. And Samael and Lilith the Elder, who is the same as Tzefonit, are referred to as the Tree of Knowledge of Good and Evil. . . . Her hair is long and red like the rose, her cheeks are white and red. . . . Lilith's epithet was "the beautiful maiden," but she was believed to have been a harlot and a vampire who, once she chose a lover, would never let him go. . . other demons as well are the bedfellows of this Lilith the Elder, who—and this is most remarkable—"is a ladder on which one can ascend to the rungs of prophecy."
—*The Hebrew Goddess,* Raphael Patai

73

From Bram Stoker's "Dracula"

Seven years ago we all went through the flames; and the happiness of some of us since then is, we think, well worth the pain we endured. It is an added joy to Mina that her son's birthday is the same day as that day long ago, when Quincy Morris sacrificed his life for her sake. The boy's mother holds, I know, the belief that some of our brave friend's spirit has passed into him. His bundle of names links all our little band of men together; but we call him Quincy.

In the summer of this year Jonathan and Mina made a journey to Transylvania, and went over the old ground which was, and is, so full of vivid and terrible memories. It was almost impossible to believe that the things that they had seen with their own eyes and heard with their own ears were living truths. Every trace of all that had been was blotted out. The castle stood as before, reared high above a waste of desolation.

When they got home we got to talking of the old time—which they could all look back on without despair. I took the papers from the safe where they have been ever since our return so long ago. We were struck with the fact, that in all the mass of material of which the record is composed, there is hardly one authentic document; nothing but a mass of type-writing, except the later notebooks of Mina and Seward. We could hardly ask any one, even did we wish to, to accept these as proofs of so wild a story. Dr. Seward summed it all up as he said, with our boy on his knee:

"We want no proofs; we ask none to believe us. This boy will some day know what a brave and gallant woman his mother is. Already he knows her sweetness and loving care; later on he will understand how some men so loved her, that they did dare much for her sake."

*Each of the Gnostic sects was founded by an initiate, and their tenets
were based upon a deep knowledge of the inner meaning of the symbolism
of all nations. The Gnostic Naaseni postulated the opposition of these two
Dragons as one of their leading tenets, and identified the radiant and
perfect Serpent with Jesus Christ, or Sophia; but Jehovah (or Ialdabaoth)
was considered by them to be the creator of, and identical with
Ophiomorphous, the Serpent of Evil, the leviathan, that crooked serpent
mentioned by Isaiah (xxvii. 1-3)*
—The Encircled Serpent, M.O. Howey

74

From "*Confessio:* Private papers of Dr. John Seward"
(1990)

[Pamphlet, privately published, Von Helsing collection]

Over the years a number of close friends have asked me about
my involvement in the famous "Dracula" case, described by Bram
Stoker in his novelization and by several others. It is for this
reason that I leave behind this final statement, with instructions
that it not be opened by anyone until 50 years have passed after
my death. The main people involved in this affair will by then be
all deceased, and no harm can come to anyone by my personal
speculations on the case.

Many people have commented on the strange role played by
the Professor in these events. Some have even suggested that the
events were cleverly stage-managed by him for some hidden
purpose. I can only concur in this opinion, for I believe that we all
were part of a strange and ghastly scientific experiment, one that
resulted in the untimely deaths of at least three people, including
Lucy Westenra and Quincy Morris.

In recent years I was able to get access to the Professor's
private papers maintained in a special collection in a library in the

Soviet Union. The papers were in code, only recently broken, and they suggest that he was working on a strange hypothesis.

The Professor was a student of religious history, psychology, biology, etc. and, after years of study, had come to the conclusion that ancient peoples living in the Middle East had discovered a technique by which the human life-span could be extended without limits. He proceeded to try to discover if any living person knew of the technique, and, after he felt he had located such a person, set in motion events that would lead to his being able to get access to this knowledge.

As part of his experiment, the Professor had introduced some heretofore unknown biochemical agent into the blood of one of his patients. He then proceeded to collect her blood for study. In order to collect enough blood for analysis and for future experiments, he even increased the quantity of her blood available to him for analysis through a series of dangerous blood transfusions. Part of his bizarre experiment appears to have involved creating a stress reaction on the part of his patient, creating a breakdown in her physiology that he believed would trigger a "metamorphosis" into a new form of life. Even more bizarre, during the blood transfusions he took the opportunity to reverse the process so that the blood donors were also affected/infected by the unknown biochemical agent.

Before his death, three years after these events, the Professor finally recognized that the experiment was a failure. He came to abandon the idea that human life could be extended beyond the known limits. After all, the progress of human evolution depends on weeding out the older inferior stock, and replacing these old individuals with newer, hardier individuals. This realization led the Professor to committ suicide in his laboratory in Berlin in 1893.

However, the story does not end here. Even though several of his subjects died, some of us lived on. We lived on with the knowledge of what had been done to us. The violence unleashed against us has indeed made us different. Even today we walk the streets of your large cities. You may know us as your neighbor, or even an acquantance. We are called many things. But do not call us friend. . . .

—J.S., London and Purfleet, 1939

Once the statue had been purified in various ways, and adored in
expiation of the violence done to it by it sculptor ("O sculptors of the
statue, stop doing disgraceful things to the father, do not strike the father,
O sculptors do not transfix his body"—this was Horus speaking and these
words clearly indicate that before the ritual started a statue was a purely
material object), the opening of the mouth took place to enable the "ka"
to enter and vitalize it: "Horus opens the mouth of his father Osiris."
Finally "he walks, he speaks," the dead man had become immortal.
—*Egyptian Art*, Francesco Abbate

75

Letter from Quincy Harker

Nov. 7, 1983

Dear Sir,

I received your letter, welcoming it with a feeling of joy and
exhilaration. For many years now I have hoped that someone
would be interested in writing a short book or memoir about my
mother. Since her death in 1911, almost all those who knew her
have moved on to the Spiritual Kingdom. As the only one who still
remains, I will describe to you in fullest detail what I can recall of
the blessed death of my mother, Mina Harker.

I had been away at school in Dublin and arrived home in the
late afternoon, leading into a rather chilly evening. Having eaten
on the wayside before undertaking the last leg of the journey, I
went directly to her room. There I found her among the gathered
flock, attending her in her last hours.

I recognized several of the women there, including her niece
and also a gentleman who had been her friend for many years—a
psychologist named Dr. John Seward. There were a few others,
including the artist Sikert, who did the painting you mentioned
seeing, and some others that I did not know.

The bedroom was on the upper floor, and in the darkness the firelight glistened off the fleur-de-lis wallpaper and dark wood panels. The bed was wrought-iron with straight starched linens neatly tucked into the feather mattress.

As darkness came, we saw her dark hair and small Irish nose set off by the deepened shadows. She spoke several times of her desire to visit Ireland and of her recent trip to the Holy Land. Her mind wandered across many things she would like to say, but as we all knew of the many trials of her long life in service to the Lord, so very much was left unsaid.

She seemed then to speak to one of us, or to some spirit standing just over her left shoulder—it was not clear by then what she wanted to convey or to whom it was intended, but I suspect that it was to the spirit of my father—gone now five years—or to the angel D'Israel who I believe was keeping his own vigil over my mother.

When at last the end was near, Dr. Seward administered to her the contents of the blue glass vial that she carried with her for so many years, tied by a black ribbon around her neck. It was strange to see death take one who was still so young. Dr. Seward pronounced her dead a few minutes later and she was immediately taken to the back room to have her body prepared for burial. It was her wish that it be done quickly. I still recall Dr. Seward climbing aboard the hearse and the sight of its black form speeding away into the darkness.

Her death marked the end of her long labour. This labour is summarized in the copy of her testament that I am enclosing with this account, and also in the many other documents and spirit writings that remained unpublished at the time of her death. Most important of all are the writings that tell of her encounter with the daemonic being "Dracula," who has since become known to the world as a monster of unparalleled evil. All of these writings convey the true story of Mina Harker, as in all its many parts it touched our lives. My fondest hope is that it touches yours also.

In memorium,
Quincy Harker
Islington and Exeter, UK

At the four corners of the bier are perched four hawks, representing the four children of Horus, each with their father's banner, keeping watch over the dead god, as they kept watch over the four quarters of the world. A fifth hawk seems to have been perched on the middle of the body of Osiris, but it had been broken off before the tomb was discovered in recent years, for only the bird's claws remain in position. . . . The scene represented is unquestionably the impregnation of Isis in the form of a hawk by the dead Osiris; the Copts who dismantled the shrine appear to have vented their pious rage on the figure of the hawk Isis by carrying it off or smashing it.
—*The Golden Bough,* Sir J.G. Fraser

76

The Last Will and Testament of Mrs. Mina Harker

This being the thirtieth day of the first month of the year nineteen hundred and eleven, I, Mina Murray Hawkins Harker, being of sound mind at the age of forty-six, do testify to the events described herein as true and factual in all details. This testament is witnessed to by my good friends, my sisters in Christ, and my beloved children, who now minister to my needs in this the hour of my illness.

I have set forth to the best of my knowledge and ability these events and here reveal many facts that have previously been hidden from you. Because my story might be used by skeptics and unbelievers to cast doubts on the sublime truths of the spirit world, I ask that these and other documents remain hidden from general view after my death, until such time as the human race will have grown to accept these spiritual truths.

My life has been solely devoted to this great work: the Ministry of Spirits to a world mired in Self-complacency and Pride.

As a child I was the passive receiver of spirit invasions; a variety of spirits manifested themselves in my presence—a Scottish Highlander in a red and white plaid kilt with white leggings appeared in my room each night to watch over me as I slept; the beauteous Woman in White who watched over me during my mother's long illness; the Spirit Children who played with me in my nursery. And, of course, the Water Sprites who danced pretty shapes in the sand on the banks of a stream near my childhood home . . . they danced until I clapped my hands with joy, whereupon they transformed into sparrows and flew away, or if they were especially mischievous they could hurl clots of mud on my clean dress while laughing with the sound of tiny glass bells.

These spirit invasions continued through my childhood, but as I grew older they came to me less often. The Highlander ceased his nocturnal watch; the Woman in White came no longer after my mother's illness ended; the Spirit Children abandoned my nursery, except for occasionally plaiting my hair in elflocks as I slept. As I entered my teens they ceased altogether. So finally I came to understand Wordsworth's belief that "We come from heaven trailing clouds of glory." With the years these clouds disperse in frail wisps, leaving only the Light of Common-day.

At this time began my psychic life. I came to meet the great spiritualist, Douglas Home, who had established a center in Birmingham. Through his efforts I discovered my own abilities as a medium. Indeed, I was a perfect vessel for these spirits, as I had been prepared throughout my childhood for this purpose.

It was as a young woman that I acted as a medium for many thousands of souls. Indeed, I became quite well known in spiritualist circles throughout England, often giving two or three seances a day, for many people were in direst need of spiritual comfort.

I continued as a medium for several years, until one day a spirit guide took possession of my body and wrote this message:

"Do not interfere with the dead. Your duty lies among the living. You must stop now, while you can."

From that day I ceased to act as a medium, for clearly these years of promiscuous seances had adversely affected my spiritual well-being. I came even to doubt the source and validity of my mediumistic and psychical powers. The only result of my six years of mediumship was the cynical belief that I had been merely giving myself up to the oblivion of a trance state, that I was a sort of prostitute for whatever spirits desired to use me for their own purposes.

Instead, I turned to a new ministry by helping those who had, like myself, become lost in occult experiences. I followed this ministry as best I could for eight years, during which time I met my future husband, Jonathan Harker, who worked as a clerk for Mr. Peter Hawkins, my step-father.

During this period in my life I began a serious study of the principles and origins of religion, and in particular the Christian faith. My own recent disillusion with spiritualism was a telling point in this inquiry, and I was determined not to be deluded by supernaturalism and pious fakery. Nevertheless, I did come to a realization, early on, that the story of the Christ bore a strange resemblance to other stories of great healers, many from distant lands who could not possibly have been influenced by the Christian faith.

Further, I eventually came to believe that the origins of many of the major religions were based on the discovery, or re-discovery, of more ancient religious practices. The story of the childhood of Christ is instructive on this point. Let us suppose that as a child, Jesus witnessed certain primitive religious rituals that were still common in the Middle East of his time. These might be holdovers of Canaanite "magical" practices, or even certain Jewish healing arts. At the time, let us suppose, he thought the practices curious, but not particularly important.

Then, some years later, during his family's sojourn into Egypt, Jesus was introduced to some Egyptian magicians and healers who showed him their temples and their art works. During the visit, Jesus is struck by the resemblance between certain practices revealed in the art works and the practices he had earlier witnessed in his homeland. He learns all he can from the Egyptians, but withholds his own growing "gnosis"—a secret knowledge and understanding of ancient practices.

At this point, the young man returns to Israel and begins to expore and investigate, and even experiment with his new knowledge. Soon he has mastered the knowledge. But what is this knowledge? I puzzled over this question for many long days and nights. I sat at my reading table, piled high with old books. Books, after all, are quite old—an ancient technique by which human memories can be transferred from person to person, or from the dead to the living. I enjoyed the fruit of their labour, as I gathered in their knowledge to put to my use. I had mastered them, as they had become me.

At the time of these speculations, I went on a tour of the British Museum with several friends, just to pass the time. I carried with me a volume of Goldsmith and a collection of faerie stories for children. The thin, elderly gentleman who was our guide had taken many thousands of people through the Egyptian exhibit over the years. As we passed a stone relief depicting the god Osiris, the guide stopped and pointed, commenting on the way Osiris held his arms crossed over his chest. "This," he said "is the sign of Osiris dead." He crossed his arms over his own chest, similarly. Then he opened his arms outward, his palms flat and his elbows rigid at his sides. "And this is the sign of Osiris resurrected."

At that moment, I saw the X-shaped Cross of St. Andrew carved into the stone breast of the god Osiris, and I knew what it was that Christ had seen in the temples of Egypt—the truth of the bodily resurrection into eternal life. The knowledge he had discovered was passed on by initiates within the Christian church through the centuries, until the suppression of the Cathar Christians in France. From that point on, the knowledge was held by only a few initiates and eventually lost altogether.

I spent the rest of my life gathering facts in support of this truth, up until the time of my meeting with Drakulya in Transylvania. The events that followed have become well known to the reading public through the imaginative narrative written by Mr. Bram Stoker. His book and these documents, letters, and spirit writings are the legacy I leave you, as I now begin my long journey. . . .

Christ is called our inward man because he communicates to us His
spirit whereby we are renewed from day to day. The more Christ renews
our spirit by the fire in His spirit, the more he insinuates Himself into
our body, the more is our inward man said to grow in Christ. . . . Our
inward man is truly heavenly, has come down from Heaven of the
substance of God, of the divine substance of Christ, not of the blood, not of
the will of the flesh but of God. Our inward man is God as Christ is God
and the Holy Spirit is God. As the psalmist said, foreshadowing this
truth, "I have said, ye are gods." As the one God in many makes them
Gods so the one Christ in many makes them both Christs and Gods.
                                                    — Michael Servetus

77

From "Spirit writings" (1954)

You may call me Lilith. Or you could call me Ishtar, or Astarte,
or Semiramis, or Pelagia, or Judithiah, or Marahianna, or even
Mina.

I found my way at last to my new home, and there I found the
50th box where the gypsies had placed it, just inside the gates of
the castle. I carried it down to the crypt, where the other boxes
lay waiting. It was the box containing the remains of Mircea
Drakulya, formerly Lord of the Undead. I added his box to the
others, so that there were fifty in all, and then I brought down the
51st box, a coffin of English manufacture and described as "luxury
itself" by the undertaker who had sold it to me.

That night I claimed my first victim: a young assistant school-
mistress. It was from her that I had learned this lesson: Life takes
on its greatest meaning where the flesh of two beings meet.

Drakulya was dead. But I was able to draw from him, as he had
drawn from the Children of the Night, a knowledge of the spirit
world that was far beyond anything I had ever known before. I

absorbed their wisdom, two by two, so that the power of healing was mine.

Many years passed—a terrible burden of war and famine destroyed all of Europe. But eventually a strange peace settled on the land and a race of new men and women came to build their lives in the valleys below. And with them came a new growth in the land: the orchards were heavy with fruit, the fields gave forth the bounty of wheat and rye, and the fish and birds were multiplied—so that the Waste-land was no more.

———————————